Swashbuckling Cats: Nine Lives on the Seven Seas

Edited by
Rhonda Parrish

SWASHBUCKLING CATS:
NINE LIVES ON THE SEVEN SEAS

EDITED BY
RHONDA PARRISH

TYCHE BOOKS LTD.

Swashbuckling Cats: Nine Lives on the Seven Seas
Edited by Rhonda Parrish

Published by Tyche Books Ltd.
Calgary, Alberta, Canada
www.TycheBooks.com

Cover Art by Sarah Dahlinger
Cover Layout by Indigo Chick Design
Interior Layout by Ryah Deines
Editorial by Rhonda Parrish

First Tyche Books Ltd Edition 2020
Print ISBN: 978-1-989407-16-5
Ebook ISBN: 978-1-989407-17-2

Author photograph: Cindy Gannon Photography

This book was funded in part by a grant from the Alberta Media Fund.

Contents

Dedicated to those furry little assholes we call cats.

And also, as always, to Jo.

INTRODUCTION

BY RHONDA PARRISH

IT BEGAN ON Twitter. Because of course it did.

May 24, 2018
@RhondaParrish: I just wrote the sentence, "Yar, if we open to submissions[date] we could do a [date] release." In an email to a publisher. Yar. I mean . . . perhaps not the best word to use in business correspondence?
@AuthorJessOwen: Unless it's a pirate themed thing?
@RhondaParrish: Alas, not this time LoL
@AuthorJessOwen: But I mean you Could
.
.
.
☺

Meanwhile . . .

@RhondaParrish: I just wrote the sentence, "Yar, if we open to submissions[date] we could do a [date] release." In an email to a publisher. Yar. I mean . . . perhaps not the best word to use in business correspondence?
@S_G_Wong: it's perfect!

@RhondaParrish: In this case the publisher in question was @TycheBooks and she's used to my little idiosyncrasies . . . but I still edited that word out before sending ;)

@TycheBooks: *GIF of a cat in a pirate costume*

@S_G_Wong: *GIF of a Viking cat weathering a storm*

@RhondaParrish: . . . I wonder if there's a market for a pirate cats anthology LoL

@TycheBooks: . . . maybe?

@S_G_Wong: mine was a Viking cat ;)

And yes, im sure there is! Maybe, to broaden the range of subs, it could be swashbuckling cats or cats on the high seas . . .

@Kristadb1: When is the submission date

@RhondaParrish: OMG.

This is just because I was bragging that my 2019 wasn't over-scheduled, isn't it?

@Krisatdb1: So 2019? Ok.

@TycheBooks: Swashbuckling cats ftw!

Swashbuckling cats ftw, indeed.

I could spend more time talking about cats, or the process by which this anthology came together. Or, I could end the Introduction now, let the stories speak for themselves, and go take a nap. I think we both know which choice a cat would make.

Rhonda Parrish
Edmonton
11/25/2019

THE PRIDE

MEGAN FENNELL

ALTHOUGH THE BARDS came to different conclusions about exactly which of the hundred port cities on the Shattered Coast was the best of all, ranked variously on food, wine, and the friendliness of their women, they all agreed there were a damned lot of them to choose from.

To Kit's mind, the fact the *Pride* had made port in his bloody town despite the bounty of other options proved Fate was a bit of a sadistic bastard.

He'd been doing his best to ignore the ship. So far his methods had involved staring at it, asking the dockmaster when it had arrived, for what purpose, and how long it intended to stay, as well as setting up his grill so he had an unobstructed view down Merchant's Line to stare at it some more. As a jackal, ignoring things was not one of Kit's particular strengths.

As the afternoon limped into a muggy evening, Kit went through the motions of running his stand for the last few folks who wanted a taste of spiced meat before they packed up for the day. A half-hearted breeze slithered up from the sea, making the heat from his grill slightly more tolerable. Down in the bay, the dark sails of the *Pride* were bundled in for the evening but their banner still snapped and fluttered in the breeze, the golden vertical-pupiled eye staring proudly out over the port. In the half-light, Kit could make out the shapes of the crew as they moved about on the deck, coming to wakeful activity after what he suspected had been a lazy afternoon of lying about and squabbling over the best sunbeams. Still no sign of Felix—not that Kit was looking specifically for him—but he was amusing himself trying to pick out the rest of the old crew based on their silhouettes when the tang of jackal-scent hit his nose.

His attention snapped back to his surroundings as three young men strutted up to his stall, cackling and bouncing off each others' shoulders, running pack colours like the city guard couldn't do a thing about it. Like they could turn the cobblestone streets of Skulduggery into hot desert sand just by wanting it hard enough. Their dark eyes were wide and glittering and the stink of drug-smoke hung about them, something that probably cost more than Kit made in a week. He could damn near feel their jackal-forms writhing beneath their skin, flirting with the idea of shredding through their human shapes and tearing through the city.

Wiping a rag over his grease-slick counter, Kit adjusted the material of his gloves so they covered up as much of the metal caps soldered around his fingertips that they could, and tilted his chin to the men in silent understanding. *I see you seeing me.* He didn't mean it as an invitation, but all three, still grinning, crowded in around the front of his stall, openly sniffing the air.

"People *pay* to eat this?" the tallest of the three said. His words rolled with a heavy accent, though he spoke the human tongue.

"When luck's with me," Kit said, his words casual but his skin prickling with tension. The tall jackal's posture was unguarded and his balance was poor. Had Kit been that careless with his safety when he'd run with a pack?

The leader looked him up and down as his cohorts skulked around the sides of the stall, visibly casing the place, circling him.

Come on, not for the twenty-five coins in my bag, Kit thought. *Don't you carrion-dogs ruin my stall for that little!*

The leader's mouth twitched into a frown. Snake-quick, he grabbed Kit's hand and yanked his leather glove down from his wrist. The bands welded around his knuckles to hold the finger-caps in place sparkled in the fading light, a silver cage to hold his claws captive under his skin, the suffocating reminder that the beast beneath the surface of his form was imprisoned. The dark X branded in the space between his thumb and forefinger stood out stark in comparison.

"A lone jackal, branded for a pirate, dressed up like a human, with capped claws," the man announced. He dropped Kit's hand in disgust. "I almost don't want any food from you. Your uselessness might be catching."

The smaller two cackled and circled back around to join their leader, eyeing the meat hungrily. Without comment, Kit set to work wrapping up three heartily-portioned kebabs for them, tense with restrained anger. They didn't pay and he didn't care, so long as they were leaving.

They jumped him in an alley half an hour later, a block away from the market, laying into him with fists and boots until he wasn't fighting back when they rifled through his pockets.

"Times are changing, boys," the leader laughed, the scent of alcohol and kebab lingering on his breath. "Cull the weak. Unite the strong." He tore Kit's coin-purse from his jacket and grumbled at its lack of weight. "Pathetic excuse for a jackal." He boasted the word jackal with enough bravado it made Kit want to vomit. "I think the catkiller would work on him too."

"Throw him on board with the others and let the hunter find out," one of the cronies snickered.

"Try it now," the third said. "I want to see. I've got some . . ."

The rustle of a bag and fear of the unknown inspired one more panicky burst of fight in Kit, but there were three of them and he was already hurt. He snarled at them as they flung a fine pale powder into his face, his claw-tips breaching his skin and pressing dangerously against the silver caps meant to shatter them if he shifted forms. The dust flew into his nose, his eyes, and sent him into a fit of coughing that brutalized his aching ribs.

"Still jackal enough to live," one of his attackers commented, sounding disappointed. He leaned down and spirited a lit match from behind his ear, dangling it dangerously near Kit's cheek.

"Enough playing," the leader said. "Let's go."

The one closest to him grinned with all his teeth, leaning in close to Kit. "Lucky day for you." He tossed the match onto a smear of powder on the cobblestone and grinned as it combusted into a flash-fire of sparks.

They moved off as one, and Kit watched through blood and dust-clouded eyes as they fell into formation with their leader and trotted out of the alley. And what hurt worse than the beating was that the emotion boiling under the surface of his skin wasn't anger, but envy.

IT WASN'T HOW he'd imagined going back to the Pride, empty-handed, hobbling, and with a burgeoning black eye to match the purple of their sails, but a painful and sleepless night had settled his mind on the matter. Whenever he'd pictured this moment—which he'd done with humiliating frequency in the last few years—he'd been dressed in elegant clothing, with a jewelled walking stick in hand, all cool ambivalence. His reputation would proceed him and the crew would be whispering about his most recent string of successes by the time Captain Garnet earnestly asked him to come back on board, to travel with them one more time . . .

"Dock-scum," someone hissed from the top of the gangplank. "Piss off. This is a private ship."

Kit squinted up at the pirate who was perched like a gargoyle on the gunnel, the morning sunlight making his eyes water and throwing the sailor into a dark silhouette. He could make out the long-limbed shape and the flash of a golden hoop through one scar-notched ear, a small feather dangling from it.

"Umber," he called up. "It's me, Kit. From . . . before."

An extended hiss slid through the air like a sharpened knife, and Umber uncoiled from her perch, stalking down the gangplank on bare feet. "Not welcome here." Her fingers twisted at her sides like her nails were threatening to stretch into deadly claws. "Jackal traitor. *Go.* Take your face away from here or Umber takes it away from you."

He found himself involuntarily backing away despite having nearly half a foot of height on her. Above, a few other crewmates had gathered along the gunnel to watch the show.

"I've got important information," he protested. "I need to speak with the Captain."

She crowded into his space, piercing him with her green eyes, her hands still twitching at her sides. She'd acquired a few more tattoos in his absence, including a stylized bird in flight high on her cheek, blue ink on sable skin.

"Captain doesn't need to speak with you," she countered, jabbing a finger into his chest. "Enemy of the *Pride*."

His stomach twisted, dragging his heart down with it. When he heard that they'd survived their tangle with the Queen's Navy he'd wept with relief and guilt. And here he was, their enemy. "Please," he said, "then can you pass him a message for me? I could write it down . . ."

"I think I'd rather hear it directly."

Kit's sinking heart lurched back into his throat, suddenly beating double-time. Captain Garnet strolled down the gangplank, his boots soundless on the boards, and put his hand on Umber's shoulder. His auburn hair hung loose around his shoulders, the sunlight picking out the gold in it that complemented the colour of his eyes, and his posture was proud and untouchable. He seemed taller than Kit remembered, and his expression that had once been so open was now unreadable.

"Whatever it is, I expect it's got to be damned important if he's bringing it here in person," he added, quirking an eyebrow and gesturing for Kit to follow him.

Scrambling for something—*anything*—to say in response, Kit hurried after him onto the *Pride*.

Everything was just like he remembered, from the faces of the crew to the placement of the barrels, and painful nostalgia coursed over him like a wave. The scent of pitch and salt-weathered wood smelled like family.

A chorus of sibilant whispers greeted him as the crew stopped what they were doing to stare at him. A few started forward in anger, until the Captain dropped back to walk at his side, his amber eyes sliding over his agitated crew.

"This information of yours," he said quietly, "is it worth the risk of mutiny I'm presently incurring on your behalf?"

Kit nodded. "It is," he said, and hoped he was telling the truth.

The Captain led him into his quarters and shut the door. The wood of the deck creaked as the crew crowded around outside, shamelessly listening in. Kit suddenly didn't know where to stand or where to look or what to do with his hands. He stared at the writing desk and the dark green jacket slung over the back of the chair, refusing to let his eyes stray even slightly towards the private area at the back of the quarters.

"Well," the Captain prompted, "what do you have for me?" Crossing the room, he unpinned a black cloth from above his wall-mounted maps with casual grace, letting it drop down over them.

"You don't need to do that," Kit said, before he could bite back the words. "I'm safe. I wouldn't . . ."

"Sell us out if you knew our routes?" His voice was smooth but Kit saw his jaw flex as he turned around, leaning against the wall with folded arms. "I don't believe I want to take that risk. You sure as hell haven't given us any reason to."

Guilt and regret burned through Kit, bringing heat to his face. He twisted his hands together like he could squeeze the nervous energy out of them, and his silvers clicked together softly beneath his gloves. The Captain's eyes snapped down at the sound, a slight frown slipping into his expression.

"There's a poison in the city," Kit blurted. "I found out about it. They're calling it 'catkiller'. It's a pale powder but I don't know exactly what it does. I . . ."

"Slow down," the Captain interrupted, his gaze mercifully moving away from Kit's marred hands. "Who are *they*?"

"A pack of jackals," Kit clarified. "They mentioned a hunter, so I think there's someone in the city going after your kind."

The Captain's eyebrows ticked upwards. "*You* run with a pack now?"

Kit stared at him. "No. Whispering Hells, Felix . . . Of course I don't. They're the ones who gave me this." He gestured at his bruised face and blackened eye.

"I never knew you as well as I thought I did," the Captain countered quietly. "I won't pretend to know what you're capable of."

Stung into silence, Kit jammed his hands into his pockets. "Not that," he muttered.

The Captain studied him for a long moment, then nodded, pushing away from the wall and moving towards the door. "I appreciate the warning about the poison, Kit. I'll keep my crew aboard and out of town until we leave." He glanced at him as he reached for the door. "Is twenty gold sufficient?"

It took Kit a moment to process his words. "What?"

The Captain shrugged. "I can make it twenty-five. You look

like you could use it."

Pain flared in Kit's hands, his claws flexing against their silver bonds, and the colours in the room sharpened as his body fought the urge to change, his blood hot with anger. "I didn't come here for your coin."

The Captain paused, reading his posture, his hand still on the door. His hearing sharpened, Kit could hear the crew outside scurrying back to their posts, pretending they hadn't been eavesdropping the entire time. The Captain leaned into his space, looming over him, sending the hairs on Kit's arms prickling up at his proximity to a larger predator.

"Then what," the Captain said quietly, "did you come here for exactly?"

Answers surged into his mind, tangling up in his throat and choking him. He'd come to apologize. To bring this information like an olive branch. To explain. To tell him that although he'd told the Queen's Navy where to find the *Pride* to save his own skin, he knew in his heart they'd be quick and clever enough to get away safely. To tell him that the dreams where he'd actually died in that slaughter-room, letting the Navy's interrogators take him apart, were the *good* dreams.

"I only came to warn you," he said. "I never wanted any of you to get hurt."

The Captain studied him for a long moment, like he was somehow reading all of those unspoken answers in his eyes. "*Want* has nothing to do with it. We're a crew. A damned pride. The weakest link breaks the chain. A single careless spark lights the powder keg." He reached past him and pushed the door open.

"Dismissed," he said. "You recall your way off the ship, I assume."

Kit left with the weight of the crew's eyes on him, soft, hissed insults chasing him down the gangplank. Umber graced him with a mocking curtsey as he passed, and a stone zipped past her shoulder, striking him on the side of the head. The smallest member of the crew had grown from a child to a teenager since his departure, and she glared at Kit, hissing with bared fangs. He still remembered the texture of her hair as he'd plaited it into the best braids he could manage and entertained her with all the stories of the desert-folk he could still recall. Imbri reloaded her slingshot, firing again, bashing his shoulder with a satisfied jeer.

When his feet touched solid ground again, it was with all the heaviness of the last time he'd left this ship.

SKULDUGGERY WOULD HAVE to do without spiced meat on Merchant's Line for a day. Kit set himself up on the steep bluffs overlooking the bay to watch the *Pride* slide out to sea, a full day before the dockmaster had told him they would. Guilt and anxiety and something like heartbreak churned in his stomach as he watched the prow of his old home slice through the waves battering the mouth of the harbour, setting a course southwards down the coast. The crew leapt and scrambled among the rigging, running the length of the yards on nimble unshod feet to secure the sails. He could see the Captain at the wheel guiding them with easy confidence through the rough waters, his long coat unfurling like a banner behind him. And it was the realization that even in the privacy of his own thoughts the man was no longer familiar enough to call "Felix" that made Kit's eyes burn with something more than the salt-stinging wind.

The quarters hadn't smelled of anyone other than the Captain. Not that Kit had any right to care or protest if it had. Not that it even really mattered.

The Shattered Coast had one hundred port cities and with odds like that, Kit would likely never see the *Pride* or her crew ever again.

He scrambled futilely at the soft earth with his capped claws and howled his frustration, his sorrow, his pain, until the ship was out of sight. One botched errand ashore and everything had been ruined. One stupid misstep . . .

He slumped against the craggy rocks that crowned the clifftop and watched the sky change colours.

Staring numbly out at the open sea, it took him a moment to even register anything significant about the next ship crossing through the mouth of the harbour and bidding Skulduggery farewell. It was a dark, full-rigged beast built for speed, riding high on the water. A chaser. As he watched, the sailor in the crow's nest vaulted from their post, landing in a crouch on the deck below, before standing and disappearing below deck as another scrambled up to take their place. Not a human crew, then.

Their banner was a curious composition of silver on sable, depicting a modified Jolly Roger with an elongated skull and long teeth grasping a femur. They were headed south as well at a fair clip. It made him smile for a moment in spite of his dark mood; even on the open seas it seemed dogs would chase cats. The name painted behind the gunports said *Hunter's Moon* in curling gilded script.

Sudden horror slithered through the heart of him.

Throw him on board with the others and let the hunter find out . . .

In his haze of pain and fear, he hadn't given much thought to what the man had been talking about. It had never occurred to him that "the hunter" might be something other than a person. And if this rig was wielding the catkiller powder, heading south on the tail of the *Pride* . . .

Not again. Not this time.

He took off sprinting down the path back to Skulduggery at breakneck speed.

PANTING, SWEATING, AND dishevelled from the run, Kit knew he wasn't making the most convincing argument. He'd stopped at his rented room long enough to grab his knives and pull his savings out of hiding, all fifty coins he'd managed to scrounge away while still keeping his grill running and himself fed. Ironically, the gold he'd refused from the Captain yesterday probably would have gone a long way in making his case.

The woman with the boat looked him up and down, methodically puffing on a pipe and somehow managing to blow streams of smoke in a judgmental fashion.

"So you don't know how far I'd be taking you or exactly where," she repeated, "But you're *not* running from the law?"

"Swear on my life," Kit pleaded, "I'm in good standing. I run a little food stand on Merchant's Line. I just need to catch up with a ship." He looked past her to the boat, a nimble little racer with silvery sails. The prow was slightly battered like it had kissed a rock or two and the whole thing was only big enough for perhaps three or four, but it might get him to the *Pride* before the *Hunter* reached it.

"Which ship?" she asked, punctuating with another long

inhale.

Well, he was in this deep. "Have you heard of the *Pride?*"

Her smoke stuttered out in bursts. "The pirate cats?" She peered at him, leaning in. "You're . . . not a cat though. Are you?" The humans had a tendency to lump species into 'humans' and 'not humans', letting the subcategories blur.

"Jackal," he clarified, trying to not imagine how far away the *Pride* had already sailed. And how much water the *Hunter's Moon* had put behind it. The woman had opened her mouth to counter, gesturing at him with her pipe, but he cut her off. "And yes, I know we're desert folk. I know we're not meant for the water. I know how all of this looks." His face was hot with frustration, his throat tight. "But please, please, if you've got a heart at all . . . I've got friends on that ship, people that I loved." He'd stuttered over the tense of the final word. "I've got to get to them, to let them know what's happening."

She eyed him dubiously a moment longer, weighing the coin purse in her hand, then gave a short nod. "All right," she said, "You're the strangest person I've met in an age, but I've done more for less. Get onboard, the name's Jess."

IT TOOK THEM less than an hour to catch up but the ride was a brutal one. Kit spent most of it ducking beneath the sweeping boom, trying not to catch too many waves in the face, and staying out of Jess's way. All things considered, he *was* a desert-dog, built for dry heat and packed sand. It had taken him weeks to grow accustomed to the bounce of the waves and everything he wore always being a little bit sodden. But one amused smile from the Captain would set him steady on his feet, one quiet compliment would deafen him to the ribbing of the crew.

As the prow of the little racer slapped over the icy rollers, he was surprised to realize he'd actually missed this part too.

There wasn't much time for reflection on the matter of aquatically-inclined jackals and whether they were mad to attempt a life on the water, as they rounded a pine-thick outcropping jutting from the coast and came into view of their quarry.

"Gods preserve us," Jess exclaimed, "you never said I was taking you into a fight!"

The *Hunter's Moon* was already barrelling down on the

Pride, which was sweeping broadside to meet them. The sound of the crews beating to quarter for battle rang out over the rough waves as gunports clattered open on both ships.

"I need to get aboard!" Kit called to Jess, who gaped at him.

"What kind of god do you think I am?"

"Just get me close enough to jump," he begged. "I can take it from there. They're too busy to notice you and you're quick enough to get back out."

She stared at him incredulously. "You're a mad dog, you are!" But the glimmer of fire sparked in her eye and she looped a coil of rope around her arm and pulled back hard, swinging the mainsail so they lurched towards the fray. The speedier boat banked to the right, making a long arc around the towering ships so they could come up behind the *Pride*. Jess's face was locked in determination as she fought against the large ship's wake to get up close. Kit clambered to the rail, slipping a knife into either hand and bracing himself to leap as they fell into the deep shadow of the *Pride's* hull.

"Go on, mad dog!" Jess yelled again. She met his eyes for a moment, offering a disbelieving shake of her head and a wicked grin of approval. The shimmer of something more than human gleamed in her eye. "Luck be with you, lunatic."

Kit gave a shaky grin, then turned and leapt with all of his strength, slamming his knives into the wood of the hull and hanging on. He scrambled for purchase with his boots, wishing like hell for claws and waiting for the roll of the ship to be in his favour before he started his climb. Hand over hand, knife over knife, he crawled his way up the side. Finally slinging his shaking arms over the railing to catch his breath, he saw Jess's racer already skipping to safety in the distance.

The deck was a flurry of activity as the crew scrambled to their battle stations. Several had already shed their clothing and were roiling into their primal forms, sleek black fur racing to cover tanned skin, fingers lengthening into wicked claws, long tails lashing. The ones not changing shape mustered cutlasses and daggers, hissing and caterwauling at the dark shape of the *Hunter's Moon* still bearing down on them. Below deck, the cannons rumbled into place, the teams hollering as they charged them with ammunition and powder. Captain Garnet stood with a team of shifted panthers prowling around him, his cutlass unsheathed, studying the other ship with the patient anticipation of a predator accustomed to victory.

A yowl of offense was the only warning Kit got before strong hands grabbed him, hauled him roughly over the gunnel, and flung him to the deck. His knives clattered out of his grasp, spinning on the boards next to him. Umber stood over him, her dark eyes wide with fury. "You! You . . ." She stammered between languages before expressing herself with another yowl. "Traitor! You do this? You set these dogs on us?"

Kit shook his head, cringing as he saw the situation through her eyes. "No! I came to help! I know what they . . ."

She sent one of his knives skittering down the length of the deck with a kick and backhanded him across the face hard enough that stars exploded into his vision. A boom from the *Hunter's Moon* echoed over the water, followed by the unmistakable splash of a cannonball falling short. He shook his head to clear it and found more of the crew had gathered around, hissing and spitting. The Captain stood among them, staring in exasperated disbelief before levelling his cutlass towards Kit's throat.

"Speak," he ordered. "And damned quick. Choose your words well."

Before Kit could open his mouth, a series of cracks sounded from the *Hunter's Moon* and projectiles whined overhead, tearing through the mainsail and splashing into the ocean on the other side. One struck the mizzenmast, but instead of splintering the wood, the ball shattered on impact, sending a cloud of pale, glittering powder falling to coat the deck and the unfortunate crewmembers below it. There was a moment of confused silence before they began to scream.

"Catkiller," Kit breathed, frozen with horror. The Captain spun to see what had happened, his cutlass slack at his side.

The crew that the powder had touched went into a frantic dance, clawing and scratching at themselves as they howled, collapsing to writhe on the deck. The dark shape of a panther's muzzle stretched the face of one of the men long enough to show sharp fangs in a wail before receding again. Their bodies twisted, half-shifting, like they were frantically trying to find a shape that wasn't in agony.

The *Pride's* cannons spat fire in return, only briefly drowning out the screams of the poisoned sailors, but the *Hunter* sent over a fresh volley. Another orb struck the gunnel, spraying the shifted boarding party with pale powder and throwing them into a panic, while another smashed against the side of the Captain's quarters, sending even more of the deadly dust into the air. The sailors that had first been touched by it now writhed in monstrous half-forms, their mouths wet with froth and blood.

"Stay away from the powder!" the Captain roared, snapping into action. "Get below deck! We'll board them from the damned gunports and tear them apart! Pip, bring us in close! We . . ."

A whistle cut the air before a fresh orb smashed against the main mast, throwing another cloud over the crew closest to Kit. The Captain threw his arm up to protect himself but it covered him like a ghostly embrace. Kit watched in horror as orange and black stripes chased each other over his face and throat as he began to scream.

Time seemed to slow down. The catkiller powder drifted down over Kit, still prone on the deck, coating his face and his clothes. The world had turned into a hellish nightmare of contorting flesh and tormented cries. Through the fog-like haze of catkiller he could see the silhouette of the *Hunter's Moon* drawing in close now, anxious jackals tossing ropes and steadying themselves on the railing with eager snarls. They wouldn't have dared a close range fight before poisoning the crew; the cats would've torn them apart. But now . . .

Felix's cutlass clattered to the deck. Kit had never once seen it leave the Captain's hand in combat, even through brutal wounds and impossible circumstances. But both of Felix's hands were scrabbling at his face, trying to wipe the powder off of his skin as he howled, the sound somewhere in between the scream of a man and the roar of a tiger. Kit lurched to his feet, picking up his remaining knife. One lone jackal, dressed as a human, branded as a pirate, with capped claws and a knife, ready to defend the might of the *Pride*. The weakest link was now the last one on his feet.

But a single careless spark lights the powder keg.

Kit whirled and slashed his knife across the metal banding at the gunnel with all his strength, throwing up the flurry of sparks he'd been looking for. There was a moment when he thought it hadn't worked, thinking the match and the jackal in the alley just a fluke, but then the fire caught and flame raced through the silvery clouds like a crimson gust. A sound like a sucking inhale followed and then a low *WHUMP* threw Kit backwards to the deck. His vision swam as pain wracked him, the sky a burning sheet overhead as the fire ate the catkiller powder out of the air in a wave. His ears were full of one long high-pitched whine but, distantly, as the fire rushed through and the sky cleared once more he could hear the shouts of the people around him.

If they were firing catkiller from their cannons, they'd have it stockpiled on the gundeck, and Kit could only think of one way to return the favour.

The crew was pouring up from below deck in a fury of yowls and screams, abandoning the gundeck for survival. Kit rushed to his feet, ricocheting off the agonized crew to find three cannons waiting to be loaded. Pirates writhed and withered, screaming in dark corners. The cannons were covered in the dusting of the white residue that had infiltrated through the gunports

Kit had never trained on guns, so he gathered everything flammable he could find and dumped it in with the cannonball, adding handfuls of waxy pitch and gunpowder—he had the ingredients but no recipe to follow.

"Light it up." From the corner of the pile, a voice strained through clenched teeth. "Burn it up, and burn the dogs!" Imbri hissed, doubled over, blood tearing from her eyes, her muzzle shaping and reshaping, stretching her muscle like rubber, caught in a waking nightmare.

Kit resisted the urge to help her. The last time they'd practiced lifting the cannonballs she'd been too young to assume her cougar form but so proud to try. Now it clawed at her from the inside, screaming like a demon to get out. He closed his eyes and grabbed a fallen torch, stuffing it into the mouth of the cannon to light the ammunition.

"The bloody fuse, dust-for-brains!"

Embarrassed, he spun around, running to the other end of the cannon, and remembered where the fuse was. He whisked the torch around to kiss the rope on each cannon and waited.

The first cannon exploded, sending the fireball streaking to the other ship with a cape of flame. The sound was so shrill Kit slapped his hands to his ears and was sent sprawling by the bounce of the cannon smashing into his hip. The next two explosions followed, and one of the hefty guns rolled backwards threatening to crush Kit, forcing him to scramble out of the way.

There was a half-breath after the blasts where fear grabbed his heart with sharpened claws, whispering that maybe they were all out of catkiller and his gamble to defeat the dog-ship was in vain, before he heard the detonation. Splinters of wood flew like daggers through the gaping gunports as the hull of the *Hunter's Moon* exploded into the *Pride*. One ragged chunk imbedded in his thigh and he ducked. More explosions followed as he crawled to Imbri and hoisted her out of the line of fire and up to the stairs to the deck.

A cacophony of explosions rang out as he stumbled out onto the deck. Out in the open there was nothing stopping the flurry of shrapnel and the impact of the blasts from battering his merchant's body. He wavered with the additional weight of the girl in his arms and fell to the side, dropping Imbri and catching himself on the gunnel, striking his silver-bound hand on the metal. Sparks shot into the air and another burst of flashfire exploded. The fire latched onto the pitch staining the metal binds over his fingers, crawling like hungry insects to find the pockets of gunpowder trapped beneath the silver. He scrambled to snuff the fire but a muted crack from under the metal and a burst of light and impossible pain sent him back to the ground.

Kit rolled to his side, gasping and choking, groping for a weapon or a miracle. He couldn't find his knife but there was a sound like dropped scattershot as the remnants of the silver claw-caps soldered onto his hand fell free. Brief elation surged through him, until he realized they were falling away with bits of bone and blood, into a mess of flesh and char on the deck. They'd detached because there were no longer any fingers to bear them.

A shadow fell over him and then a dirk, his dirk, clattered down dangerously close to his face. Umber was peering down at him, blood at the corners of her mouth. Her hair was singed and her vest was in tatters, but her form was stable. She gave him a nod, touched the pommel of her sabre to her forehead, and then leapt over him, charging towards the side of the ship where the *Hunter* had been closing. Through the buzz in his ears, he could make out the snarls and yowls of the *Pride's* crew, all fury now, and the clatter of grappling hooks. There was a jolting boom as the ships collided broadside.

The image of Felix was in his mind, years younger, back when the only thing he looked at Kit with was fond amusement and faint worry. *If we go ship-to-ship, you arm up and stay near Umber. I've asked her to keep an eye on you, just until you get your feet under you. Stay near her and watch her back for me, will you?*

Kit dragged himself to his feet, clumsily taking the dirk in his remaining hand. He would fight with his damned teeth, with a musket if he could find one. The only thing he knew for sure as he watched the crew leap across the space between the locked ships, shining blades clutched in clawed hands, white fangs bared and brazen against singed faces, was that he wouldn't leave the *Pride* to fight without him again.

With the manic cackling cry of his people, Kit charged towards the dog-ship, setting a boot onto the railing and leaping towards the fray on the other side.

A musket cracked from the deck of the *Hunter's Moon* and it felt like being struck in the chest by a plank of wood. Kit dropped, splashing into the icy churning water between the massive ships. Above him, he saw Captain Felix Garnet leap across the gap of sky, his long jacket streaming with smoke, his face and chest still a riot of orange and black stripes.

When the dark water closed over Kit's head, no regret followed him down.

LIVING, IT SEEMED, was a painful affair.

He found himself drawn back to consciousness by the thrumming ache in his right hand and the sound of methodical scraping. When he opened his eyes and blearily made out dark wood above his head, his stomach lurched, thinking that he was in a casket and being buried. But the world gently rocked and the supposed casket smelled of nothing but Felix and a bit of blood, and his heart settled again.

"Ah, good. You should have some input on this, I imagine. Hand, hook, or paw? Suppose we could put claws on it too, if we went that way."

Felix was seated next to the bed, having pulled the chair from his desk up beside it. The view from the private alcove in the back of the Captain's quarters was otherwise unchanged.

"What?" Kit croaked. He lifted his right arm and found it was shorter than it had been, the end of his wrist capped with a tight bandage.

Felix held up the piece of wood for him to see before going back to scraping slivers of it away with a small knife. "Hand, hook, or paw? You certainly don't do things by halves, do you? There are easier ways of getting rid of capped claws. Water's on the table. Rum's next to it if the pain's too much."

Kit pushed himself gingerly upright, reaching for the bottle next to the bed with a burned but intact left hand. The damned silvers had stayed on *that* one, unfortunately. He took a moment to swallow some water before speaking again.

"Easier ways?" he asked hesitantly.

Felix's mouth twitched as he kept whittling. "Depends, doesn't it? With some careful tools, they come off easily enough and you can stretch your claws again. I've done it before myself. But if a man were to walk back into a civilized town where there's more guards than common sense, he'll find himself right back in them. Waste of time. My time."

Kit followed the water with a healthy swallow of rum, staring at his abridged right arm. "Career choices might be limited for a lame jackal."

"From my experience, you've always been adept with either hand." He glanced up, meeting Kit's stare. His face had been lightly burned as the powder had seared off of it and it made his eyes as vibrant as polished gold in comparison. "But if a man were still intent on being a pirate, it might be worth our time."

Kit's face burned with more than the signature that flame had left on his chin. "What does it take to be a pirate?"

"Courage," Felix said. He rested his elbows on his knees, turning the carving over in his fingers thoughtfully. "You seem to have found yours. And trust. The trust of a cat's hard enough to earn the first time around. The second time's nearly impossible. You'd have a hell of a fight on your hands to work your way back in with the crew, every damned day." A faint smile ghosted over his mouth. "Though I've heard jackals are all a little bit mad, so perhaps that's no deterrent."

Kit opened his mouth to speak and Felix shook his head, holding up a hand to stop him.

"Don't say anything now," he warned. "Rest and think it over so you can tell me true where you're headed, Kit."

Kit nodded, finding a smile. "All right." He gestured towards the carving, determination blossoming in his chest, along with something like hope. "But make that a paw," he said, "with claws."

THE COMEBACK KITTY

S.G. WONG

THE QUEEN DEMANDS satisfaction.

Every one of them had that drilled into their soft little skulls from the very first. When you come to the end of one path, the start of the next requires a visit to the Queen. And only once—only *if*—She deems your gift worthy will you be released to begin your new life.

Kit knew all this, though it did not make being a ghost in the meantime any easier.

She shook herself harshly. Now was no time to lose oneself in complaints and regrets. She was *this close* to securing the treasure she knew would be her best chance at winning the Queen's regard.

If only Ying, her person, would stop shivering and focus.

Kit permitted herself one long-suffering sigh before returning to the business at hand.

"Ying, girl, pay attention. We're down to days now, remember? If you miss your mark, we'll lose our only chance to see me whole again."

"I'm sorry, kitty. It's just so cold out here." Ying held herself even more tightly, staring balefully at the rigging of the junk across the dock from them. It was a three-mast'er, made for the lower skies and fast freight. Its berth assignment had placed it just low enough from Ying's position that she could see downward onto it. With sails furled, the tall masts cast long shadows against the deck and the single, rectangular cabin at its centre.

A mechanical deck sweeper plodded its way port to starboard, over and over, grinding its gears with a silent pop of air. The whirring of its exposed cogs changed to a loud clank for a few cycles before catching their teeth properly once more, accompanied by curses from the off-duty crew. Puffs of steam escaped from the sweeper's rear hatch, as it swept around and around and around the few deckhands still setting the airskimmer to rights for the night.

"I can hear its brushes. Shush shish shush shish shush." Ying giggled. "It's like a funny little dog, but it looks like a giant beetle."

Kit bit back her retort, judging it prudent to let the girl get out her nerves with silliness. For now. Ying was no longer the scared orphan peasant girl of three months ago, but she was nonetheless not yet grown. They'd only been in Kamtien City a month. Signing on with a raggedy airskimmer that had seen better days was understandably a new thing for the girl. Kit narrowed her eyes to slits and practiced patience, giving a small swish of her tail now and again.

The moon hid behind its monthly veil, an omen sure to augur success, and Kit would take all the good fortune she could amass, however haphazardly it got tossed her way.

"Enough giggling, Ying. Focus now. The gods would not gift us this junk's proximity if they did not wish us to succeed. We have been hunting for The Sky Lion *for weeks, have we not? And just as we sign on with your new Captain, with* The Sky Pearl, *here is our prey, berthed only a stone's throw away. I told you this was an auspicious post."*

"Easy for you to say, kitty," muttered Ying. "You're not the junior coaler."

"You cannot expect to hire on as senior anything on an airskimmer, girl. You did a fine job at Master Hui's warehouse, yes, but that's now done and behind us. I told you that position was only one step along our journey. It was never meant to be permanent. We found the information we needed from Master Hui's manifests. We found The Sea Lion. *And now, this is the*

next step. We retrieve the item."

Ying made a face. "But they were teaching me to read. I liked it," she finished in a sulk.

"Hush now. No more complaining. If you enact my plan to completion, you shall learn to read and more. You shall become a true adventurer, Ying, free as any of those pirates in your beloved tales. Save your strength now. Be disciplined and we will succeed."

The night stretched on and the berths around them grew steadily quieter.

At her perch in the shadows below the fore bow, her legs and arms wrapped securely around one of the thick anchor cables, Ying kept sullenly silent while Kit stayed vigilant for them both. Finally, the single guard on deck propped herself up against the centre cabin fore wall, and dropped into a doze, one hand on her cutlass. The guard would be thus until the water clocks struck two, signalling this watch's end.

Or so Kit had overheard earlier in the night as she floated in and out and around the portholes of *The Sky Lion,* gleaning information like a fisher netting bright silver prey, plotting and planning.

"Quickly now, girl. The crew sleeps in that cabin there. The deck's clear save for the one asleep on duty. Check your glider gear. We go now."

"You promise they're asleep, kitty?" Ying's voice shrank. "I'm frightened."

"I promise, Ying. Just as kitty trusts you to be strong and agile, you must trust kitty to take care of you."

Ying sniffled one last time, the motion sending the cable swaying in the air. She bit her lip, guilt written across the broad planes of her begrimed face. Then she hoisted her thin body off the cable and let herself fall, unfurling her purloined silk wings with an outward flick of her arms. Kit trailed after, invisible to all, wafting through the cool air without so much as a whisper, watching for unwanted attention and the unseen dangers of errant ropes or cables. As she watched over the girl, Kit thanked the gods for Ying's natural curiosity and athleticism. This would not have worked if she had not picked up so deftly the handful of lessons given her by *The Sky Pearl*'s kindly, maternal second mate.

After a breathtaking few minutes, Ying landed soundlessly aft of the cabin, out of the line of sight of the dozing guard. She grinned, wide and bright, ready for praise.

"Good girl. Stow your wings. That way now, the hatch closest to the stern. They don't post guards belowdecks, but I shall be your lookout nonetheless."

Ying's eyes sparkled with wonder and excitement. "Kitty!" she whispered. "Did you see—"

"Hush. No speaking aloud. Mind only, Ying. Even a whisper could be the end of us here." Kit tempered her tone, reminding herself she needed Ying chastened, not terrified. *"Remember, dear girl? Think of me as you speak and I will hear. We shall have our own secret speech."*

Ying deflated. *"Yes, kitty. I'm sorry. I forgot."*

"You're a brave girl, Ying. Quietly now. Listen to my directions."

Kit led Ying away from the cabin, sending another prayer of thanks to the unseen powers that the item they required had been stowed far from the sleeping crew. Ying's lean arms carried additional muscle built by two weeks shovelling coal into *The Sky Pearl*'s greedy firebox and she had no problem lifting the tight hatch—though the scrape of wood sounded like a cannon shot to Kit's sensitive ears. Ying froze at Kit's warning, her gaze darting to the cabin only twelve feet from her, then away, futilely, for a place to hide.

The creaking of wood and ropes, as the junk swayed gently in the night breeze, held aloft by the engine's lowest output and a touch of dock magic to prevent accidental collisions with neighbouring berths.

"Kitty?"

"It's all right, Ying. No one awakened."

Ying looked down at the section revealed by the open hatchway.

Their luck had run out.

"Everything's packed up to the top! How do I find the treasure, kitty?"

Kit bared her teeth and flattened her ears, cursing her now useless insubstantial form.

"I don't think I can unpack everything without making any noise, kitty. What should we do now? I don't suppose the

treasure is right at the top . . .”

Hearing Ying's unanticipated calm, Kit brought herself up short. She could not allow a farmgirl-turned-junk-coaler of thirteen to show her up. Dignity was the benchmark of superior breeding.

“Unfortunately, Ying, it is not.” Kit spared a glance at the central cabin. *“We shall have to wait until they unload the ship. I'll follow. Perhaps it will be stored in a nearby warehouse and we can obtain it then. Captain said we don't leave Kamtien until day after next.”*

“I guess the gods are having their fun with us, aren't they, kitty. They made retrieving it tonight impossible for us, but they also made The Sea Lion *late into docks so we wouldn't miss the unloading tomorrow. So we'd have another chance. Is that what you mean when you say we should be grateful for what the gods give us?”*

It took Kit a moment to reply. *“Yes, I suppose it is.”* She shook herself all over, resettling her fur. *“Replace the hatch and let's be gone.”*

“I'M TIRED, KITTY. Fei fell asleep again on duty. I was so busy doing double the work again, I didn't even see when Boss sent him packing. But she promoted me to assistant coaler. Even got my extra ration tonight.” Ying dropped onto her meagre pallet, patting her concave stomach, and let out an enormous yawn. “I just want to sleep now.”

“We cannot leave without the treasure.” Kit sniffed, lashing her tail in a slow sinuous arc. *“Or should I say,* I? *Are you no longer concerned with my situation?”*

Ying's eyes opened, widening until Kit could make out each individual blood vessel. She sprang up to sitting, one hand automatically bracing against the low cabin ceiling to avoid hitting her head. “No, kitty. That's not what I—”

“I have mere hours left now to finish my quest, Ying. Hours. There is no time to find someone else to help me. If you refuse me, I am done. I will fade away. A disgrace to my line.” Beyond redemption. Kit twitched her ears, violently.

Ying's mouth hardened as she frowned. “Stop saying things like that. I am not abandoning you, kitty. I'm just tired. That's all. Can't I have a few minutes' sleep before—” She pulled up short. "*Before we sneak off again?*"

"*You're right.*" Kit relaxed her ears and tail. "*Either I trust you or I don't. I apologize, Ying. I'm afraid the . . . timeline has me on edge.*"

"*Oh, kitty, I'm so sorry. I wish I could hold you right now and cuddle you like I used to.*"

Kit shuddered. "*As do I.*" She stretched herself, low and long. "*There's no time for sleep.*"

Ying rubbed at her eyes and put on her third-hand glider gear. "*Are you sure I can't just glide down? That would definitely wake me up.*" She gave a mischievous grin.

Kit reached for patience. "*No, Ying. Between airships is one thing. Out in the open, down to the docks is quite another. The gear is only meant to be used in emergency—*"

"*It's not a toy, I know, I know.*" Ying grumbled to herself as she finished fastening the two belts around her torso, then pulled a pilot's cap on, the leather scraping against her head, newly re-shorn just that morning to combat the heat of the engine room. Kit swivelled her ears at the irritating sound.

Relying on Kit's scouting to avoid her crewmates, Ying slid over the side of the hull and clambered down one of the anchor cables to reach the dock tower and its exterior ladder to the ground. From there, she crept from shadow to shadow, passing warehouses, a tea house, and a noodle shop along her careful path, all dark and shuttered for the night.

"*You're watching for patrols, aren't you, kitty?*"

"*No need, girl. Kamtien City is known to be friendly with pirates. They will not patrol the docks for fear of hurting their coffers.*" Kit registered Ying's uncertain expression. "*Never mind. I promised you adventure, did I not? And here we are, in the heart of pirate territory.*"

"*On land, at least.*" Ying flashed a brief grin.

Kit stopped Ying at a medium-sized warehouse, deep within the maze of the dock area, its massive front door lit variously by handheld lanterns in the grip of what appeared to be guards overseeing a little hive of activity.

"*The gods smile upon us again, Ying. The window's open and the workers are busy at the front. No, don't look. Better you know nothing of shipments moving under cover of night, girl.*"

Ying hauled her slender frame up and through the ground-floor opening, then pressed against the inside wall. The warehouse was really nothing more than an enormous rectangular room, with a high bank of windows, doors at either end, and two set of offices.

Kit thanked the gods the warehouse owner still preferred gas lanterns. It allowed for patchy illumination, which allowed for stealth.

Ying cautiously exited the side office, and Kit led her through stacked wooden crates and barrels, to a flight of stairs at the back wall, retracing her steps from earlier as she followed their prize, unloaded from *The Sky Lion* into its current space. At Kit's insistence, Ying crawled upward on all fours, keeping her profile low. The stairway continued upward to the roof, but Kit directed Ying to stop at the third level, and to enter the room here, the foreman's aerie which spanned the width of the warehouse. Inside, Ying crept, hunchbacked, past one desk and a few hard chairs, toward a low shelf of jute bags in a corner.

"There, Ying. That chest. That's the one."

"It looks like a toy chest, kitty. Like the one a-Ma had a-Bah make for us. There's not even a lock." At a sudden, far off shout, Ying looked over her shoulder at the open doorway. Kit saw the gleam of unshed tears, then decided to ignore it. If the girl was trying not to cry, Kit would not tip the balance.

Ying turned back, sniffling quietly once, and lifted the lid of the chest. She gently rummaged through the jumble, setting items carefully onto the cool floor. Kit's avid gaze combed over each object. Children's clothing, some of it threadbare. Old shoes. Carved toys. Fabric scraps.

"There. That's it. Tuck it inside your shirt and we can go."

Ying frowned. *"But whose toys are these? And the clothes? Why would this chest be here? These are no trade goods. You said we would find treasure fit for a queen. This isn't—"*

"Hush, girl. Didn't I tell you to trust kitty? You must be gone before anyone finds you here. No one will miss it, but we need it to make me whole again."

Ying clamped her lips tight, her expression turning stony, and replaced every article back into the wooden chest, then closed it with a cautious thump. As she turned to exit, she caught the glimmer of a pair of eyes from between two misshapen bags beside the door. She gasped, startling.

"Ignore it." Kit gave a sniff of disdain. *"It is only a clockwork. I heard one of the dockworkers grumble that the warehouse owner can't maintain his clockworks. You're safe."*

Ying nonetheless reached out to touch the riveted metallic frame. "*It doesn't even reach my knees.*" She pivoted one way then the other, trying to measure its dimensions in the tight space. "*I think it's meant to look like a mantis, it even has delicate little antennae and its eyes are faceted. Oh, except it has wheels. How intriguing*!"

"Gods, girl, we do not have time for this. You do not *wish to be caught by workers transferring shipments to a* pirate's *hold."* Kit hissed, she couldn't help it.

"Oh la, uninvited guests." A dark shape stepped out from the shadows, from behind the clockwork guardian, revealing sleek fur, narrowed eyes, and twitching ears. "Shall I tell my owners you're here?"

Ying's face softened in the dim light. "*But kitty, he calls so sweetly. Doesn't he look adorable?"* She stepped toward him, whispering low. "Hello, miao-jai, you meow so prettily. Are you lonely in this big old place? Do you need a cuddle?"

"No need to throw threats, brother." Kit stared, imperiously. "The girl was only exploring. She found some old toys, but she's taken nothing and we are leaving."

"You'd better. We don't suffer invaders here, ghost. Move on. There's nothing for you here. And my owners prefer to keep what's theirs." His tail swished, from one side to the other. "From the ragged look of you, you don't have much time left. I suggest you not waste it fighting my little friend here." His tail caressed the metal guardian's jointed shoulder.

Kit hissed again, keeping her glowering gaze on him though she addressed the girl. *"Ying. Out. Now. He threatens to awaken the clockwork beast."*

Ying snatched back her reaching hand with a startled jump and ran, as light on her feet as any feline might wish. Kit threw a prideful look at the other as she faded out of the room after Ying.

He pinned his ears back and yowled, raising the alarm.

The clockwork beast sprang to life with a whirring whistle and a plume of steam. Its hooded eyes glowed yellow as its head swivelled with eerie grace, antennae twirling to search the reason for its awakening. The dun cat stared at Ying, unblinking, ears still flat against his skull.

Knowing she was useless to defend against his attack, Kit lashed her tail in frustration. *"Ying, away now, quickly. It comes for you."*

Ying scrambled through the doorway. The sawing of her breath grated in Kit's ears.

"Up, you must go up. The clockwork may not be able to climb and the workers are coming this way. Hurry, Ying."

The girl turned right and ran, her feet slapping against the wooden stairs like thunder echoing in the skies. Two flights up, Kit passed through the sole door at the top of the stairway even as Ying yanked it open and tumbled back out into the moonless night. She recovered from her stumble and ran toward the closest edge, untying the straps that kept her wings furled tightly against her arms and sides.

"Stop, Ying! No."

"We're only five floors up." Her chest heaved with every laboured breath. *"I know I can make it, kitty."*

Kit howled and ran ahead of Ying, placing herself in the girl's path, for all that Kit remained invisible to non-feline senses. *"No, foolish girl! There's not enough height for you to catch the wind. You'd be throwing your life away."*

Ying strode through Kit, and shivered to an abrupt halt.

Kit jumped aside, trembling. She looked about in desperation. *"There. The flyers. Take one, Ying, my brave girl. It's your only escape."*

Ying hesitated at the edge of the roof, staring back over her shoulder at the single-person flying mechanicals, parked neatly in a row beneath an awning of bamboo and waxed jute. *"I'd just as likely crash if I tried."* She swivelled to scan the surrounding rooftops. Kit saw her young face clarify with determination. Ying shook out her wings.

"I'm jumping to the next building. It's the only one below this one. The gear will help me, I think. At least I know how to use it. It's the better chance by far."

Kit followed, helpless once more, as Ying launched herself over the edge of the warehouse, heading for the neighbouring rooftop, at least a dozen feet away. The silk wings fluttered uncertainly for a moment. Then two. Ying fell.

Abruptly, she rotated her shoulders and tilted her torso and legs. The wings billowed out, accompanied by Ying's short *whoop.* Just as she spanned the gap, the wind disappeared and the wings reverted to nothing but two bits of fabric strung together with thread and strapped on with hope.

Ying twisted desperately, stretching out to her full length, scrabbling at the overlapping lacquered tiles that created the overhang around the building's four walls. At the last moment, she snagged the head of the sculpted dragon set where two corners of the sloping overhang met. Kit thanked the gods it was sturdily attached to its own beam. It held Ying's weight—though it provided no further solution to her predicament.

"How far up am I, kitty?" Ying's breathing came fast and shallow. *"I can't see the ground in this darkness."*

Kit looked in her stead, noting the girl was right. The ground had all but disappeared in the night's murkiness. *"Too far. You . . . would not land on your feet well."*

Ying sent no reply, but the choking feeling of fear struck Kit in her deepest heart. She startled as though stung by a wasp, then shook herself from ears to tail.

"Well this looks like a difficult spot to get out of."

The voice came from behind Kit. She whirled, cursing her distracted focus. *Of course* the warehouse workers would come searching for Ying. How could Kit forget that?

But it was no common dockworker who met Kit's narrowed green gaze.

"Who's there?" asked Ying, voice wound tight.

"You may call me Leung, little one." The figure sat her flying mechanical with the easy grace of a seasoned flyer. "Though it's lovely of you to ask, I suspect your manners may be misplaced. How will you get down from there, do you suppose?" To Kit's astonishment, the figure shifted as though to look over at Kit herself, her opaque goggles hiding much of her face, as well. "Or are you the one with the plan, cat? Are you spying on my shipments, then?"

"You . . . you can see me?"

"Hmm? Oh, my apologies. I cannot hear your thoughts. But yes, I think I can guess your immediate question. Yes, I see you."

"Please," Ying gasped. "Please, Mistress Leung, can you help me get down?" Ying's hand slipped from the snout of the dragon to its stone pedestal. She fell those scant inches with a little scream, her dangling legs windmilling in alarm.

"Safely," added Kit hastily. *"Say you want to get down* safely, *Ying."*

The girl did as instructed, her voice tremulous and small. Leung shook her head, though only Kit could see it. "No, but I can help you up." She pointed skyward as she looked at Kit with the edges of an amused expression around her goggles.

Above them, a dark shape hovered silently. The bottom of an airship, its engines muffled with magic—expensive magic. Kit's ears swivelled, one pointing slightly forward while the other faced backward. How had she missed this? The ship was small, probably no more than a two-mast'er, but even so . . . She tucked her tail into her body, flicking her gaze back to the mysterious figure.

"Come aboard, little one, and we'll talk."

The end of a rope ladder dropped down, landing on Ying's shoulder with a thud, then fell to a swaying stop just past her feet. The girl let go one hand with a gasp and hooked an elbow over one rung. Huffing with effort, she swung one foot onto another rung, then pushed off the ornamental dragon, motions clumsy from fatigue. The rope ladder swung wide with her momentum. Ying's foot slipped from the ladder, and she jerked to a jarring halt, crying out as her elbow took on her full weight against the pull of gravity.

"Help her," called Kit, though she knew the single-flyer could not support nor fit another person. Nor could her cry reach the mysterious flyer. She whipped her tail in a frenzy of impotence.

Nevertheless, the flyer, Leung, deftly manoeuvred close, angling sideways to keep the various hot pipes of her mechanical away from vulnerable flesh, and reached across to grab the girl's flailing arm, directing it to the ladder. Once Ying was secure, Leung steered away with a small puff of steam, a startling white in the gloom.

After taking a few trembling breaths, Ying began the climb. Kit resisted the insistent urge to travel ahead and scout the airship properly. The stranger had helped Ying, yes, but that did not mean all was safe. Kit's instincts advised her to stay close to the girl.

As soon as Ying came level with the side of the ship, a strong arm curled around her shoulder and pulled her on board in one smooth motion, though Ying's foot caught for a moment on the hull, a dull thud quickly lost to the wind at their altitude. Deposited on the deck by a beefy crew member, Ying slid into a boneless heap. Kit watched, tense, whiskers vibrating, as the crewperson swept the girl up and carried her to the aft cabin, really nothing more than a covered, three-walled shelter. Kit distractedly registered that her estimate of the junk's size was indeed correct.

Despite the lack of ship's running lanterns and moonlight, Kit was confident the crewperson who helped Ying was the only other on board. With a buzzing and whirring, the flyer landed on the foredeck with the softest of thuds. The crewperson hustled over to help their captain divest flying leathers and cap. Kit felt the fur on her tail stand up as Leung approached, still wearing her goggles.

"Ying, stand up, girl. Ying!"

The girl managed to pull herself up to sitting. "What's going on? Ma'am," she added, a clear afterthought.

"You're exhausted, poor thing." Leung settled with an easy litheness on the low-slung camper's chair next to Ying's makeshift pallet of blankets. Ying shifted away slightly.

After a moment, Leung returned her attention to Kit. "You've run her ragged these past weeks, haven't you? Forcing her to join a coaler crew, and she small for her age to begin with. A lonely peasant girl who lost her entire family and her home, victims of plague. And then her favourite barn cat went and got herself killed. A shame how that axe fell right on top of you, wasn't it? But you know, you ought not to have stuck your nose where it didn't belong." She cocked her head to one side. "Didn't anyone ever teach you the limits of curiosity? One would think you'd have learned that lesson the first time."

"I don't understand." Ying wrapped her arms around her up-bent knees, sounding small and wary.

Kit stared at Leung, hard and long, fur and whiskers bristling with outrage and threat.

Leung's lips twitched, just a little. "Oh no, cat, don't misunderstand me. I'm no enemy. In fact, I'm here to do you a favour, one you'd do well to accept, given how little time you have left to claim your next life. Number three, isn't it?" She settled more comfortably. "I do apologize about these," she pointed to her goggles, "but they help me see you better and I'm sure we can agree it's in your best interests that I know where you are at all times, no? Now, what was I saying . . . Oh yes." She folded her hands primly on her lap, though a smirk played around the edges of her expression. "I'm here to take you to your Queen."

The airship shot upward with a purr of its engine. Kit knew that if she were solid, she would have felt the vibrations beneath her paws like a captured sparrow's heartbeats, almost too swift to differentiate one from another. Or perhaps she was feeling her own heart, for real, right now, floundering like a trapped bird.

Kit looked from Ying's shadowed face to the black goggles.

Leung's face smoothed out. "Go ahead. Feel free to explore the ship. It won't take long, but neither will our trip to my fleet." She gestured airily. "Ying can tell me all about herself."

The girl's eyes widened. *"Kitty? What is ma'am talking about?"*

"It's complicated. We don't have time for explanations." Kit paused. *"I apologize. I must determine if we can trust this woman. Trust kitty for now, yes? As kitty trusts you to take care of yourself?"*

Ying straightened her spine, rearranging to sit tailor fashion, arms crossing. "What do you wish to know?" she asked Leung.

Kit lifted her nose and stepped lightly through the aft wall of the sheltered structure, her tail held high, with the smallest of lilts at its very black-tipped end. A low chuckle drifted out to her. Kit prowled around the stern, needled on by something . . . familiar, a scent that caused her to freeze, in order to confirm its origin. There. Yes. Kit puffed up her chest with pride. The Queen knew this junk. She had been here. Leung was telling the truth.

Soon enough, the two-mast'er pulled to a halt at a starboard hull longer than any Kit had ever seen or heard rumour of. The bosun greeted Leung with a crisp salute and a curt "Captain," while a five-person crew swarmed the smaller junk, untying its temporary moorings and puttering off at a steep angle to disappear into the dark sky. Kit perched on the edge of the railing, marvelling at the ship's nine sails and three deck cabins, at its exceedingly efficient—and mostly silent—crew, at the sheer number of able bodies scurrying to and fro on the visible decks. This mighty airship was more than worthy of Kit's admiration. Behind, she heard Ying's exclamation of wonder. Kit alighted on the deck, her insides filling with a burst of pride at the girl's earlier poise and grit.

Leung finished her exchange with the bosun and gestured to her guests before turning on her heel. Trailing after the captain, Ying's gaze darted every which way, her mouth agape and her hands clasped in front of her, knuckles white with the tightness of her grip. Kit followed closely beside, though no one but Leung had marked her presence.

As they descended belowdecks, toward the bow, Kit shook off her maudlin leanings with a tic of her whiskers. Such dramatics were beneath her. They had succeeded, against long odds. Ying was fine, safe as could be expected, a young girl without family nor connections. And this stranger, with her magical crew and magnificent airship, was taking Kit straight to her Queen. Kit would fulfil her quest and claim her right to a third life, with hours to spare, no less.

This was as it should be.

Their strange procession ended inside a cabin that Kit calculated took up a good portion of the bow, with a luxurious profusion of portholes on both walls, and plump furnishings in sumptuous fabrics and exquisite craftmanship. Ying came to an abrupt stop in the middle of the cabin, uncertainty in the line of her bowed shoulders.

"Before you spear me with your glare, cat," said Leung, "you shall know my business with your girl only after your audience with your Queen. It would be tiresome for me to explain anything until afterward, frankly."

Kit swished her tail, whipfast.

Leung motioned with her chin toward a wall. "That way. You'll find her quarters through there. I believe they've started without you."

Kit kept her nose up as she neared Ying. *"My time is here, Ying. Will you keep yourself safe until my return?"*

Leung gestured to the smaller table, topped with stacks of

bound volumes and loose papers. "Take a seat, Ying."

"It's all right, kitty. You can trust me to take care of myself." Ying offered their host a tentative smile as she sat. "Thank you, ma'am."

Leung leaned against the edge of the table, crossing her arms, and looked down at the girl. "Now tell me why you didn't go for one of the flyers on that warehouse roof."

Ying met the captain's intensity with an open and clear expression. "I don't know how to fly one, ma'am. It would've taken far too long to figure it out."

Satisfied, Kit approached the designated wall and walked through without further delay. Leung's low laugh floated to her ears as she exited fully into a narrow compartment, luxuriously appointed. Kit looked upward to find the ceiling just as high as in the captain's quarters, with a few shelves jutting out on opposing walls, just within jumping distance of each other to make a ladder of sorts, if one were in the mood for a challenge. The wood panelling here was just as richly varnished as in the previous room, though one large cushion and a scattering of thick blankets took the place of bed and chairs and tables and desk. Two portholes, set in a vertical line, would give plenty of daylight, Kit saw. For now, however, two small lanterns, set like sconces up high, gave the walls a rich golden glow.

"Nice of you to finally join us."

Kit froze, laying her ears flat against her head. After a breath, she turned slowly to face the interior of the room, tucking her tail in tightly to her feet. A grey cat with black stripes and jade green eyes sat upon a raised dais, watching Kit with cool disdain.

"You certainly like cutting it close, Kit, but you should know One does not like to be kept waiting."

Realizing she was staring, Kit slowly relaxed her entire body and blinked, slowly. "I apologize, my Queen."

"Sit over there, like a good kitty. You are not the only ghost clamouring for an audience tonight."

Kit moved to the side, as commanded, knowing the Queen would brook no more nonsense from her. She settled down with her paws folded underneath herself, and kept her nose up and her spine straight, then artfully curled her tail around herself until the black tip peeked out from her front right paw.

Four ghosts watched Kit for another beat, before turning their attention back to the Queen. She nodded at them in turn, and they each stepped forward to sit behind one object apiece. Kit felt calm envelope her, even as she assessed the black pearl necklace, the fire opal broach, the golden dagger, and the walrus tusk which comprised the other supplicants' offerings. These treasures were all fine and good, of course, but they would not carry the past with them. They did not hold all the cherished memories of one's happiest childhood.

Kit found her patience and waited her turn. She was confident as only a feline could be after a good hunt that she had made the right choice for her tribute.

The Queen stepped down lightly to inspect the treasures before her. Though in reality only medium-sized, She nevertheless seemed to crowd the ghosts as She examined each item with intelligent, green-eyed intensity. Returning to the first ghost and his item, She signalled for him to tell Her his tale.

Kit had eyes only for the Queen, focussing with a force that entirely shut out the stories told by the others in the hopes of winning their Queen's regard. Kit had no interest in comparing herself to them. She wished only to prove herself to the One who truly mattered.

"Kit."

"Yes, my Queen." Kit bowed her head.

"Where is your tribute?"

"With my person, my Queen."

"Go fetch it."

"My apologies, my Queen, but I cannot."

A pause. A heartbeat. A twitch of whiskers.

Kit heard tittering from the others. Her tail lashed, once, twice. The murmurs abated.

"One would think, as your end time dawns tomorrow, that you would have the foresight to bring it with you."

"Yes, my Queen. My apologies, my Queen. In my condition, at this late hour, I am no longer able to carry anything myself."

"Imbecile. Go back and get One's captain to fetch it."

"My Queen, I'm afraid I cannot make myself heard by the captain."

"No matter. She will know what you need."

Kit hesitated for a moment, confused. Then she recalled

herself and gave another bow of her head. The Queen stared, her ears standing straight up. Nevertheless, Kit kept her nose high as she turned and re-entered the captain's quarters through the special hinged door.

Ying now sat with Leung at the dining table, in front of a platter of fruit and an honest-to-gods porcelain tea service. The captain took a sip from a teacup so finely wrought, the dark tea within shaded the outside of the porcelain. As she replaced the cup on its dish, she said, "It's time, Ying."

"Oh! Kitty, Captain says you need this?" Ying pulled out the worn grey scrap secreted in her tunic, then seemed to realize she could not hand it to Kit. The girl looked uncertainly at Leung.

The captain smiled, showing tobacco-stained teeth. "Push it through that cat door, there, the one cut near the bottom of the wall, if you please, Ying, and then our two cats will continue their business and we may continue ours."

"Kitty, oh kitty, Captain says they're the biggest pirate fleet in the skies, kitty! And Captain heads it all! One hundred airships! All kinds of airships!" Ying jumped up and all but skipped over to the wall, shoving Kit's offering through the little swinging door, hinged at its top. *"Captain said if you decide to stay, then I can stay, too! As long as I prove my worth. She said they have need of smart girls who can be quiet and fit into tight spaces. But it all depends on your Queen, she says."*

Kit shook her head, trying to clear her ears of Ying's mental shouts. *"Didn't kitty promise you a life of adventure?"* she replied distractedly, exiting back into her audience with the Queen. Ying's cry of glee cut off abruptly as the door swung shut once more.

Kit found herself alone with the Queen. She peered at the back of the space, discovering a normal door with another hinged opening inset near the bottom. Oh. Regaining her composure, Kit ventured to speak. "Were they deemed worthy, then, my Queen? Have they been restored to their next lives?"

But the Queen ignored Kit, focussing instead on the ragged grey scrap in front of Her paws. "You did it." She looked up, turning her head to one side. "You found it. You found One's Mischief."

Kit approached, tail rising cautiously. "Yes, my Queen." She gathered her courage. "When the family died, I became the only one who remembered where it was, and I knew it was my last chance to right a wrong I'd done to Your Majesty—" Kit hesitated, gathering her resolve to speak only the truth to her Queen. "The very best of friends, all those years ago."

The Queen remained silent, though her ears relaxed a fraction. The left one even pointed forward slightly.

Kit continued. "So I . . . Forgive me, my Queen. It seemed appropriate that I be the one to retrieve it from the family's things—Ying's family. Though the girl was too young to remember me, from before, and I saw no need to tell her. I guided the poor girl to leave her family's farm, after their terrible deaths, to follow the trail to Kamtien City, where I knew a distant cousin resided. Ying's mother had sent them a trunk of old things for their little ones, but we discovered that the trunk had been sold at auction, contents sight unseen. That led us to a merchant named Hui and then to a three-masted airskimmer, a trading junk that plied the routes between Kamtien and the smaller coastal towns, named *The Sky Lion*. We found Ying a post on another trader junk and—"

"One finds that your tale leaves a lot to be desired, Kit. Though One may be persuaded that the closeness to your fading is the cause for your haste." The Queen paused. "But let One be frank. You cajoled and terrorized the girl in order to manipulate her into doing your bidding. Is that not accurate?"

"Yes, my Queen."

"You caused the illness of a boy in order to get the girl onto that junk and take his place, is that not correct? And then bullied the girl into disobeying captain's orders and crew curfew, and to committing theft?"

"Yes, my Queen. If I may, my Queen, I did hear that the boy recovered rather quickly. Just not quickly enough to regain his position."

"And One supposes that was part of your plan, as well?"

"Yes, my Queen."

The Queen assessed Kit in a weighted silence. Finally, She twitched her nose. "Though you have clearly grown soft, coddling children and such, One is willing to admit to being impressed with the breadth of your plans and the lengths to which you went in order to secure One's tribute."

Kit straightened up infinitesimally, careful to keep her ears and tail still.

"But hear One carefully, Kit. One will not forget your foolishness."

"My Queen?" Kit could not keep her ears from flicking. "Forgive me, I do not understand."

The Queen blinked at Kit. "You say it was all a life time ago, but not for *me*, Kit. I reached eighteen years on my *first* life, which is precisely why I was made Queen—while you attained your second life and stayed busy pretending to be a barn cat. Hiding from my wrath. And rightfully so. We were supposed to rule together, that was our pact. You foolish, vainglorious thing, dying for a whim of curiosity and losing me my little Mischief in the bargain."

Kit took heart from the change in address. The queen spoke as herself.

Still, Kit remained wary. Her friendship with the other cat was a long time ago now.

The queen rubbed her nose and then her forehead against Mischief. Kit took up her courage once more. "Forgive me, my . . . friend. I should never have left you to see what those boys were up to. I was ignorant and arrogant in that ignorance, and it cost me not only my first life and the pact we made—but also, you."

Kit weighed her natural pride and arrogance against the possibility before her, and abruptly realized how insubstantial the former were, how misleading. For all that she'd planned this very reunion for months, Kit only now registered the very real pain in her oldest friend's eyes. "Please. Please forgive me."

The Queen looked down and batted her toy mouse between her paws a few times, seemingly content to let Kit stew in uncertainty. "I lead a charmed life here, you know, Kit, for all that pirate ships are not always the safest. I won't have you challenge that with your recklessness and pure irrational need for adventure."

Kit softened her ears. "I imagine a pirate fleet ought to see more than a lifetime's worth of adventure, my Queen. I would stay, if you allow it."

Kit's best friend met her gaze. "Then, yes, you are forgiven."

Between one blink and the next, Kit came back.

"Welcome back, Kit."

"Thank you, my Queen." Kit paused. "Thank you, Kat."

They entered the captain's quarters, one after the other.

"Kitty!" With a *whoop*, Ying scooped Kit up into her arms and stroked Kit's black-striped grey flanks with affection, rubbing her face against her beloved barn cat's velvety dark pink nose. "I missed you so much."

The Queen was satisfied.

Kit's world was made right once again.

THE MOTLEY CREW

REBECCA BRAE

CAPTAIN NEREYDA HAD just relieved a merchant ship of its cargo of spices and cloth. It was a short haul vessel, small and only half stocked. Still, it was a bloodless exchange for a moderate profit and a bonus find on the way to a bigger prize. There were rumours of a ship carrying a healthy church tithe in these waters. Sadly, she wasn't the only one looking. They'd already avoided one piratical associate.

Her crew was prying open the last big crate in their hold when there was a thud from inside and it suddenly shifted sideways, knocking two crew off their feet. The lid slid half off on its own. Nereyda stepped back, eyes narrowed.

"Thundering Gods!" Old Sumati, her quartermaster, swore as he dusted himself off. "I told you I heard something in there."

A low growl crept between the wooden slats. Nereyda met each of the nearby crew members' eyes, pressed a silencing finger to her lips, and gestured for everyone to get out. Whatever was in there, it was big enough to move a solid wooden crate and clearly agitated. This was not the kind of loot anyone needed.

Captain Nereyda waited for her six crew to evacuate the hold before following them up the ladder. As they retreated, so did the light from their lanterns. A dark shape crept from shadow to shadow, gaining ground, silently and quickly. The growling had stopped, but the fine hairs prickling the back of Nereyda's neck warned that death was only a breath away. Twin emerald stars flashed in the darkness just below her feet.

She leapt up the last few rungs, rolling onto the deck as her crew slammed the hatch door closed. There was a solid *thunk* as the creature rammed the weather-hardened wood. The hinges groaned but held as Nereyda slipped the iron lock into place and sat on the door when it bucked under the onslaught. Others joined to weigh it down until the banging stopped and the only sounds were the wind in the canvas and the comforting creak of the ship's old boards.

The other hatches to the ship's belly had been closed for the raid. Nereyda made sure they were secure and gathered her crew at the main mast. All but the galley and captain's quarters were below deck, along with most of their food and water stocks. They could last three, maybe four days on what they had above. Shore was four days away if the wind remained fair and no detours were necessary, but it wasn't a settled coast, nor one she was familiar with. Dangers all around and most certainly below. Finding that tithe ship would have to wait.

"Right. New rule. We open all crates on deck, with weapons ready." Nereyda nodded to her quartermaster. "And when Old Sumati says he hears something, we bloody believe him."

There were some snickers and jibes about the wisdom of the ancients before the old pirate in question shushed them. "Cap, what in the nine hells was that big bastard?"

"Thundering Ass. Where's me cap. Balls to the boards." Zahmet, a mangy black bird, landed awkwardly on Nereyda's shoulder and continued to spout profanities until she gently grabbed its beak and gave it the stink-eye. It uttered a quiet "awk" as she released it and judiciously decided to preen the few wing feathers it had.

"Best guess . . . some kind of jungle cat. I've seen a few dead ones. Never heard of one that can meld with shadows the way that one can. But those eyes . . . even on the dead. Unmistakable." She shook her head and refocused on her crew. "We'll set armed watches at the hatches. Two crew at all times. It's four days to shore. We'll ration, sleep in my quarters and the galley in shifts, and stay ready. You know from the wounds

Limpy Jo inflicts, even small cats aren't to be messed with. I've heard tales of these big ones wiping out whole villages . . . as in, multiple villages. Their hides are thick and they're quick as lightning. Even if you're lucky enough to land a shot, chances are you'll only piss it off."

Sumati organized the crew into watch and work shifts while Nereyda took directional readings and plotted a course. By the time night fell, they were under way, wind filling their sails, even if a measly chip of hard tack and swig of rum did nothing for their stomachs. They were on edge, jumping at every break of wave on the bow and snap of rope. Every so often there was a croaking "Bung the bilge" or "Curse me timbers" from above. Captain Nereyda manned the helm, fingers wrapped protectively around the smooth-worn handles on the ship's wheel, eyes locked on the stars marking their way. She'd made it, lashed to the wheel pedestal, for three days without sleep in a spring storm not that long ago. She could do four.

Though the moon was only a sharp sliver, its light reflected off the water's surface and diffused a soft glow over the *Destiny's Scourge*. From her elevated vantage point, Nereyda could see everyone, sleeping or working on deck or in the masts. She loved nights when the wind was steady and the sky cloudless. Her world, both sea and sky, was endless and beautiful. It felt as though she could steer the ship up into the stars and beyond.

An ice-cold shiver ran down her spine and she focused her attention on the deck. A sleek, black shape slid over the railing near where Sumati was sleeping. The old man flicked a hand across his cheek to wipe away a stray drop of water. Nereyda held her breath as the cat crouched and bared its teeth. Sumati slept on and the creature melded into the next shadow.

The beast was wet and left behind a shining pool of water—it must have squeezed out of one of their bilge pump holes and then waited until dark to climb up the damn side. It was wily and much bigger than expected. How it had made it out of a hole that could barely fit a child, she'd never know. The dead jungle cats she'd seen were lean, orange and black spotted creatures, the size of an average woman. This one was powerfully muscled and longer than Sumati, who was six feet tall.

If she raised the alarm now, the cat would spook and her crew wouldn't have time to find it, let alone kill it before it killed them. She saw one of the hatch watch groups notice its movement and quickly motioned for them to stay still and silent. The great cat slunk by them, noting their awareness, but only letting out a huff of warning. It kept raising its head to sniff the air. It couldn't be looking for their salt pork barrels, as those had all been in the hold. Unless it had finished them and was after more . . .

The cat moved swiftly and deliberately from end to end of the ship, following the railing with nose to the wind. It climbed the masts and walked along the yard beams as if it had been born on a ship, instantly compensating for every wave and gust with no pause in its gait. Each watch and work party passed on the captain's cue not to engage.

An expectant silence pervaded the deck. Passersby would have believed it a ghost ship, afloat only to carry its dead to a lonely port. Nereyda whispered a prayer to the gods of the sea that their fate would not be so.

The crew balanced on knife-edge tension, hearts thundering in their chests as they clutched swords, daggers, and the few pistols they had. Nereyda's heart thudded along with theirs as the cat deftly maneuvered around and over each person. Her pistols hung heavy and useless at her sides. The sea was not rough, but the rolling waves this far out meant that the wheel had to be held constantly to keep their rudder true.

She studied their uninvited guest. It wasn't behaving like a creature stalking prey. She'd seen Limpy Jo hunting mice. Cats were stealth killers, sneaking up, pouncing with deadly precision, then maybe playing with their dinner a bit before the inevitable carnage. This giant of the species was keenly aware of the crew, defensive and certainly nervous, but it wasn't hunting any of them.

It was tracking something though. She was certain of it. The way it occasionally stopped and stared intensely in a direction, mouth open, sensing with its nose and tongue as if it could already taste its quarry.

Nereyda stiffened as it passed by her for the third time. It kept returning to the same spot at the railing on the quarterdeck. Stretching as far over the side as it could, sniffing, growling. She briefly contemplated pushing it off, but there was no way she was fast enough, and the cat could obviously swim. It would find a way back on, probably in a worse mood.

The cat's huge black head turned and glared as if privy to her thoughts.

Nereyda tore her gaze away from the emerald eyes and focussed on the wheel. Some creatures considered direct eye contact a challenge and that was not a fight she wanted to pick in the middle of the sea. Her three-masted ship had never felt like a confined space before.

The cat growled when she looked away. The deep rumble reverberated through Nereyda's body, rousing a primal fear rooted in the ancestral soul of every prey animal. She risked a glance back. It briefly held her gaze, swung its head to focus on the same point on the shifting horizon, then turned back to stare at her, blinking slowly without fully closing its eyes. There was an unexpected level of intelligence within, belying its animal form.

On a whim, she set a course in its direction of interest. The cat sat on its haunches, head raised, sniffing, whiskers twitching. The muscles under its gleaming coat remained taut, but the cat's tail curled around to cover its front paws. From her time with Limpy Jo, Nereyda recognized it as a sign of relaxed waiting.

She carried on that bearing for a good while, then veered off, back to her original course. The tail stiffened and twitched. The fur on its back bristled as the cat peered over its shoulder and let out a piercing snarl. Nereyda resumed the cat's course.

Maybe it could smell land. Maybe its home was near. She'd come across one uncharted island that seemed to spring whole-formed from the depths. Maybe there was another just over the horizon. Whatever it was, it had to be closer than four days. Even the gods' noses wouldn't smell anything four days out.

Dawn broke, red as blood smeared across the horizon, and the crew was able to move around, slowly and at a respectable distance from the furry stowaway. No one dared approach the quarterdeck where the captain and cat were holed up. The cat shifted position every so often, making it loudly clear when Nereyda needed to adjust their bearing.

The day wore on in this uneasy truce, with the crew and

captain using hand signals and short whistles to communicate. The cat's ears flicked back at the sounds and movement, but it remained fixated on a mysterious destination. Through a stroke of luck or, as some crew believed, through their witch captain's powers, Zahmet stole a chunk of hard tack and stayed airborne long enough to drop it on the wheel's pedestal. Nereyda shooed the bird away before the cat's interest was piqued, and gratefully ate the crunchy offering as quietly as possible.

By dusk, a low bank of clouds gathered overhead and the wind picked up. Though cold and blustery, it was just the weather Nereyda wanted. More wind in their sails meant quick travel, and as long as the storm didn't grow enough to kick up monstrous waves, they were golden. A whistle from the crow's nest signalled a ship sighting, and her lookout pointed to a dark spot on the horizon.

Nereyda stared at the cat whose nose was aimed at the other ship. Its posture was rigid, lip slightly curled with one long, sharp fang gleaming in the dying light.

"Well, blast me, you furry bastard. Is that what you've got us headed for?"

The cat ignored her, its whole being focused on the distant dot.

Few ships could outrun the *Destiny's Scourge* and even fewer had captains more savvy than Nereyda about the ways of the sea. She was confident she could run down any ship in the long chase but eyeing the bristling cat focused on its prize, she was also certain she didn't want to test its patience.

She passed a quiet word to get Glivers positioned at the bow watch. It would be a long cold night for him, but he had the best ear for waves breaking across a shoal. She steadied her own nerves with another nip of rum and let her ship run with full canvas into the night, tacking for as long as the cat would allow to gain speed. Its questing nose was the truest compass she'd ever used.

Dawn whispered over calm waters before they fully caught up with the ship. The crew of the small bilander were frantically adding sail, but it made little difference at this gentle hour.

Nereyda ordered their Old Roger raised atop the main mast. Its rich black background emphasized the white dagger piercing a scarlet heart with three drops of blood. Sumati was ready at the bow with the nine-pounders loaded and primed. As the bow rose on a swelling wave, his arm dropped abruptly and the cannon belched a broad plume of smoke, hammering backwards in its cradle.

Thankfully, the great cat took this onslaught of sound and fury in stride. It practically vibrated as it stared at the target ship, unconcerned about anything the captain or her crew did. Small mercies. Nereyda eagerly scanned the rigging of the bilander through her glass as the last of the smoke cleared.

The grapeshot load had mostly missed, as to be expected at this range, though she was gratified to note the yard arm of the top sail listing at an odd angle, and a flurry of sailors grappling with dangling ropes that had been in well enough order a few seconds before. As she watched, the sailors abandoned the rigging and the ship struck its colours.

She flashed Sumati a high sign, indicating another successful surrender. Some of the knots in her gut loosened. She'd built her success using speed and timing to put their targets in no-win positions fast enough that they surrendered without any blood shed on either side. Much of her crew's loyalty relied on her ability to bring them coin and not bloody deaths at sea.

With well-timed hand signals to her crew, and their deft adjustments to the hundreds of lines controlling the sails, she brought her ship to within a stone's throw of the bilander's rail. Every free hand not occupied on the sails was armed and ready. Three of the huskiest brandished grappling hooks that would be used to lock the ships together for the raid.

Lightly loaded, the smaller ship's rail was almost level with their own, but her elevated position on the quarterdeck gave her a split second's advance warning as canvas covered bundles on the decks shifted and revealed a full squad of soldiers, lifting heavy muskets.

She shouted a warning and flattened herself to the deck behind the heavy pedestal that backed the ship's wheel. Chips of solid oak peppered her, and she heard one shot whip by her head. She pulled out her pistols, flipped open the priming pan covers, and cocked the hammers. Screams broke out on the deck below and aloft. They were shooting her sailors!

A snarl like the sound of ripping canvas under gale-force winds echoed her fury, and she turned to see the cat rise from its crouch by the rail and leap over the side. It hung in midair, seemingly defying gravity. The bilander's soldiers were busy reloading. Someone on their quarterdeck raised a pistol. She rose and fired on the run. Once, twice. They went down, either hit or taking cover.

The cat landed, not with a furious splash in the water as she'd expected, but by digging its claws into the side of the rail. One paw after the other failed to find solid purchase and gouged pale lines in the sea-rotted wood—all but the last foreleg. Several hundred pounds of cat dangled improbably over the heaving sea.

She dove again for cover behind the solid bulk of a capstan as the first shot of the next musket volley rang out. A little more ragged than the first, but still tight and fast. No merchant carried this many trained soldiers. What in Poseidon's darkest realms had they stumbled on? She hurriedly reloaded and primed her pistols. More shrieks rang out across the water. She tried to close her ears to the sounds of her crew's slaughter. But the screams continued well past the end of the volley. And kept going.

She popped up for a quick glance and stayed up. There would be no third volley. None aimed their way, at least. The cat scythed through the massed soldiers on deck. Blood sprayed and bodies dropped as it passed. A few managed to draw swords and strike. Two closest to the bow actually got shots off, but nothing slowed the cat's onslaught. Everyone that had been standing on the quarterdeck was already dead.

A few of her crew returned fire, but most realized, as she had, that this was no longer their fight. Finished with the soldiers, the cat took to the rigging and systematically hunted down all the sailors. A couple leapt to temporary safety in the sea. One hit the water badly and never resurfaced. The cat disappeared below-decks, where muffled screams tracked its progress.

Nereyda joined her crew on the deck as Sumati directed those unhurt to help the wounded to the galley and start repairs. There was a caw from the mast followed by, "Swab the decks and blow your holes."

"Shut up, you daft bird," hissed Old Sumati. "If that beast comes back up, I swear I'll make sure it eats you first." He turned to Nereyda, eyes wide with shock. "Reckon we'd better push off and haul sail while we can. Forget the loot. I'll be fine with keeping my life."

"Agreed." Nereyda flinched as a sailor erupted from a hatch on the bilander and threw himself overboard. The screams were swiftly abating, and a terrible silence settled over the ship. "Well, a few got away." She glanced overboard and grimaced at the bloodied water and circling fins. "Briefly."

She watched as Mad Gilly tried to rouse Auntul, one of their new recruits from the last port. She rolled him over and Nereyda stared for a long time at the gaping hole where his face used to be. "Get everyone to their posts, Sumati."

Nereyda piloted the *Destiny's Scourge* a few hundred yards away and signalled for her crew to drop sails again. Sumati joined her on the quarterdeck. A worried frown creased his leathery forehead when she motioned for him to take the helm.

"Hold her here. I'm taking the ship's boat over." His frown deepened and she sighed. "Look, I saw the cat's wounds. It's not long for this world and I doubt there's anyone left to give me trouble."

One of her quartermaster's bushy grey eyebrows shot up. "It's not worth it. I . . ."

"Oh, it will be." She ground her teeth. "It has to be carrying something valuable that someone thought they could slip by us on an unassuming vessel."

Sumati's disapproval remained unchanged and she spat out, "They signalled surrender, dammit! Then they did this . . ." She swept her hand to indicate their deck, slick with her crew's blood. "There's something there and I'll be damned if I'm leaving without it. Auntul's dead. Iylena took a bad shot to the leg. At best she'll only lose it and not her life. How many others? The crew needs this. I need this. Besides, when have you ever known me to pass up an opportunity or mystery? If I die, the ship's yours. How's that for incentive?"

Sumati blew out an exasperated breath and shook his head. "You'll never live to see my age if you keep this up, Cap."

"Who wants to live forever?" Nereyda patted his shoulder and called Mad Gilly over, her consummate partner in crime and other fun things.

On hearing the plan, a wide grin emphasized the rakish scar running down Gilly's cheek and across her lips. "You're my favourite captain."

"I'm the only captain crazy enough to hold your interest for longer than one voyage."

"Aye." Gilly paused. "We'll blow the hull too, right? If someone happens across this massacre and it gets tied to us, it could put a real damper on business. With this rep, we'd have to fight every bloody time we take a ship." She pulled a sizable gunpowder pouch and long fuse from somewhere in her skirts. "I came prepared."

"I expected nothing less." Nereyda snorted and took her arm. "We can scuttle it from the hold. Let's get Auntul onto the boat. Lad deserves a proper send off."

They made it over to the bilander in good time and hefted Auntul's body onto the deck. They unceremoniously dumped the dead soldiers overboard to clear the quarterdeck and gently laid Auntul beside the wheel.

"Fair winds and calm seas." Nereyda tucked a gold coin into his pocket.

Gilly held his hand and said a prayer to her god.

Night fell as they worked, and the wind began to pick up. Nereyda lit a small lantern, which she held far away from Gilly's volatile skirts while they searched for the hatch to the cargo hold. It didn't take long to find, and when no signs of life, human or catlike, presented themselves, Mad Gilly led the way down.

There were a few bodies scattered about. From the bloodied clothing, it looked like a well-off merchant and a couple of sailors had tried to hide, pushing a crate against a man-door leading to the rest of the lower deck. The door was shattered at waist height. Gilly stopped to investigate the crate, studiously ignoring the severed arm to one side, while Nereyda moved to a larger crate at the other end. She froze when her light picked up the edge of a large paw.

When the limb didn't move, she raised her lantern and saw the jungle cat sprawled on a heap of splintered wood and black hides. It was nearly invisible amongst the furs, its blood-caked chest raising and lowering unevenly, nose burrowed in the pelts. There were ones as large as it, and tiny ones, belonging to youngsters who must have been barely out of the womb. It was then that Nereyda noticed the cat's belly, teats swollen and unused.

The cat made no move toward her. Indeed, it seemed to have lost track of anything but those barren remnants of once vibrant lives and times.

Nereyda's heart gave an extra hard thump and sunk in her chest. The poor thing must have been tracking the scent of these pelts, either hoping to find her family and friends alive, or knowing they were dead and seeking vengeance. Both possibilities were tragic.

She glanced at Gilly. Her companion had seen their erstwhile guest and was making her way to the ladder dragging a nondescript chest. She was straining under the weight.

Nereyda turned back to the cat and, against her better judgement, spoke. "I know I'm crazy, but I'd feel bad not saying something after what you've been through. It isn't fair to you—and your family or whoever they were, didn't deserve their ends either—but I'm sending this ship to the bottom of the sea, along with all its horrors and sorrow. For what it's worth, I'm sorry."

The cat grunted and pawed at a hide, digging itself deeper into the pile.

Nereyda took that as acceptance, slowly laid a gold coin on the floor as near as she dared, and then walked away. They could blow the hull from another cabin before they left. The fuse should be long enough to allow time to get out of the immediate blast zone and hopefully onto their boat. There was no need to disturb the cat's vigil.

Gilly grabbed her arms as soon as she saw them on the ladder, hauled her out of the hold, and dropped the hatch door closed. "I've secured the other doors and hatches. Let's blow this rotten bucket."

Nereyda snorted and decided not to remind her how well the securing had gone last time. Gilly wasn't happy about the change in location for the scuttling but had worked with the captain long enough to recognise when she wasn't open to discussion.

They set the charge under the crew quarters in the cable store, tucked between a coil of thick rope and the hull. It was more forward than they wanted, but still a vulnerable area and well below the water line. Nereyda ordered Gilly back to the deck before she lit the fuse and then sprinted for the ladder. She was halfway up when the shockwave slammed into her. Nereyda's head cracked one of the rungs as she fell. Before she could sit up, Gilly appeared out of the smoke and tossed her over her shoulder. She climbed the half-broken ladder and made it topside before the ship had even begun to list.

The sea was rough and climbing down the wet rope to the boat was touchy work. Nereyda's vision was swimming from the knock to her head. Twice she slipped and barely caught herself before sliding into Gilly, who had gone first with the chest firmly lashed to her waist. They eventually clambered aboard the rocking vessel, thankful the storm had forced the sharks deeper.

Nereyda grabbed an oar and rowed alongside Gilly, watching the merchant ship slowly keel and begin to sink. The swells grew until she could only intermittently see the hull, and then finally, night and the sea swallowed all trace of the doomed ship. The journey back was challenging, and their muscles burned by the time they set foot on their own deck.

Mad Gilly triumphantly opened the chest she had rescued and the crew ooed and awwed over the glistening contents—all finely cut gems and gold bars. It wasn't a royal fortune, but certainly wealth enough to keep the ship running and crew happy for a long while. No loot could erase all that had happened, but maybe it would buy them some good memories to replace this day, and enough rum to deaden the rest.

Nereyda collapsed on her bed, soaking wet and fully clothed. She had neither the energy nor will to pluck the slivers of wood from her calf that she'd acquired in the explosion or examine the swelling lump on her forehead. A deep, exhausted sleep overwhelmed her the moment she dragged the blanket over her shivering body.

NEREYDA AWOKE IN darkness with a great weight pressing on her legs. Thinking it was a nightmare, she didn't struggle, but closed her eyes and whispered, "Wake up. Wake up. Wake up."

She cracked an eye open and was greeted with the same darkness and weight. The ship rocked back and forth, so the storm was ongoing. The wet shirtsleeves clinging to her skin implied she hadn't been asleep long. Had a beam cracked and fallen on her?

The lantern fixed to the post beside her bed was just within reach. She lit it, prepared for the worst, and saw the unimaginable. The damn jungle cat was sprawled across the bottom half of her bed, drenched torso and head resting on her legs. It blinked in the light, stuck its back leg straight up in the air, turned to lick a wound there, and then settled down on top of her again.

A rumbling purr vibrated her legs, and the bed, and probably half her ship. How in the deepest hells was she supposed to explain this new crewmate to the rest, let alone the disreputable port authorities they dealt with? Nereyda snuffed the lantern and decided that was a problem for another day.

WHITI TE RA
(LET THE SUN SHINE)

GRACE BRIDGES

THE YELLOW CAT balanced in the bottom of the gently swaying boat. It was a fine summer day on Lake Rotorua; little clouds scudded by far above in the endless firmament. Sunshine herself kept her eyes on the three humans who watched the fishing rods braced against the stern. One of the humans was Sunshine's own person, which was why she'd come along. Well, that, and the potential offerings of fish guts.

The sun grew warm and she lidded her eyes for a moment. Light filtered strong and red. Then something shifted, and she observed the humans to see if they'd noticed.

Graeme gestured towards the city shoreline. "I say we should go back and grab some fish and chips, or maybe one of those fancy chicken and brie pies they have on the corner of the park."

"You're making me hungry!" Tiger rubbed at his stomach and laughed. "But the last time I went in there, the Aussie tourists had been through and eaten everything except the rum balls."

"To be fair, we don't always have marauding bands of Aussie tourists," said Graeme.

Harley eyed the surface of the lake. "I haven't tried raking up the fish with my feet yet."

"We've got time. Do you want to?" said Graeme. "It's January, after all, there should be something here to catch. The lake is warm enough."

"Should be, yeah, with the sun shining on it all day. Not warm enough to get in, though. I brought my swimming togs for nothing." Tiger shaded his eyes and stared out at the water. "I think I see more fish activity a little farther over that way."

Harley nodded. "Let me try it with Sunshine."

"You're having me on. Cats don't like water." Graeme side-eyed Sunshine and she ignored him deliberately.

"She has the same gift as I do, from the taniwha. We were running around on the lake earlier today. My cat is a water-walker, just like me."

Tiger frowned. "Your cat? I thought she was a stray."

"I've been feeding her," said Harley, "and then I found out she has this gift, y'see. We belong together."

Sunshine's heart grew oddly warm and she rubbed her face on Harley's ankle.

"This I'd like to see." Graeme clambered forward and flicked at the controls—turning the start dial so the engine purred like a huge cat. Then he pulled the little steering wheel to one side. The floor tilted to a slight angle, and Sunshine leaned into it to stay firmly upright as the breeze picked up with their movement.

In a few minutes, the motor eased off, and the boat fell silent, settling into the rhythm of the lapping waves. Graeme turned from the controls and grinned.

Harley sighed, sat on the stern, and looked at Sunshine. "Our turn for a run out."

Sunshine didn't fully understand what the words meant, but she knew what Harley had in mind. Her person's wrinkly bare feet slid from their jandals, swung over the edge and touched the water, dipping in and out a little—until Harley stood up and in one fluid movement launched into a run across the waves, never wetting more than the soles of the feet.

The cat blinked and bounded in pursuit. One great leap landed her on the water, where she sank in only a little, but still shuddered. She coiled her powerful hind legs and leaped again in the ballet of a feline gallop.

Gallop is such an unsophisticated word. I'm not a horse,

after all.

Oh. The words were back again in full force, because she was using her gift. She sped up and ran circles around Harley, who laughed.

"Where are the fish, my Sunshine? Let's scare some up for our tea."

Back in the boat, Tiger and Graeme pointed and stared.

The two of them continued their swift dance on the water as Sunshine's mind grew sharp. When she blinked, the sunlight made her eyelids glow again, and she recognised the same fire from the distinctly cat-like creature of flame who gave her this ability.

She looked around her as she frisked on the waves, peering at the distant lakeshores and Graeme's boat, the *Funky Pūkeko*. They scared a pair of black swans into flight, and Harley giggled again.

Where are the fish? Sunshine glanced down into the water she skimmed over. Silver glints passed far below, not near enough to catch, but perhaps they could be herded back towards the *Pūkeko* and the fishing rods. She dodged back and forth on the surface, never once stopping because she would sink, and the trout flipped around, reflecting from their shiny scales.

"I'm done," Harley huffed between panting breaths. "Back to the boat for me."

Good idea. Sunshine followed along and leaped onto the prow as Harley gripped the ladder on the stern and rolled over into the floor, curling up and forcing long, slow inhalations and exhalations. Easing her way around the little windshield, Sunshine joined the humans, taking her place on the pilot's seat, and watched as Graeme and Tiger set up their rods again. Carefully, she licked every drop of lakewater from her feet, and cleaned the places where it had splashed her belly fur. *Yuck.*

Presently, Harley sat up. "I'm too old for these sorts of shenanigans. I'll admit, sometimes I wonder why I have to run to make it work."

A rumble sounded across the lake and echoed between the low hills of the caldera's circle. All three humans and the cat glanced up. Mount Ngongotaha brooded darkly as it always did in the afternoon, and farther away, fearsome Tarawera basked in its dose of sun. Both volcanoes were quiet; the rumbling did not come from them. The sky was clear of all but the tiny white clouds here and there.

Good, we're not going to get rained on. Sunshine paused to lick her shoulder.

Graeme gripped his rod. "That wasn't the sky."

Harley frowned and looked to Tiger. "What do your eyes tell you?"

"I saw something move, but it was somehow below." He leaned over and peered into the depths of the water. "But it's too dark to see very far down."

Tiger's gift of powerful sight was still dependent on human levels of light, unlike cat eyes. Sunshine preened. *I'm the only actual feline here, Tiger-boy.*

There was another rumble, closer this time, from directly below. Harley staggered upright to join the others. "Quake!"

The water heaved and the boat tipped almost perpendicular. The three humans in the stern vanished, upended into the water, but Sunshine dug her claws into the seat cushion and hung on as the world spun.

In moments, gravity reasserted itself. The boat splashed back down on its hull, empty now except for Sunshine herself. She raised herself cautiously on all fours. Waves still pitched this way and that, but what had caused them to tip up so badly?

Sunshine turned towards the front of the boat.

A creature rose before the bow, a delicate vision in swirling water, the shape of a sea-dragon, a manaia, formed entirely of the hated aqueous liquid. It towered high, its neck curving back around while it inspected Sunshine. Its beak was almost as big as the *Funky Pūkeko.*

"Taniwha!" Tiger's scream carried across the water.

Sunshine licked her lips and stared wide-eyed. The great head bent closer to the *Pūkeko's* blue and black trim, and the cat reverted to pure instinct and panicked. She bounced around the cockpit, seeking escape; there was none except over water, and her cat-brain screamed a determined *no* to that option even though part of her remembered it held no danger for her.

Careening across the dashboard, her back legs hit something that clicked. The engine hummed to life and the little motorboat spun into a circle. Sunshine clung to the pilot's seat, mindless fear engulfing her spirit.

A flash of gold passed by above—was it the sun, whirling in the sky?

Sunshine blinked, and clarity returned, even in the midst of the motor's struggling roar, the water sluicing by too close for comfort, the unpleasant G-forces exerted by the spinning.

It was the dragon. Tama-Nui-te-Ra, Sunshine called him, or just Te Ra, though she had no proof he was really the sun-god. Golden wings whooshed by her, and this time she distinctly felt their breeze although the creature was more or less incorporeal.

"Haere atu koe!" roared the golden taniwha. *Be gone.*

The water manaia rumbled something back that was lost in the sound of rushing waves. It opened its beak, and a long tongue of liquid snaked out above the *Pūkeko*, aiming for the dragon.

Te Ra breathed fire. Hot and cold met in a hiss of steam right above where Sunshine held the bucking boat by her claws.

Let the taniwha fight, Sunshine had other things to worry about. Glancing over the edge of the boat, she spied two swimmers in the water—Tiger and Graeme. They were strong young men and they could swim. Harley, of course, must have started running to keep above water, but it was a long way to shore for all three of them.

The *Pūkeko* swung around again. Tiger and Graeme's heads loomed closer in the water. They were swimming away, but Graeme kept looking back to see the fate of his boat. Sunshine peered at them, then at the dials on the dashboard.

The next circle came even closer to the humans in the water. Then the boat veered again, uncontrolled. *I have to do something.*

Sunshine launched herself at the steering wheel and caught hold, but her body hanging from it forced the *Pūkeko* into an even tighter spin.

Her brain rattled inside her skull. The G-forces made her dizzy.

Tiger shouted close by. "Harley's dang cat is turning that thing into a—a—a Death Pūkeko."

It was nice that he maintained his sense of humour, but he was legitimately in danger. Sunshine dangled from the wheel by her front claws, let go, then fell undaintily on her rear. She picked herself up, still shaken. At least no one had seen her tumble.

Tiger's voice came again, more garbled this time.

I need to be taller! Sunshine narrowed her eyes and stared up at the steering wheel. Maybe she could try reaching it from the chair, like the humans did. It was a difficult proposition with everything still spinning around. She leaped. One claw snagged and lost hold, flinging her against the inside wall. *No!*

Another holler. "What are they fighting for?"

It was Graeme this time, she thought, then Harley called out from slightly farther away. She jumped again and gained the seat, clinging on in the centre of the boat as the spin pulled her. Now if only she could reach the controls somehow from here . . . if only she had long arms like the humans.

She squeezed her eyes shut and extended a paw. Golden light flashed in her eyelids and she peeked; everything looked different somehow, the details were fuzzy, but what she saw in that moment was that she indeed had human arms.

What? She trembled and looked down at herself. She appeared to possess a complete female human form. Fingers stretched out from her new hands and grasped the wheel, as long, strong legs balanced her flat-footed on the floor. *Huh.*

First things first.

She twisted at the dials until the motor ebbed to a gentle hum, and straightened the steering wheel to bring the vessel out of its almighty spin. The forces on her eased immediately, and she hung her head and breathed.

Long golden hair fell down around her face, and she reached for a strand of it. *What's happened to me?*

She looked up, surprised to see that there was no longer any sign of the warring taniwha. The lake was calm but for Harley running towards the boat.

Sunshine gulped, for real this time. What would Harley say? What was she going to do?

She stood on her human feet for the first time, a little unsteady, still gripping the steering wheel, and looked out over the lake. Beyond Harley, she spied Tiger and Graeme swimming. They would be here soon too.

"Who the heck are you?" Clearly, Harley was close enough to see her.

I'm Sunshine. No, no. She had to speak the words out loud.

How hard could it be?

Harley grabbed the side of the boat and vaulted in, glaring at her. "Well?"

"S—shi—ine." Her name came out all mangled.

Tiger and Graeme reached the stern and clambered in, panting. The three humans—the three *other* humans, Sunshine reminded herself—all stared at her, gaping.

"Wha . . . wha ye lookin at?" she managed finally.

Tiger gestured at her and averted his eyes. "What's with the fur mini?"

Sunshine looked at herself again—a human body, with new sensations, new dimensions, new balance.

Oh. Instead of clothes like the humans wore, she was covered with bright golden fire that flickered with soft light. The effect reminded her of the fur that was her greatest pride—was it gone forever?—and of the sun. *Te korowai o Tama-nui-te-Ra . . . the cloak of the sun himself.*

"I—I'm a cat."

Her friends looked at her blankly, and Graeme's expression grew sceptical.

These people are impossible. Sunshine stomped her foot and licked her teeth. "I—am—the cat."

"Excuse me," said Graeme. "Did you just say you *are* the cat?"

Sunshine nodded. "I—I was, until just now. The—the taniwha, Tama-nui-te-Ra . . ." Words tripped more easily from her tongue. She stared at her own hands, flexed the fingers like she would if they were claws. "He's made me human!" As if it was something she wanted. Meh.

"Naaaah," said Tiger. "Pull the other one."

Graeme nodded. "He's right. I mean, I know we see a lot of weird stuff with the taniwha and all, but this just doesn't seem like something they'd do, you know?"

Harley stared silently at Sunshine, not speaking a word in her defence.

Feral anger boiled within her and she let out what she intended to be a ferocious hiss.

Dangit. That didn't work well with a human mouth. "Ugh!"

Sunshine turned towards the side of the boat, momentarily surprised at her new lack of distaste for wetness, and swung her legs over. She looked back once at Harley, who could still only gape at her. *You had your chance to help.* If no one believed her, she'd be better off on her own until she could figure things out.

Her new legs launched her into a run that kept her safely far above the surface of the water. Movements came instinctually and she settled into a comfortable pace. *I'm a human. But I'm a cat. How is this possible?* She glanced back at the boat, now just a dot in the distance and the three figures barely distinguishable inside it. Suddenly wistful, she longed for her own self. "Te Ra, would you change me again?"

In a breath and a flash of golden light, she blinked and fell on all fours to the water. Her paws swam into view. *Paws! What a relief.* Sunshine the cat was back again. But *ew*, the water slipped between her clawed toes. That part was much more bearable as a human, for sure.

She loped across the lake, only slightly choppy from its taniwha upheaval. The sun beat down and she stretched her shoulders as she ran, enjoying the warmth of Te Ra. Reaching the shore at Sulphur Point, she eyed the small boats that people eased into the water from their trailers. It had been scary to have to control the *Pūkeko* when her friends were in danger, but if there was no danger it might actually be really fun.

Shaking each paw as she left the water, she picked a boat on a trailer clearly waiting to use the ramp and go out on the lake. While the people weren't looking, she leaped up into it and curled up out of the way behind a chilly bin. Once they were out on the water, she'd change into a human and take the helm. After all, she understood about boats now, and wanted to repeat the experience under less stressful circumstances before she went on to explore all the other nuances of being human and feline at the same time. She closed her eyes in a smile to herself, and dreamed.

It was her time to shine.

The Growing of the Green

Lizz Donnelly

Saviour. Tyrant. Monarch. Friend. Pirate.

O'Malley had been called many things in her nine lives. She embraced them all and even added one of her own: Master Gardener. It had been her father's title before her, and when he passed over the rainbow bridge it had become hers. She took it seriously.

Their kin lived on a small but hardy world—Planet Emerald I-SLE on the northern edge of the 2-DOR solar system. They were a poor planet, but fierce and free. They had precisely one export, also known by many names: 'nip, grass, veg, sweet stuff from Sligo, or simply, the green.

The green grew in abundance on Emerald I-SLE and the cats that lived on the planet relied on its continued sustainable growth and export to trade for the things they needed to survive. O'Malley's father had been responsible for the creation and implementation of a long-term plan for their desirable product, and as a result, the population had looked to him as de facto leader in times of crisis. But as her father had so often told O'Malley, "the best laid plans of mice and cats gang aft a-gley," whatever that meant. He was usually well into his cups by then.

For O'Malley, it meant that wherever there was a demand for something, there was also a black market. Since the ascension of

Elizahiss the First to the neighbouring throne, there had been more and more breaches—unauthorized ships landing on Emerald I-SLE, gathering as much of the green as they could before they were caught, and sailing away into deep space to turn a profit for themselves, at the expense of the native population.

It also meant that O'Malley spent a lot of her time in low orbit, in her father's old ship, *The Rockfleet*, trying to chase off poachers before they were able to land. She was most comfortable in space; zero gravity made her graceful in ways land never did, and the gentle rocking of her ship as it spun was like floating on an ocean.

She was dozing in her pilot's chair, whiskers drooping and tail twitching half-heartedly when the alarm sounded. The voice of Silver, her second-in-command, came over the radio immediately.

"Captain!" O'Malley's orange tail fluffed out like a bottle brush at the urgency in Silver's voice.

"Hi-ho, Silver," O'Malley responded, doing her best to remain calm. She'd just caught sight of the screen in front of her that contained an image of the incoming craft, and she had a feeling she knew the source of her first mate's panic.

"Are you seeing this?" Silver asked. "It's an absolute monster. It's going to destroy half a season of crop just landing."

"I see it," O'Malley said. "Let's not let it land. Silver, I need you to deploy some backup. I'm good but this thing is a little much for my guns alone."

"Roger that, good buddy," Silver said.

O'Malley growled in response as she strapped into her pilot's chair and set her sights on the large ship that had just appeared on the outer edge of her atmosphere. It would be a dog day in heck before she let them land on her planet. She fired up her engines and set her course for the intruders. She sent out a message on every radio channel that she had, ordering them to halt their course. The ship ignored her.

As she zoomed closer, O'Malley could see the markings on the flank of the ship. She cursed under her breath and kept calling on the radio, though she knew that they wouldn't respond. The ship bore the mark of Her Majesty Elizahiss the First, and O'Malley had a sinking suspicion that the Captain was her arch-nemesis, Bingham, a pompous little tuxedo cat and Elizahiss' pet starship trooper.

O'Malley's ears flattened angrily against her head as Bingham's smug whiskers appeared on her screen. "Top o' the morning to you, O'Malley," he said. "Her Majesty sends her regards and has requested a rather large shipment of green to be sent to her colonies. She didn't think you'd be able to handle it by yourself so she sent me to get the job done."

O'Malley didn't listen to the rest of his prepared speech, instead she fired off a warning shot in the direction of his bridge, hoping she'd hit him. She was also hoping that her backup was on its way.

"Oh come on, O'Malley," Bingham said. "That wasn't very nice. I'm only trying to help."

"Keep your filthy paws off my planet, Bingham, or I'll take a matching chunk out of your other ear," O'Malley snarled. "That goes for your ship, too. Clear off and send me an ambassador. Elizahiss and Emerald I-SLE have come to terms in the past, we can do it again."

"But there's such a lovely boxy field down there," Bingham continued. "I can see it from here, and I'm just itching to land my ship in it."

"You will do no such thing," O'Malley said. "I said scram." She fired another shot, and watched in satisfaction as a piece of Bingham's ship went sailing off into space. It was a small piece, but it was better than nothing. At the same moment, O'Malley became aware of other small blips on her screen. Finally, her back up had arrived.

Bingham's chirping laugh came through the radio. "You call this an army, O'Malley? You're a rag tag bunch of kittens playing at war."

"Go hack up a hairball, Bingham," she said, but he didn't hear her because he was still talking.

"This is a royal warship. Do you want to see the latest invention? It's this funny little electromagnetic beam that allows me to pull anything metallic I want wherever I want. And I think I'll take this ship with me."

The beam locked onto one of the small single occupant fighter ships that O'Malley's team had arrived in.

"I've lost control!" Silver's voice came through the radio.

"The beam has knocked out my controls but locked onto my ship. O'Malley, he's pulling me out of orbit and I can't get away!"

"Think of this as your first and only warning, O'Malley," Bingham continued. "I'll be back tomorrow to land and collect my green, and if you'd like your friend back you won't get in my way."

O'Malley continued to fire on his ship, but she barely made a dent. She didn't want to disrupt the beam that had Silver's craft in its clutches. If it had knocked out the power, then with luck Silver would fall into a low planet orbit, but there was a chance she could plummet straight through the atmosphere with no way to brake or land. It was a risk O'Malley wouldn't take. Once he'd dragged Silver, figher craft and all, into the docking bay and secured his prisoner, Bingham turned the behemoth of a ship with a surprising amount of agility and blasted off into deep space. O'Malley's smaller ship rocked with the force of his engine blast.

Her security team was waiting at their landing site when O'Malley touched down. She took a moment to remove her helmet, and licked her right paw, smoothing her fur down and patting her whiskers into place, stalling while she figured out what she was going to say to them.

O'Malley was greeted with a chorus of yowls, growls and general caterwauling the moment she stepped off her ship. She held up a paw for silence.

"Of course we're going to get Silver back," she said.

"How?" they chorused.

"Guns!"

"Swords!"

"Lasers!"

"Claws!"

A cheer of approval went up from the crowd at this suggestion but O'Malley held up a paw for quiet. Tails twitched impatiently and someone hissed softly at the back of the group. They were anxious, and O'Malley understood that, but they had one chance to get this right. One chance to free their First Mate, and one chance to retake their land from Elizahiss and her advancing army. This had to be played very carefully.

"Parlay," O'Malley said at length. There was a collective gasp and she stalled their complaints with a low growl, deep in her throat. The auburn hairs on the back of her neck stood straight up. "That is my decision. I will inform you in one hour which of you will come with me to meet the queen."

"You've got to be kitten me," a grumble came from the back of the group.

"I am not. Not everything can be settled with swords and claws. Sometimes, the most important rope you can pounce on is strategy."

O'MALLEY APPROACHED THE planet Windsor cautiously. She had heard tales of Elizahiss' personal guard, who, according to all stories, had little tolerance for intruders and even less sense of humour.

"Captain, they're closing in."

"I see them," O'Malley said calmly. She pressed a button to send up a small white flare from the back of her ship. Bingham's face appeared a moment later on her screen. His whiskers twitched in annoyance.

"O'Malley, do you really expect me to believe that you're surrendering?"

"I'm not surrendering, fuzz face, I'm requesting a parlay with Her Majesty. Be a good pet and let her know that I've arrived."

"Her Majesty doesn't deal with pirates."

"That's not what I hear," O'Malley said. "And anyway, you came into my atmosphere, threatened to steal my crops, and cat burgled my first mate. If anyone is a pirate here it's you."

"You have taken countless shots at my ships every time I'm nearby your planet."

"Then stay out of my airspace, Bingham. It's very simple, as is my request. Alert Elizahiss that I'd like to speak to her. Immediately."

O'Malley batted off her screen with a lazy paw to sever the connection with Bingham, and stretched out in her chair. She knew that they wouldn't have to wait long for a response. There were whispers around the ship, but none of her selected crew dared to question whether or not O'Malley was doing the right thing. She was their Captain, and she hadn't steered them wrong so far, even if they were currently in the middle of a battalion of enemy ships.

O'Malley didn't look scared. Her ears swivelled lazily, listening to the hushed whispers of her crew. Bingham would be back any minute; she was confident.

A few moments later, Bingham's moustachioed whiskers were indeed back on her screen. He looked sour.

"Land your craft on the pad next to the palace and disembark unarmed. Her Majesty will see you."

O'Malley left her ship alone to meet with the Queen. Her crew had strict instructions to remain on board and ready to go in case they needed to make a quick getaway. They were not, under any circumstances, to come in after her, no matter what happened with the Queen.

Bingham was waiting for her with a cutlass when she came down the steps of her ship. O'Malley advanced with the Claymore that had belonged to her father. He'd trained her to use it when she was barely more than a kitten, though the sword had nearly outweighed her, and it was still her best defensive tactic. She was more adept with it than any saber or rapier she'd ever tried. O'Malley lunged and Bingham dodged the unexpected advance. He parried and she deflected easily. Her sword was longer, and Bingham couldn't get close enough to strike. The clink of metal on metal and the low growls of O'Malley and Bingham echoed around the landing pad. Both crews were crouched, tense, and ready to intervene for their respective captain.

It didn't take long for O'Malley to send Bingham's sword flying; it clattered to the deck of the landing pad. He was frozen for a moment, prepared for his demise, but O'Malley calmly handed off her Claymore to the nearest member of her crew for safekeeping.

"I said no weapons," Bingham said.

"A similar courtesy from you would have been diplomatic, but I fully expected you had no manners."

O'Malley flexed her claws as his soldiers patted her down for additional weapons. She smirked when they didn't find the dagger in her boot. She'd sewn in the invisible pocket herself.

"You look taller on a screen," she said. For all of their battles over the green, they'd never been face-to-face before today. They'd always fought from their ships.

"And you look less mangy," he replied. "I can't wait for Her

Majesty to put you in your place and secure my commission to your relaxing and profitable little planet."

"Don't get your hopes up, Bingham," O'Malley snapped. "The only thing that's going to be smoking is your designs on my planet when you crash and burn."

Bingham coiled back, preparing to pounce, but was interrupted by the palace doors opening and Elizahiss herself standing just inside them. She was as tall as O'Malley, her long tawny orange fur perfectly brushed, with the telltale markings on her forehead that all of her ancestors had shared. Divine right, they said. Small gene pool, O'Malley thought to herself. Around her neck was a starched and frilly white collar that O'Malley thought was entirely over the top.

Bingham bent over into a bow before his Queen. O'Malley stood tall and looked Elizahiss directly in the eye.

"Bow," Bingham hissed at her.

"No, thank you," O'Malley said. Elizahiss looked momentarily flummoxed. She recovered quickly.

"Rise, Lord Bingham," she said. "Welcome, Captain O'Malley. Will you join me inside for our discussion?"

"I'd like to be reassured that no harm has come to my first mate, first."

"She will join us in the drawing-room. Bingham, fetch the prisoner."

Bingham protested immediately. "Your Majesty, surely it would be best if I stayed here to protect you. O'Malley is a pirate!"

Elizahiss looked amused. "Yes, I know. You have your orders, Bingham."

"Yes, Your Majesty." With one last hiss at O'Malley, Bingham was gone.

Elizahiss led O'Malley into her drawing-room, where there was a table set out with a variety of tea and snacks. O'Malley could smell her favourites—the breaded, fish-flavoured kind—and wondered if the Queen had been doing a little recon on her. Without a lot of open water on Emerald I-SLE, and almost none of it saltwater, fish sticks were one of their most desired imports. There was also a small pot of a familiar green leaf, as if O'Malley needed a reminder why they were there. She reached out a paw and batted it gently.

"Seems you have no trouble growing your own," O'Malley said. "I'm not sure why you feel the need to steal mine."

"Supply and demand," Elizahiss purred. "My demand is exceeding my supply at the moment. Soil conditions, you know. Your soil is much more hospitable."

"It is," O'Malley agreed. "But we're not. Especially not when you launch the first attack and take my first mate hostage. I know you have a little empire going over here, but we're not a part of it and we have no plans to be."

"More than a little empire," Elizahiss said.

"Not so big that you can get away with sending kittens like Bingham to intimidate me and steal my crops."

Elizahiss trilled a laugh. "I like you," she said. "Bingham was so sure that you were here to kill me, but I'm glad I gave you the benefit of the doubt, even though you did bring a dagger in your boot."

O'Malley stared at the monarch in surprise. She was usually in control of a situation, but she wasn't sure where this was going at all. The hairs on her back were tingling, and lifted a fraction in defence.

"I have a similar pair of boots," Elizahiss continued. "And a similar dagger."

O'Malley's whiskers twitched, and her eyes darted around the room before she gave a small chuckle. "Strangely, I like you, too."

"Then I'm confident that we can come to some agreement." The queen was all business now. "I'm in need of a large quantity of green. The colonies demand it. They're rather fond of it, and when they're happy, I'm happy."

"I bet," said O'Malley. Elizahiss pointedly ignored her cynicism.

"I know you have enough to supply my colonies. The question is do you have the cat power to orchestrate the harvesting? I'm not interested in stale green."

"You're suggesting some of your own soldiers to, what, supervise?" O'Malley asked. "Unnecessary. We'll manage."

"And if you don't?"

"We will."

Elizahiss was quiet for a moment, as she weighed O'Malley's answer. O'Malley fought the urge to lash her tail in annoyance.

She could rein in her temper for a little while longer.

"Acceptable," Elizahiss said at last. She didn't mask the threat in her tone. "We can always renegotiate. If it becomes an issue."

"In return you release my first mate to me, unharmed, and you make sure Bingham keeps his grubby little paws out of my airspace. I will shoot him down. If it becomes an issue." O'Malley parroted the queen's words back to her with a smirk.

Elizahiss waved a dismissive paw. "Deal. I have plenty of other commanders."

"Are we finished here?"

Elizahiss flexed one claw. "One other tiny matter, speaking of Bingham. It will have no bearing on our previous deal, should you choose to decline, but I hope you'll accept. As you've no doubt noticed, dear Bingham is . . . inadequate. I find myself in need of someone with a good command of her ship and her dagger to run some interference for me on a little matter of fish shipments from my saltwater colony. I've had a few instances of lost cargo in the farther reaches of my empire."

O'Malley smoothed back her whiskers with one paw, and bared her teeth in a grin. "You want to hire a pirate."

O'MALLEY'S RETURN TO her ship, with Silver at her side, was met with cheers and shouted questions from the whole crew. She didn't answer them, just settled into her captain's chair and fired up the engines.

"Set the coordinates for Emerald I-SLE?" Silver asked, taking her place at the navigation controls.

"We have one small stop to make first," O'Malley said, and gave Silver the coordinates for the saltwater planet on the other side of the solar system.

"Why are we going there?" The question came from Mia, the little tabby, on her first real trip with O'Malley.

"Because it turns out parlay can be a very profitable strategy."

"I've heard stories about that planet," Silver said. "There are monsters in those waters."

"And all the fish sticks you can eat," countered O'Malley. "We've never let monsters scare us before, have we?"

The crew shrugged. They'd never really encountered sea

creatures. However, their ears had collectively perked up at the mention of fish sticks. O'Malley could see their pupils dilating in anticipation of the hunt; the beginning stage of what O'Malley called "pirate eyes."

"Have we ever run from a challenge?" O'Malley tried again.

"No!" they shouted.

"Then gather your swords and spears, me hearties. We're going fishing."

The Cat and the Cook

Blake Liddell

If a ship wants to stay on the right side of the waves, it must have a cat onboard. When *The Slippery Haddock*'s cat was lost, the ship stopped at the first island on the horizon. Sailors were sent ashore with orders to catch a cat and bring it onboard.

When Ruby and Mayhew came striding back to the jolly boat, their wide grins flashed in the afternoon sun. Their faces were shining with sweat and crosshatched with welts, the bloody tracks of claw-swipes beaded red on their cheeks, hands, and forearms. Ruby dumped a heavy sack caked with sand into the bottom of the jolly boat.

"There's the cat, my friends," Mayhew drawled, wiping pink sweat from his face with a filthy neckerchief. "Feisty beastie, real ornery, but we got it in the end."

The sack was very still.

Another sailor peered at it, dubious. "This is a cat? Still alive?"

"Oh aye, it's alive. Just real angry. Word of honour."

The sack lay still as the rest of the sailors gathered, as the oars began to dance through the bright blue waves, and the jolly boat nosed up to the side of *The Slippery Haddock*. Ruby had the honour of hauling the sack up onto the deck. Sailors milled around, murmuring. Nothing moved in the sack, nothing.

The Captain came striding through the unsettled crowd, his head wreathed in the bluish smoke of his fat cigar. He pulled a knife from his belt and sliced open the sack. After a moment, the mass in the sack shifted and stretched. From the mouth of hessian, a cat uncurled. Pure white, golden eyed, thick, fluffy tail. The biggest cat any of them had ever seen.

Without stretching, the cat could have taken a bite of the flesh above the Captain's knee. Its tail tip was level with the Captain's belt buckle. It arched its back and flexed its paws to show hooked claws an inch long.

The Captain drew on his cigar then exhaled, and a long plume of smoke drifted towards the cat. He grinned, showing his yellowed teeth.

"That, my good men, is a cat! Get the jolly boat shipped and the anchor raised. It's time for us to sail!" The Captain turned on his heel and strode away. Mayhew began to shout orders, the sailors moved to follow them, and the giant white cat narrowed its golden eyes, watching them all.

The Slippery Haddock ploughed through the waves, her square-rigged sails belling out fat with wind. The Captain expected to deliver the cargo on time, making port within the contracted three weeks. The sun shone, dolphins danced in the ship's wake, and the sailors sang as they worked amongst the rigging.

The youngest sailor, a dark haired boy called Toby, was meant to be sanding the deck but he abandoned the sandstone and sidled up to Mayhew, who was expertly coiling ropes.

"Mayhew," the boy whispered. "Mayhew, I don't like it."

"Eh? Like what?"

"That cat. It keeps . . ." Toby trailed off, fidgeting with some tufts of oakum loosened from the rope.

"What? Boy, spit it out."

"It keeps on stamping near me. Everywhere I start sanding, it stamps on past."

Mayhew raised a shaggy eyebrow. "Boy, cats don't stamp. They sleep and they sneak and that's about it. I s'pose they eat too. But they don't stamp."

"This one does. Around and around the deck. Like it is angry. Like it wants to stamp on me."

Mayhew spat over the side of the deck and shook his head. "Get back to work, boy. Sand the bloody deck. If you're scared of a fluffy kitten, you ain't going to last at sea."

Toby slunk back to the sandstone, ears hot. Kneeling on the deck, ready to start scrubbing, he looked up. The cat was perched on the forecastle. Its thick tail was switching back and forth, white fur glittering in the sun. It narrowed its golden eyes at him. Toby swallowed and put his head down. He began to sand, working the stone back and forth, determined not to look at the cat again.

BELOW DECK, IN the ship's galley, garlands of garlic and strings of dried sausages hung from the ceiling beams and swung with the constant roll of the sea. The most light in the tiny room came from the coals, glowing red in the bed of sand that passed for a stove. The floor was covered with a layer of tin, scorched here and there from an escaped ember. The ship's cook, Tabitha, muttered to herself as she added a handful of dried peas to a pot.

Lifting her ladle, she paused. Had she seen something? A slight movement, a waft of something white past the open doorway. Tabitha squinted, rubbed her eyes with the back of her hand. No, nothing. Nothing at all.

It stayed in her thoughts, though, that white wispy thing. Distracted her as she chopped wizened carrots, crumbled herbs, and stirred the simmering pot.

When she slipped out to the pantry, a tight, dim nook next to the galley, she found a flour sack pulled open and powdery white paw prints over the casks and jars and bottles. A wheel of cheese high on the shelf had deep, needle-like holes pressed into the wax. Like bite marks, Tabitha realised. Like long, sharp teeth.

She knew of the cat, of course. She hadn't seen it—or perhaps now she had seen a glimpse of its tail as it slipped on past—but she had seen the cat's handiwork. The crosshatched tracks of claws left in the skin of Ruby and Mayhew.

As ship's cook, Tabitha had somehow also become the ship's doctor. Some bemusing logic of working with meat and knives and herbs had bestowed upon her the responsibility of the healing salves, a set of shiny needles, and a reel of gut thread.

The needles hadn't been necessary for Ruby and Mayhew, and Tabitha had been relieved. She did not enjoy the drag of gut thread through flesh, or the deep fear that she was stitching badly, that her poor sewing would cost a sailor their hand, their foot, their life at sea.

While the tracks of the cat's claws had split the skin and spilled blood, all that was required from Tabitha was a gentle washcloth and a thick layer of salve. Ruby sat still, stoic, as the salve was worked into the red wounds. She was known for her silence, Ruby. Tall and wiry, with dark skin and cropped hair burnt white from sunshine, she spoke little. She offered quiet thanks before slipping away. Mayhew lingered, having grunted and muttered through the salve, ready to spin the tale of the catching of the cat. Having found it asleep in the sun, trying to be stealthy only to end in a violent wrestle, fur and claws and teeth flying.

Tabitha shook her head and tied the flour sack closed. She dusted off the paw prints. She rewound the headscarf that kept her hair up and out of her eyes, and returned to the hot, dark galley to stir the stew.

RUBY LOVED TO be up high in the rigging, swinging in the sky, the rolling, dancing ocean laid out beneath her. Fast, fearless, she was the silent queen of the ropes. So, when she tumbled gracelessly from above, thumping onto the deck with string of curses pouring from her lips, the rest of the crew stopped and stared.

Ruby struggled to her feet, still swearing, running her hands over knees and ankles and ribs, checking herself for injury. Mayhew ran to her.

"What is it?" His voice seemed weak and frail against the tide of Ruby's yells.

"That cat," she spat. "That cat is up there. Up in the rigging. Up on the mast. Hanging from the yardarm, upside down. Claws sunk into the wood and hanging there like some fat, rotten fruit, some poisonous flower."

Mayhew rubbed the back of his neck. The watching crew stared.

"I saw it," Ruby hissed. "Saw it hanging and it saw me and I fell."

"Ruby," Mayhew said, spreading his hands in front of him, "please, calm down."

She stamped her foot, jerked her arms, and howled with rage.

"Ruby, you can't have seen the cat. Look," he pointed, a slight tremor in his hands. "Look, Ruby, the cat is over there, sleeping on the forecastle."

It was there. Stretched out in the sunlight, fur flashing brilliant white, deeply asleep.

Ruby's mouth fell open and her face flushed a sickly grey. She blinked, once, twice, and then turned on her heel and strode away.

AFTER THE SUN had set that day, young Toby sought her out. Ruby was curled on top of a rain barrel, knees drawn up, arms wrapped around them. Her eyes glittered as she stared out at the star lit waves.

"I believe you." He shuffled his bare feet on the deck. "I know you saw it, Ruby. That cat . . ." He trailed off and Ruby shifted her gaze from the sea to the boy.

"They think I'm wrong. That I fell. That I imagined it." Her words were low and bitter.

"I know. I believe you, though. I do. That cat is something else. Something wrong. I don't think it likes being on our ship. I don't think it likes us at all."

Ruby reached out, wrapped her arm around the boy's skinny shoulders. He shivered, pressing close to her side. Together, they watched the rise and fall of the silvered sea.

TABITHA HAD JUST finished stirring hunks of dried sausage into the day's stew when the cat strolled into the galley.

In the heavy darkness, the cat looked very large, as big as a goat, and its fur shone like moonlight.

The ladle fell from Tabitha's hand and clattered onto the tin floor. She stepped back, then stepped forward again. The stew bubbled. The cat's golden gaze caught her pale blue eyes and they stared at one another in the gloom.

"Hello," meowed the cat.

"Hello," answered Tabitha.

The cat narrowed its eyes, flicked its ears back, lashed its tail.

"Is that it? Just hello?" The cat's voice was feminine and husky, with the smoky hint of a purr or a growl.

"Oh. Well. How do you do, my lady?" Tabitha bobbed a quick curtsy, something she hadn't done in years, not since leaving the land to work at sea.

The cat's tail lashed faster.

"Really? No yelling or screaming? No throwing things? No fainting or wailing or shouting *good grief, a talking cat*?"

Tabitha blinked. "I could do that if you like." She rubbed her eyes. "I could yell a bit if that would make you happy."

The cat yawned, stretching open a wide, pink mouth full of sharp teeth. "No. No. It isn't fun if you are doing it on purpose."

Silence fell. The cat and the cook eyed one another. The hanging garlands of garlic swung above their heads with the roll of the waves.

The cat narrowed her eyes. "So why aren't you yelling and fainting and throwing things?"

Tabitha twisted her hands into her apron. "There are two explanations for this. The first is that I have been in this room stirring boring pots for so long that I have begun to see things that aren't there, which is curious. The other explanation is that I have just met a talking cat and that is the most interesting and exciting thing to have ever happened in my life. I'm not going to waste it with noise and silliness and carry on."

"Very well." The cat paused to stretch, arching her back, and then settling back on her haunches. "Can I have some cheese?"

MAYHEW'S BELLOWS FILLED the ship's belly.

He flailed his arms and legs, still shouting, until his hammock twisted and dumped him out. He lay, chest heaving, in his drawers and undershirt.

Bleary-eyed, other sailors swung from their hammocks. A match flared and a lantern was lit. Mayhew's face was pale and shiny, beads of sweat or tears standing out on his cheeks.

"Oh mercy," he wheezed, levering himself upright. "Oh mercy on us all."

"What is it? What is wrong?" asked a sailor.

"The dream I had, my friends. A terrible dream." Mayhew shook his head. "I dreamed I was watching the waves under the full moon, and out there in the water was a person. A person gone overboard! So I threw out the line, and shouted for help. I called and called and nobody came. I hauled that person up all by myself, near breaking my back. When they got onto the deck, though, it wasn't a person at all. It was the cat, huge and white and terrible. And everywhere its paws touched, the wood rotted and split. The sea began to rush in. The ship broke up, coming apart like splinters, and it was my fault because I had brought that cat on board."

To the horror of the watching sailors, Mayhew began to weep.

"YOU AREN'T REALLY a cat, are you?" Tabitha eyed the sprawled creature.

"Of course I am. I'm just more than that. A cat with a little extra." The cat narrowed her eyes. "Just like you are more than just a cook."

Tabitha snorted. Her knife rapped on the board as she diced a chunk of salt pork.

"I never meant to be a cook, cat. I was born in a village, and when I was old enough, my parents sent me up to the Big House to work. I scrubbed pots and plates until I was big enough to start filling pots and plates instead. No-one ever asked if that was what I wanted. That kitchen, it was always full of steam and bad temper and smacks on the back of my head."

The cat rolled extravagantly, and Tabitha's knife flashed as she continued to chop.

"I was lonely and unhappy and always tired. The years rolled past and I started to think about my Pa. My father's father. He'd died when I was still a wee girl but he had told me tales, sitting by the hearth fire on winter nights. Stories of adventure at sea, of lands of sparkling ice and pure white bears, of witches who turned into seals, and nights that lasted months. I thought of all those things and places I would never go to and never see. So I ran away. I ran away from the kitchen and the Big House and headed off to sea." The knife stilled in her hand. Tabitha lowered her head, her headscarf obscuring her face.

"Cat, the truth is, it was too late. Boys and girls start to learn the sea life at age nine. I was too old. I had no skill at fishing or navigating or reading the waves. The only thing I knew was how to cook.

"So into the dim, hot galley I went. And here I am today. Just a cook."

"Come here," the cat demanded. Tabitha stepped from her bench and eased down onto the tin floor beside the creature. "Now, scratch my back." Tabitha's fingers sank into the silken white fur. A deep, growling purr began in the cat's chest. "Now, if you could have anything, Tabitha, what would you want?"

"Snow and ice." Tabitha's fingers massaged the cat's back, tears rolling down her cheeks. The cat ignored the wet spots spreading in its fur. "Seals and white bears. A starry sky dancing with magic, in a night that lasts half a year. Adventure."

The cat purred on.

"I had an island once," the cat chirped.

"I know. Mayhew told me about catching you."

"No, not that one. I had my own island. A long time ago. Lovely place, lots of delicious birds. There was an abandoned temple there, the old altar slab still in place, the perfect place to sleep in the afternoon sun. Wonderful. Only the people on the island were so noisy and nosy. I didn't want them annoying me, or finding my wonderful sleeping stone. So I drove them away. It took a long time, oh fifteen years of bad dreams and curses and ghostly cats landing on them from above. They left though, said the island was cursed. I had it all to myself, to sleep and dream and eat birds for as long as I cared."

Tabitha's hand stilled in the cat's fur.

"I don't like this story very much."

"Be quiet. Keep rubbing my back. As I was saying, I did that. Sunshine and birds left me plump and dreamy and happy. A good long rest after a hard time driving all those people away. I stayed there for years. In the end though, it all got terribly boring."

"I don't understand, Cat."

The cat huffed, flicking an ear back.

"I don't like being bored. I don't like this ship. What I do like though, is the thought of an adventure."

THERE IS ONE word, above all, that is feared on a ship. Not shark or cyclone or pirates, but *fire*. On the ocean, floating in a wooden ship, fire is certain death.

And *fire* is exactly what was being shouted in the night.

Thick, curling smoke billowed from the door of the Captain's quarters. Sailors ran to draw up buckets of sand, of sea water. The alarm bell clanged, Toby beat the brass bell.

When the first wave of sailors burst into the Captain's quarters, the smoke was thick enough to choke. Coughing, eyes streaming, they staggered about. The smoke slithered out the door, thick and white, leaving as quickly as it had appeared.

Mayhew dropped his bucket, sand spilling onto the Captain's fine rug.

The Captain stood in the centre of the room, still and silent.

"Captain?" Mayhew rumbled.

"Mayhew, my good man. My good man." The Captain's hands plucked at his belt. His eyes showed white all around, his pupils tight, tiny dots. "Calamity. Calamity has come to us."

"What is it?"

"The fire. I had no fire in the grate, I swear it, but it roared up with flames. Somehow, I can't say, somehow into the fire leapt the ship's logs, and the maps, and the times and tides and moon charts. I tried to stop them, I did, but the fire just ate them, ate up our maps and charts."

Mayhew guided the Captain to a chair, pushing down on his shoulders until he sat. Turning to the milling sailors, Mayhew waved his hands.

"Clear out. There's no fire. Get back to work."

The room emptied and the Captain reached for the nearby bottle of liquor.

"I'm sure, Captain, it isn't all that bad." Mayhew patted the man's shoulder.

The Captain laughed, or perhaps sobbed, exhaling the stinging scent of rum.

"Mayhew, without those maps, we can't sail, can't plot a course, can't find a port. Without those maps, we are just as lost as we would be if we had been transported to the desert. Without those maps, we are doomed."

TABITHA WAS DREAMING. She was filling the cook pot, handful after handful, and the more she threw into the pot, the larger it became. She emptied sacks and jars and barrels, and still the pot grew. As it loomed, mouth opening hungrily, she teetered on the rim. Her ladle fell into the giant pot's maw and with a gasp of fear, she realised that the pot would only be satisfied if she threw herself in, to be boiled away into stew.

She woke with a jolt. A large, white paw jabbed at her nose. She blinked, heart racing. The cat poked her again, pushing the soft, pink pad of her paw against Tabitha's cheek.

"Wake up, lazy. It is time."

"What? Time for what?" Tabitha rubbed her bleary eyes.

"Time for you to get up and do as I say. I have a plan." The cat's golden eyes glowed like amber in the low light, and she began to purr.

MAYHEW STARED OUT at the sea. Dawn painted the waves red and the cresting sun stained the sky bloody orange. Mayhew had watched the Captain drain his bottle, swallowing mouthful after mouthful until the liquor had drowned his horror. The Captain had slipped from his chair, head lolling, and Mayhew covered the man with his blanket, left him in the oblivion of sleep.

There was no oblivion for Mayhew.

His thoughts churned until he felt he might vomit. The other sailors began to gather around him. He closed his eyes, feeling very old and yet somehow young, as frightened as a child, waiting for an adult to tell him what to do.

"Mayhew," murmured Ruby, "what do we do?"

He turned his back on the rising sun, looking to the men and women of the ship, the crew that was his family, his friends, the folk he loved and trusted without hesitation.

He cleared his throat, ready to speak, when the door from belowdecks crashed open. The crew turned to stare as the ship's cook strode out. Tabitha, with her stained apron and headscarf, stood squinting in the morning light. From behind her, uncurled the cat, white and shining, as big as a donkey.

"Hello." Tabitha twisted her hands into her apron. "I think we are all in a bit of a situation and we have a proposal."

Toby shrieked, pushing to the front of the gathered sailors.

"That cat," he cried, "it did this. I told you all. We need to throw it off the ship." He was shaking, panting, his face blotchy and swollen. "We have to get rid of it!"

"That," growled the cat, "would be a very bad idea."

The sailors recoiled and began shouting. Through the mix of

voices, Tabitha picked out words. *Demon. Monster. Evil.* The cat began to delicately wash her paw.

"This is how people usually react," the cat purred, winking at Tabitha.

"Enough," bellowed Mayhew. He raised his hands, calloused palms out. "Enough."

The cat yawned, showing off her pink tongue and sharp, white fangs. She rose and stretched, arching her back and looping her tail.

"As Tabitha said," the cat purred, "we have a proposal. Fetch the Captain. Now."

THE CAPTAIN STUMBLED onto the deck, without his customary cigar. Mayhew had managed to rouse him, had helped him wash his face and dress in fresh clothes.

The Captain leaned against the mast. The cat prowled across the deck to sit before him.

"It seems we have a predicament." The cat paused and casually unsheathed her claws. "You have somehow lost your charts and are in dire strife."

"Lost?" The Captain grimaced, his hand straying to the handle of his belt knife.

"Yes, lost. Rather careless." The cat's claws glittered in the light. "However, I may just have a way to help. For a price."

"What price?" The Captain was gripping his knife, his knuckles white with tension.

"Not much." The cat preened. "All I ask in exchange is your jolly boat. And all of your cheese. And your cook."

THE JOLLY BOAT was lowered, four and a half wheels of cheese stacked in the prow. Mayhew took Tabitha's arm, drawing her away from the crowd.

"Lass, slip away now and hide in the bilges. We'll deal with the cat."

Tabitha shook her head, easing her arm from his gentle hold.

"Thank you, but no. I will go."

Mayhew's shaggy eyebrows knotted. "Don't be foolish. You don't have to go with that creature."

Tabitha sighed, shaking her head. "I want to. I'm happy to. I've had enough of pots and pans, enough of being belowdecks, of waiting for something to happen." She smiled, sadness in her eyes. "I don't want to wait too long."

She untied the strings of her apron, pulled it off, and dropped it onto the deck. She unwound the scarf from her head, and out spilled her long, red hair. The strands glittered in the sun. She grinned, her teeth flashing white.

"I'm going now."

She climbed over the ship's rail and dropped down into the jolly boat.

"VERY GOOD," DECLARED the cat, whipping her tail with satisfaction.

"Your side of the deal, now, demon," snarled the Captain.

The cat flourished her paws and somehow beneath them was a stack of papers. A stack of maps and star charts and tides. The Captain blinked.

"It seems you misplaced these. Lucky I found them and kept them safe, yes?" The cat's golden eyes shone with glee.

The Captain bent and snatched up the papers, rifling through and seeing that they were indeed his missing maps.

"Good travels, Captain. Perhaps we will meet again?"

Before the Captain could reply, the cat leapt from the deck, landing effortlessly in the jolly boat. Tabitha already had the oars in place and she began to row.

Ruby and Mayhew stepped to the rail. Ruby ran her hand through her hair, sun-bleached tufts sticking out in every direction. The Captain moved to stand between them and Mayhew clapped him on the back.

"I declare, if that bloody thing ever comes back, I'm quitting the sea and becoming a tailor."

The Captain nodded, his face an unpleasant shade of green.

"Me too, Mayhew. Me too."

TABITHA ROWED UNTIL her arms ached and *The Slippery Haddock* was below the horizon. The cat nibbled a wedge of cheese.

"What now, Cat?"

"Well," the cat meowed through a mouth of cheese, "we can't row all the way to the north ice. Too far and too much work."

Tabitha nodded, rubbing her biceps.

"We need to summon the Wave Wives," the cat said, cleaning cheese from her whiskers.

"I've never heard of the Wave Wives."

"You wouldn't have. Now scratch behind my ears." Tabitha, her hair shining riot red in the sunlight, sank her fingers into the cat's plush fur. "To summon the Wave Wives, we first have to find a flute made from the bones of a leviathan."

The sea sparkled sapphire around the jolly boat, and the cat who was more than just a cat and the woman who was more than just a cook, began to plan their first adventure.

Pirates Only Love Treasure

Frances Pauli

Alex the Red leaned his paws on the gunwale and listened to the sea lap against the hull. Salt air curled his tongue, clung in thick droplets to his whiskers. He narrowed green eyes at the horizon, at a dark strip that marked the island where he meant to die.

"Should be there before dusk." A purring voice boomed behind him. The captain, a black-and-white tom who'd only been sailing one tenth of Alex's years, joined him at the railing. "She's a pretty sight, no?"

"Pretty enough." Alex let his irritation show in the flicking of his striped tail. He wanted solitude now, and that was the last thing a cat found on a ship at sea.

The captain failed to take the hint. "They say she's swimming in pirate gold. More than one Jolly Roger has flown over those beaches. They say she's laying lower in the water for all the chests in her belly."

The other cat gave a jovial laugh and placed a fuzzy paw on Alex's shoulder.

"I've no interest in treasure," Alex said. "Nor any need for it at my age."

"Sure. Sure." The weight of the captain's paw seemed to increase. His throat rumbled, and he looked to the horizon for a time. When he spoke again, the words were soft and loaded with suspicion. “But you won’t be wanting us to come back for you?”

“No.” Alex sighed. They’d been over this when he hired the lugger, two weeks ago back in Ravensport. Two weeks of ship life behind them and the captain still wanted to know his business. “I mean to stay here indefinitely.”

“Right.” The weight lifted from his shoulder, but not from the other tom’s words. “So you’ve said.”

The years behind Alex the Red seemed to echo in that statement. He’d had his life already, his adventure, and his quest for pirate gold. He’d done all there was to do. Alex could sleep through a typhoon. He could tie the rigging with his eyes closed.

And he could see straight through the *Peahen’s* captain.

“I’ve no interest in treasure.” He asserted it and knew the tom beside him paid his words no heed at all.

“Well, we’ll be there tonight regardless,” the captain said. “And we’ll be leaving soon as you’re off. I’ve no desire to sacrifice the *Peahen* to some *brigand’s* greed.”

Alex said nothing. It was possible the captain knew his history, but it might just as easily be a natural aversion to piracy. It made no difference to his future. The other cat sighed and stamped back to his crew, and Alex the Red stared out at a shadow which grew larger, longer by the second.

He hadn’t lied. All the treasure he needed was behind him. What lay on the island ahead was an ending, and all he required was solitude and time to meet it.

“I see you out there,” he whispered. “You know my name, and you know my purpose. I’m coming for you as surely as death is coming for me.”

It was an old tradition, sailing away at the end of one’s life, and one rarely practiced these days. Customs died, he supposed, as easily as old cats did. But fashionable or not, he felt the years behind him more heavily than the days ahead. He was ready to lie down and rest, and if that made him old-fashioned, he could live with it . . . or just the opposite.

The island lay, blackened by the sun’s position, neither large enough nor near enough anything civilized to be noteworthy. The *Peahen* surged over the waves, as if the boat itself hurried to be done with him. Alex leaned on her gunwale and sighed.

It was as good a place as any to die. It was as good as any in memory, and he still had plenty of those. He still had his wits, and a good measure of his strength. The fur might be greying, but time had not yet enfeebled him.

"Better that way," he told the island. "Always better to get out while you're ahead."

The sea rocked the *Peahen*, answering only with the lapping of wave against wood.

THE SAILORS DUMPED his trunks just a few steps past the high tide line and then filed back aboard the *Peahen's* yawl as quickly as their paws could carry them. The captain observed from the waterline, posing beside the little craft and casting nervous glances at the palm jungle waving beyond the stretch of sand.

Once his men were ready to row him back to his ship, he addressed Alex a final time.

"You're certain you don't require a return trip?"

"I am."

The black-and-white cat frowned, adjusted his hat, and then sighed. "So be it."

Alex waited while they pushed out to sea. He watched the yawl bob over the waves, angling toward the anchored lugger. If the captain looked back, he didn't catch it, and once the crew had rowed the small craft to her parent's side, he washed them all from his thoughts and focused on his next goal.

They'd landed him in a sheltered cove, a curving arc of beach backed by dense foliage. A small scattering of stones reached into the sea at one end, and at the other, the land rose into a narrow cliff. The trees atop this reached their tangled roots directly into the open sea air.

It would make a suitable campsite, a perfectly obvious place to come to land, and so he'd need to settle somewhere else as soon as possible. As the captain had predicted, the day already passed. The sky had turned to slate, and the jungle was a blotted silhouette behind him.

Alex trudged to the smaller of his trunks, pried open the latches, and lifted the lid. He'd miss the evening meal aboard the *Peahen*. Her galley had been the best part of his final journey. He unrolled a cloth from around his silverware, laid out the matching plate he'd packed, and proceeded to open and serve himself a tin of sardines.

The trunks had enough food and supplies to keep him alive a solid month, and Alex planned to die long before that time had ended.

He ate half the tin before his anxiety trumped the needs of his belly. Leaving the rest for his return, Alex heaved the largest of the trunks onto its end. He picked an unlikely place, an area where the palms grew close together and the passage inland would take some effort. Aiming for that target, he dragged the trunk up the sand to the spot where the first fronds sprouted.

Once all his possessions lay inside the jungle's shelter, he'd erase the tracks and be able to watch the beach from relative invisibility.

Alex returned to the sand, selected his next trunk, and had heaved it to his shoulder before he noticed his plate. The remaining sardines no longer lay in their oil. The tin had been emptied and, if he correctly judged the mark left in the residue, licked clean.

Alex reached for his belt. A pair of pistols hung there, and his paws flirted with the butts without drawing them. He eyed the sand but found no prints except his own.

Not a wild animal. Not, as he'd first hoped, a lizard or some island bird. Whatever finished his dinner had had the foresight to erase their trail.

Alex the Red folded his napkin and repacked his soiled dishes. He lifted the next trunk onto his furry shoulders and gave the beach a glare that had sent many a sailor fleeing overboard.

Even his death, it seemed, would not be had in peace. He'd meant to leave the subterfuge, theft, and murder in his past, but he was not alone on the island. And if he was to find his end in solitude, first he'd have to clean a little house.

THE FIRE BARELY smoked. Alex built a mound of dirt and damp leaves around it, and kept the flames low and sporadic, only cooking when he had no other option. He'd settled down inside the trees, closer than he'd meant to but in a gap that gave him a solid vantage, a clear view of the sand and the cliff.

And anyone approaching from the open.

Behind his lean-to, he'd fashioned a row of spiked staves,

buried half into the sandy soil and pointing toward the deeper jungle. It made a poor defence against anything as savvy as his sardine thief but was better than nothing at all.

He'd considered an alarm of tins and string, something to alert him before the danger arrived, but he had it in mind to catch the thief in the act, and scaring it away only meant it would continue to lurk around the edges of his camp, an unknown factor that would most certainly spoil his last days if not dealt with appropriately.

He inhaled the scent of seared fish, closing his eyes long enough to savour the aroma and to switch his focus. His triangular ears swivelled toward the jungle palms, and somewhere beyond his spikes, a branch snapped.

Fronds rustled so softly he never would have heard them had he not been actively listening. The fish, it seemed, had been too tempting, and his trap was effectively set.

Certain that his thief was about again, Alex yawned, stretching his paws over his head and letting his pink tongue curl over his teeth. He rubbed his ears, lashed his tail, and stood, leaving the fish in its pan beside his dying fire.

Alex yawned again, scanning the jungle under the cover of that gesture. No visible movement. No more sound at all. Either he'd spooked his thief, or they were very good at what they did.

He stamped a few paces to the edge of the beach. A step out onto the sand and he paused, picking up the faintest of rustling from the palms behind him. He took his time, stretching and rubbing his belly before he strode away, leaving the camp and the jungle to his invisible watcher.

Once he'd cleared the trees, Alex shifted his path to parallel the jungle. He took long strides that made too much noise, and then, satisfied he'd made his exit clear, ducked low and crept back into the foliage. Placing each paw with silent deliberation, Alex the Red stalked back to his camp, creeping and on all fours for the first time in a decade.

All of this was supposed to be behind him. He wanted nothing of it, only the sun and the sands and a little silence in which to die. Despite this, a rush of adrenaline coursed beneath his fur. His whiskers tightened. His tail straightened out behind him, and his vision sharpened to a deadly point.

Claws that had remained sheathed for longer than he cared

to count prickled now, digging into the sand and giving each step leverage.

He circled inland, coming upon his row of spikes and peering through them with his belly pressed tight against the vine-encrusted ground. His ears swivelled forward. Alex held his breath and listened to his thief.

Soft paws padded across the camp. The pan rattled as it was lifted, and a drop of grease fell into the fire with a sizzle. His trunk creaked, and the scent of the fish wafted on the next breeze as the interloper sat down to dine on his dinner.

Alex reached one paw slowly for the belt around his hips. He drew the smaller of his pistols, the newer one that fired faster and with greater accuracy. Moving so that the vines cushioned any sound, he painstakingly primed the weapon, un-stoppering a miniature horn that dangled around his neck on a thong with his igniter and a brass box containing spare flints.

The sounds in camp had died, but he'd heard no footfalls, no indication his thief had abandoned their meal. Alex lifted the muzzle of his flintlock, steadying it against the nearest pointed spike. He exhaled and let his nerves become iron.

The pan pinged as it was set back down. The trunk creaked again. Alex's paw flirted with the trigger. Steady on. One shot should solve all his problems. One round to get his vigil back on track.

A flash of dark fur passed between his lean-to and the largest trunk. Low to the ground. Bastard was crawling, no doubt, sulking like the cur he was. Alex shifted his angle and trained the weapon on the far side of the trunk.

Something behind him rustled. Fronds rattled and snapped. Alex rolled over, swinging his pistol and catching the muzzle on the next spike. His heart did the tarantella in his fuzzy chest. He wrenched the weapon free and aimed it at the jungle where only the soft rippling of fronds gave away the second enemy.

Long gone now. Skittered back into the palms, or else training a weapon on his exposed chest. Two thieves, and either way he turned, one of them would have a clear shot at his back.

He'd meant to die on the island, but not this way. Not shot in the back like a dog. Alex aimed his pistol toward the canopy above, bet his life on the enemy's cowardice, and fired a round into the fronds.

His ears pressed flat against his head, and his heartbeat seemed to play from directly between his eyes. He shook his head to drown it out, to clear away the echo of the gunshot and his own nerves. The jungle blurred, and just as he'd decided a knife would land between his shoulder blades, he caught the distant padding of soft feet.

Retreating, vanishing into the foliage, until next time.

HE MADE PREPARATIONS all through the night. His thief had finished off the fish, stolen nothing else, and left something unthinkable behind before fleeing. Alex turned the gemstone over in his paws, leaning against the big trunk and trying not to check the jungle every three breaths.

His ears pointed in that direction, alert but doing his best not to appear so. He'd laid a different sort of trap, under the cover of darkness, and now he only had to wait until whoever hid inside the jungle got hungry enough to return.

Simple really, straightforward as an arrow. Except for the gem.

They'd only stolen his food, which he found ultimately foolish. His fishing kit would have served a hungry castaway a great deal better. A bottle of rum would have assuaged an exiled criminal far more than a piece of cooked fish. But all his sundries were untouched. The net unmolested.

And they'd left a fat blue stone in his frying pan.

Alex turned it over again, let the light from his fire refract through the careful facets. Treasure as payment? No thief worth his salt would pay for a meal fairly stolen. No pirate in exile would part with even one gem for something he could take for free.

And so, Alex stewed over the puzzle of it. He had multiple trespassers. At least two. They were small and silent, skilful even though it pained him to admit it. And they'd either left the gem in payment for what they took, or to taunt him into madness.

Likely the latter.

He snorted and tossed the sapphire into the air, watching the flash of colour as it tumbled and almost forgetting to catch it again. A lovely stone, worth far more than a tin of sardines and half a fish.

Did someone mean to lure him out? To fill him with the old lusts so he'd search the island for its hidden hoard? He thought of the black-and-white tom again. The *Peahen's* crew believed this island heavy with pirate loot. Perhaps they played a game with him now.

If they meant for Alex to lead them to the treasure, they'd suffer more than disappointment. With some effort, he set the stone down and forced his eyes away from its sparkle.

Pirates or thieves, either way, his peaceful death would be hard won. His deserted island hadn't the decency to remain deserted, and Alex the Red would have one final show before he could settle in to rest.

HE'D MEANT TO *feign* sleep, but then, his body showed its years more than his mind. He'd been snoring when the ruckus jerked him back awake and it took him several breaths to realize his trap had sprung.

Alex rolled to his feet, crouching in the shade of his trunk, and inhaled the scent of faded charcoal, old fish, and fresh fear. His ears turned, catching the sounds of struggle and a soft, high-pitched whimper.

He'd placed the net on the beach side of camp, buried it in the loose sand, and left a pile of sardine tins in the middle. Only one had been opened, just enough to let the scent free and give the illusion that he'd abandoned his meal to drunkenness.

For effect, he'd drizzled a trail of prize rum from the heap to his lean-to before sitting to wait. Though he'd had no intentions of sleeping, it seemed the plan had worked regardless of his lapse.

Alex flexed his toes and crept around the end of his trunk. He sniffed, and kept his ears moving, certain that his thief's partner was still about and currently contemplating a rescue attempt.

Nighttime made shadows of the camp, long stripes of black and paler greys. The net had been pulled tight and lifted from the ground, not as high as he'd hoped, for the trees at the fringe of the beach were thin and bent beneath the weight of his captive. Even so, that squirming mass seemed far too small.

Alex eased nearer, squinting at the struggling silhouette. He'd almost decided he'd inadvertently caught some wild thing, a pig or feral dog, until his prisoner spoke, hissing and whining in a voice that was a good decade shy of mature.

"Let me go." The sniffle behind the words cemented his first impression.

Alex stood and brushed the sand from his trousers. He approached the trap with his tail high and his ears pressed flat to his skull.

"What do you think you're doing?" A deserted island was no place for kittens, and this one had nearly gotten himself shot or gutted twice already. "I might have killed you."

"I paid for the fish," the voice turned sullen, echoed with the trace of a pout. "We only took a little."

We. Alex spun just in time to take a hit to the chest. He stumbled back, more from shock than the impact, and a second projectile arched through the thinning shadows to smack him on the cheek.

"Ouch." He caught the rock and scowled across his camp at the newcomer.

"Let him go." The kitten stalking across his campsite had more fluff than most dandelions. Her fur stood out in all directions, but her frame was lean and gaunt. One paw held another rock, ready to fire at him again, and the other was clutched tightly around something he couldn't see.

Alex put up both his paws in mock surrender. "Don't shoot," he said.

The kitten stopped in her tracks. The fire had long since died, and the first of dawn's rays were only flirting with the beach, but his eyes had adjusted quickly, and the ambient light paled by the second. His thief's partner was barely old enough to be off her mother's breast, but she had a fierce spark to her, and she'd proven her aim was better than her choice of weapons.

"Let my brother go." She kept the sniffle out of her demands too, though he saw the shimmer of it in her eyes. "I can pay you."

"With what, little one?" Alex dropped to a crouch again, aware that the net still squirmed behind him but certain the boy, at least, was well caught.

His partner in crime thrust out her closed paw, turned it pads up, and revealed a short stack of gold doubloons.

"Where did you get those?" He thought of the sapphire then, and of the *Peahen's* captain and his theories.

"Let him go and you can have them." This time, there was a tremble to her words.

Two kittens alone on the island made no sense, and he frowned and rubbed at one ear as if to dislodge the thought. It had been years since he'd landed on these shores, but if the taint of civilization had sprouted in the interim, surely the *Peahen's* men would have known about it.

"Here." The fluffy kitten waved the gold closer. She wore tattered shorts and a shirt that was held together by determination alone. "You want the gold?"

"Keep it," Alex said. "I've no use for doubloons now."

"My brother . . ." The sniffles caught her, and she dissolved into a fit of sobs, sitting on her tail in the sand beside his dead fire and letting the gold drop uselessly from her paw.

"Easy," Alex said. "Just let me cut him down, and we'll sort this all out."

Louder sniffles answered, as if the tide had broken and would not be stopped by mere reassurance. Alex sighed and turned back to the boy, half-certain he would take a rock to the back for his trouble.

Inside his net, the first kitten had grown still and sullen. When Alex reached for the rope, the little devil hissed at him, spitting and snarling through the mesh.

"Hold still and behave or I'll leave you in there." Alex barked it, using a voice he'd left behind with his old crew, with rank and obedience and all the things he'd meant to cast away forever. It worked on the kitten, who fell silent immediately. They both watched him, as he loosened his knots and eased the net back to the sand, big eyes in round faces.

When the net fell away, the boy scrambled free of it, bounded toward his sister, and then sat down beside her. Neither fled into the jungle, and Alex regarded them across the gap, filled in his details while the light grew and revealed more of their condition.

Half-starved perhaps. Certainly bonier than any kitten had a right to be. The female was fluffier, but likely just from more attention to grooming. Both their coats were duller than healthy and thin in places, and as he watched the boy began to scratch at his belly as some unseen parasite wandered beneath his fur.

"What are you doing here?" Alex heard the gruffness in his

own voice and cringed along with his audience. His anger was not aimed at them but at wherever the fault for their condition lay.

They exchanged a look and said absolutely nothing. Not that he needed an immediate answer. They'd come to his camp for food, and the need for it was as plain to see as his own whiskers. It wouldn't matter how many traps he set. He'd have no peaceful ending so long as these two were nearby with empty bellies.

"You're hungry," he said. "I'll make breakfast."

He left them where they sat, gave enough berth not to spook them as he returned to stoke the fire and dig through his supplies. He'd brought more than he needed, just in case, hadn't enjoyed the idea of ending his days in hunger. So now he cracked two tins of sardines and set them atop one of his trunks. Then he drizzled some oil into his pan and opened one of two bags of gizzards he'd indulged in at the last minute in Ravensport.

"Start with the fish," he said. "These will take a while."

For a moment, nothing moved. Alex drew his boot knife and began to slice the organs into the pan. He didn't look up once, and eventually heard the padding of paws, the soft rustling as the kittens approached the crate and dove on the proffered fish. He fried his gizzards to the smacking of lips and the scuffling of tin against wood.

By the time they'd quieted down, his first slices were golden brown. "Keep the tins handy. I've only the one plate."

"Why don't you want our gold?" The girl stood beside the trunk, holding her empty sardine tin in one paw. The gold, she'd retrieved and stacked upon the trunk beside his sapphire. "Do you like gems more?"

"I've no need for either." Alex spooned half the slices into her tin, and the other half into her brother's.

The boy had sat on the sand and held his breakfast in his lap. His tail curled around his feet, and he was busy scratching again. "Why not?" he asked.

His sister chimed in on his heels. "Mamma said pirates only love treasure."

"Your mother," Alex fit the pieces together in his mind, "isn't with you any longer?"

"She died." The boy spat it as fiercely as he'd hissed from the netting.

"Is there anyone else to care for you?"

"It was just us and Mamma," the female kitten informed him around a mouthful of gizzard.

"How long has she been gone?" Alex put his pan back in the fire and began slicing again. A cat with kittens alone on an island, on this particular island, told a clear enough story. Either she'd escaped while her ship was moored here, or she'd been deliberately abandoned to her fate. Both possibilities would explain her opinion of pirates.

The kittens exchanged a look and shrugged without answering him.

Alex turned back to his cooking, mulling over his own past, over the whole of piracy and its atrocities, and doing his best not to imagine the circumstances which would leave a new or expecting mother alone on the island. He sat back when the gizzards were finished and decided to eat them straight from the pan.

"Why are you here?"

Alex looked up from his meal to find both kittens had crept to the far side of the fire. They watched him with gleaming eyes and oily faces.

"I'm here to die," he said.

"How come?" the boy asked.

"Are you sick?" The female scooted back a pace.

"No." Alex sighed and swallowed a too-hot bite. "Damn. No. I'm not sick, I'm old. My glory days are finished, and I can feel the years catching up with me. It's my time to go, and I'd like very much to do it in peace and quiet."

If they noticed his sarcasm, it rolled right off them.

"So you're just gonna give up?" The boy sat and scratched his belly. "That's stupid."

"Shh." His sister poked him in the ribs. "That's rude, Toby."

"It's all right," Alex said. "When you're old enough to feel your bones creaking, you'll understand, Toby."

"I'm gonna live til I'm a hundred." Toby glared defiance across the fire.

Alex laughed. He'd thought no different as a kitten. "Tell me your sister's name, then, so we can be properly introduced."

“Tabitha,” Toby said, earning another rib jab for his trouble.

“And I’m Alex.”

“Are you a pirate?” Tabitha ceased abusing her brother and turned her attention to him.

“I might have been once,” Alex answered. “But in the course of a life, you’ll find, you can be many things.”

“That’s why he don’t want our gold,” Tabitha said. “He ain’t a pirate no more.”

“Also debatable,” Alex said. “Though I am curious how two kittens all on their own managed to come upon six gold doubloons and a sapphire worth more than all our heads together.”

“Three,” Tabitha said.

Both kittens drooped visibly, hung their heads, and let their tails shrink and fall to the sands. Their wide eyes turned glossy enough to spawn a lump of certain dread in Alex’s belly. He felt it coming like a punch, like a surprise uppercut just when you think you’ve got your opponent on the ropes.

“Three.” She repeated it. “There are three of us.”

THE LITTLE CAVE lay inland from his camp, tucked against the rising island interior and secreted beneath a denser mat of foliage and a canopy of thick palms.

The kittens led him to it, darting through the brush with practiced expertise that more than convinced Alex the little rats held total dominion over his “deserted” island.

He had to scramble to keep up with them. By the time they reached the crack in the ground that was their home, his chest complained, and his breath came in heavy shudders.

A small pack slung over his shoulder, filled with sardine tins and tobacco which, if the symptoms Tabitha described and the way Toby itched were any indication, should fix what ailed them. Provided they’d fetched him in time.

Toby vanished into the cave, but Tabitha waited primly for Alex to disentangle himself from the brush. Her dull fur was pale grey in the light, touched with faint stripes. She was even skinnier than he’d first expected, though her belly was round and distended.

A sure sign of worms.

He followed her into the crack, squeezing to fit and half

afraid the room beyond could not contain him. Surprisingly, the cave opened into a domed chamber big enough for him to stand erect. It was lit by a single, guttering candle stump. Crates piled against one wall, and a heap of clothing and blankets made a filthy mountain in the room's centre.

Atop these, the third kitten slept, and were it not for the soft rise and fall of his sunken in chest, Alex would have believed they'd arrived too late. The smell coming from the blankets could have choked a sewer rat.

"That's Thomas," Tabitha whispered.

The sick boy was a near twin to his brother, pure black of fur but with a softer grey underbelly. This was distended and raw, showing skin where the hair had thinned too much and the only part of the boy's body that didn't look emaciated.

"Worms," Alex said, "from the fleas."

"We don't have fleas," Toby insisted, simultaneously scratching at his belly.

"It's the same thing that happened to Mamma," Tabitha whispered.

"Can you boil water?" Alex scanned the cave more closely. The crates were battered, showing signs both of age and of water damage. He guessed the castaway cats had salvaged them from the beaches, as well as the blankets, which reeked of mould beneath the odour of urine and feces. "I'd like to make a tea, but if we can't cook, he can always just chew this."

He slung his pack to the floor and untied it while Tabitha scurried to the crates. When he stood, tobacco pouch in hand, the kitten had vanished into the nearest box. Only her tail tip showed over the rim, and the sound of metal clanking filled the dim cave.

Toby sulked in a far corner, scratching until Alex looked in his direction. Then his paws dropped to his sides and his big eyes glared defiance.

"Can you make a fire, son?"

"Mamma taught us all how."

"Get to it then. Take my waterskin."

"There's a basin," Tabitha poked her head up and scrambled out of the crate with a copper pot in one hand. "Collects rainwater."

"Good. Use that. Get it good and boiling and then come and

fetch me."

Toby wanted to argue, but his sister had more sense. She shooed him out ahead of her, and Alex was left alone to inspect Thomas and see just how bad things had gotten. The kitten moaned when he palpated the belly. His eyes fluttered but looked glazed and distant. The sounds that tumbled from the kitten's lips were incoherent, delirious.

"Hang in there, son," Alex said. "Just need to get you cleaned out, eh?"

Of course, everything in the cave was contaminated. The fleas would not vanish just because the worms were dead. Alex feared the whole litter would be re-infested in a week if left to their own devices.

The alternative, of course, was to get involved. Standing in the filthy cave, the weight of what that would entail pressed his ears flat. There was no peace and quiet here. He'd chosen a very poor place to die.

Unless he wanted to go out with a belly full of parasites.

Shuddering, Alex smoothed the fur back from the kitten's face and probed around his neck until he found a steady pulse. He found no mites inside the boy's ears, but more than one flea bounced away from his attentions.

Which made him want to scratch . . . and run.

Instead, he lifted the blanket, confirmed his diagnosis with one glance at the boy's posterior, and shivered again before dropping the cover back into place.

Thomas groaned softly, and Alex the Red, former pirate and seafarer, iron stomach of the high seas, retched and barely made it out of the cave before losing his breakfast.

The kittens had a respectable fire going, and once the water bubbled, Alex dropped in a handful of tobacco. He steeped a strong tea and then insisted on three cups despite the kittens' protests. They'd all need to drink it, and then to bathe and burn just about everything inside their home.

"He's going to vomit," he told them. "And worse. You lot too, most likely. Do your best to keep yourselves clean, and make sure he drinks water. As much as you can keep down him."

"It tastes foul," Toby said. "Like poison."

"Because it is," Alex levelled with them. They'd survived this long on their own. Coddling was far behind them. "Enough to kill the worms but not the kitten. You'll drink it if you want to live. And burn those linens as soon as possible."

"Where are you going?" Toby stared into his cup and let his tail drag.

"Back to camp to fetch some decent food."

"We got lots of treasure," Toby said. He didn't look up, and his ears sagged. "Tabby knows where the big cave is."

"I'm coming back, Toby."

Alex forced as much of the tea down Thomas's muzzle as he could. The sick kitten thrashed at first, then swallowed obediently until half the cup was emptied. "He'll need another dose, and you'll need help with the cleaning. You can tell me all about it then."

Their eyes met, just for a breath before the kitten stared at his cup again.

"Drink your tea while I'm gone. Every drop if you can."

"Yes, sir."

He left them at the cave mouth, almost certain they would obey his orders. His mind fished about for his next move, which most likely involved moving three kittens into his camp and simultaneously derailing the plan for his own demise.

Part of him argued that they'd survived alone so far, that they might just make it without his help. The rest of him knew too much of the world to believe it. Another voice whispered of hidden chests and a cave somewhere filled to the brim with booty.

Just loud enough to make him feel guilty.

He worked his way back through the jungle, focused on the next six steps, on impossible implications and non-existent options. Wrapped so tightly in his own dilemma, Alex stumbled back into camp without even noticing it had been infiltrated.

It wasn't until he stared down the business end of a blunderbuss that Alex jerked to attention. It wasn't until the familiar, black-and-white tom emerged from behind his lean-to that Alex the Red knew he'd been betrayed.

"WHERE'S THE TREASURE?" The *Peahen's* captain paced from the sand to the firepit and back while his men helped themselves to Alex's rum and sardines. "You've been on the island less than three days, and already your camp is glittering with pirate gold."

They'd found the sapphire and the doubloons, of course. Alex had left them atop his trunk for all the world to see. He cursed his lapse now and twisted against the ropes holding his paws together behind his back.

"Where is it?" the captain growled. "You came here to fetch your booty, yes?"

"No." Alex shrugged. "But you'll never believe me."

One of the sailors planted a boot in his side, and he curled around the pain, rolling onto the sand and staying there until rough paws righted him again. The same paws which had liberated him of his pistols.

Alex squinted at the sea and tried to gauge how many hours they had til sundown. If the kittens burned their linens in daylight, the plume would certainly give them away. Even at night, the smell might sink them.

"Where's the treasure," the captain snarled.

"You sound like a parrot," Alex answered. "Same thing over and over."

The slap came far too quickly to dodge, not that he had anywhere to go. The back of the captain's paw cracked him across the jaw, and Alex's head snapped to one side.

"Let him think on it." The *Peahen*'s captain shrugged and waved a gesture to his cats that Alex couldn't decipher. "We have time."

They kicked him again for good measure. Alex endured the blows and curled around the pain. He'd fared worse in his days, but then, his body had been far more supple once. Each bruise would linger now, but any attention they lavished on him kept their focus away from the sky, from whatever the kittens were up to in their infested cave.

The pirates of the *Peahen*—and he was certain they were pirates now—settled into his camp, drank his rum, ate his food, and ransacked his trunks for any trace of a map. The kittens' treasure had convinced them Alex knew the island's secrets, and nothing they would or wouldn't find among his things could prove otherwise.

But as the rum took them, they staggered, paws churning up the vines and sands until one by one they passed out where they fell. Only the captain and a few cats remained alert. Dangerous.

Alex sat up. "Save me some rum," he said. "Have mercy. At

least leave the catnip alone."

The black-and-white tom's eyes narrowed. He left the lean-to and returned to Alex. "Where is it?"

He might be tough, but no cat alive could resist the nip.

Alex shook his head, earned another slap before pretending to fold. He hung his head and whispered, "Sewn into the pillow."

They took a knife to his bedding, sent down fluttering on the breeze, and settled in with his best pipe and the finest catnip in the southern seas.

Alex watched them, breath hitching around the pain in his ribs. Once they'd succumbed to the nip, he'd have to get free, get to the kittens, and then . . . His mind churned for a plan of action, but the island was too large a temptation to just hide and wait out the pirates.

The *Peahen*'s master would never leave empty-handed.

Alex flattened his ears and hissed softly. Someone belched nearby and soft laughter spread from the cats in his lean-to. The night wrapped the camp in a veil, and behind it, Alex heard the softest of rustling from the palms.

No.

He held his breath and caught the next flutter of movement through the jungle. Unmistakable. The approach of a small body stealing through the fronds.

Alex looked to the lean-to. The captain still sat upright. In the firelight, his eyes shone. A cloud of smoke dulled the scene, obscuring the companions who seemed to have fallen over or lain down willingly. Only the captain remained, and as Alex watched, his fat head lolled forward before jerking back to attention.

Their eyes met. For a breath Alex believed the other cat would cross the camp and slit his throat. He'd have welcomed that quick a death yesterday, but the sounds from the jungle changed his mind now.

There was more than his hide to worry about.

As if on cue, the soft padding of little paws sounded behind him. Alex watched the captain, waiting for the other cat to notice. But even as Toby's low purring reached him, Alex saw the *Peahen*'s master succumb to the nip. The black-and-white fur rippled, and the big tom fell onto his side.

“Hurry, little one,” Alex whispered. “They’ve all gone to their dreams now.”

He imagined the kitten meant to untie him, but the cool press of a blade brushed against his paw pads, and with three sharp jerks, the ropes fell free.

Alex scooted back, easing toward the foliage and keeping his eye on the lean-to, his ears swivelling. When no one twitched, he rolled to all fours and faced a grinning Toby.

“You didn’t wait for me,” he said.

“Come on.” The kitten bounced in place and then wiggled back into the vines.

Alex followed his puff tail. They crawled through the jungle, bellies down and tails snaking behind them. He listened for any sound of pursuit, and once they’d left the camp far enough behind, lifted into a crouch and tried to get his bearing.

“Toby?”

The kitten popped up from a bunch of ferns.

“Where are we going?” The little cave lay sharply to their left, yet the kitten led him determinedly away from the previous trail.

“To meet up with Tabby,” the kitten answered. “She’s helping Thomas.”

“They’ll follow us,” Alex said. “We should lead them to the cave. Maybe we can set a trap.”

“This way’s better.” Toby grinned and bounced again. “You’ll see.”

He bounded off, but Alex stopped him, pouncing despite the aches in his bones and dragging the kitten around by his collar.

“Wait,” he hissed. “Do you have any of that gold on you, son?”

Toby’s eyes stretched wide. A tickle of fear crossed his features, but he nodded and shoved his paws into his trouser pockets. Alex took a handful of doubloons from him and then, while the kitten watched, flung one back the way they’d come. Then he then hurled the rest toward the cave.

“They’ll follow that for a ways,” he said. “Slow them down at least.”

“I knew you weren’t a pirate.” The kitten grinned back at him.

ALEX CARRIED THOMAS in his arms after the boy stumbled for the third time. Tabitha had helped him as far as she could, and by the time they reunited in the jungle, all three kittens looked weaker, haggard.

They'd been through hell tonight already, and Alex couldn't promise it wasn't about to get worse. The rum and nip would wear off eventually, and there was only so much island he could put between them and the *Peahen*'s crew. With the cave abandoned and his camp destroyed, they had no supplies, no weapons.

He carried the boy and kept his fears to himself, following the littlest of guides and trusting in the kittens' intimate knowledge of the landscape to keep them alive.

They crossed the island to a point nearly opposite his camp. Here the cliffs rose high above the sea and a trail like a twisting hair wound along the top of the rocks. Far below them, the sea churned and beat against the land, deep and wild and studded with jagged rock.

Moonlight lit their way, but Alex cursed it. The jungle fell to leggy brush here and the light would make them an easy target from the shelter of the palms. He followed behind Toby—who followed Tabitha—crouching over the boy in his arms and darting continual nervous looks behind them.

Any minute now, a shot could ring out.

Death by bullet would also be acceptable, and yet, the kittens would be left to the *Peahen*'s crew, end up as slaves at best, dead most likely.

"Where are we going?" His nerves came out in a hissed protest.

"Not far," Toby called back.

Alex rumbled in his throat and checked the trees again. Three more paces, however, and Tabitha vanished. His heart stalled, certain the girl had tumbled from the cliff, but Toby bounded after her and out of view just as quickly.

Alex scooted to the spot and found a crack in the trail. A narrow passage led into the cliff itself, barely large enough for him to squeeze inside. He had to adjust his cargo, sling the half-conscious Thomas over his shoulder to pass through, but once he did, the way opened.

He stood inside a tunnel, tall enough for a grown cat and

clearly not fashioned by nature's paw. The floor sloped downward and curved deeper into the cliff, and a clear pattern of tiny pawprints marred the layer of sand and dust inside the passage.

Alex eased Thomas back across his chest and checked the kitten's breathing. The boy would have a long recovery, and yet, when he cracked an eye and grinned up at Alex, the glassy look had passed.

Only trust remained, a blind acceptance that made Alex's belly squirm as if *he* had the worms now.

The other two returned from around a curve in the path. They stared at him expectantly, waiting with the same naïve expressions.

Alex swallowed and gave a stern nod. Then he marched after them, down the twist of tunnel and around, spiralling toward sea level and what he suspected would be the mother of all pirate troves.

The tunnel turned again, snaked to the left and right, and then stretched its mouth wide and spat them out in a sea cave lined with stone teeth and a tongue of sloping sand. The ocean thrashed in that maw, carrying the sting of salt and moistening the air until it dripped from every hair in Alex's pelt.

He stood where the path ended, staring. Every shelf and cranny in the cave gleamed. Chests perched on both rock and sand, some closed tight but many more overflowing with doubloons and gemstones. Jewellery sparkled from every corner. Gold plates and goblets tumbled through the tide of coins, strewn from their chests by nature or the tiny paws of three little kittens.

Alex surveyed it all, gold reflecting in his pupils. He scanned the treasure of all treasures, but in the end his eyes landed on the centrepiece of the cave, a slope of sand built into a ramp, a stout post wound round with rope, and tethered like a crown jewel atop the makeshift launch pad, a sleek wooden sloop.

Alex the Red stared at the ship, the stones, and the open sea and laughed.

"STAY DOWN." ALEX waved to Toby and ducked behind the gunwale while the sound of many boots rang through the tunnels. "Hold steady, son."

They crouched in the bow of the little sloop, tucked behind the railing and armed only with two knives that had more decoration than blade and a single matchlock pistol Alex scavenged from below deck.

The stores there were sparser than he'd hoped, and they'd dumped more than one barrel of rot over the side before finding tins that might still be edible. Tabitha and Thomas were safely below deck, but Toby had insisted on remaining with Alex despite the sound of many pirates descending upon them.

The treasure gleamed. The ocean heaved. The rope holding the sloop in place creaked and strained. It was a fine place for a last stand, a magnificent arena in which to die had that still been his intention.

"Hold," he whispered. "Wait for my mark."

Alex the Red watched the tunnel opening, listened to the boots, and prayed the *Peahen*'s captain would continue to be predictable. When the black-and-white cat led his pirates into the sea cave, Alex grinned.

"Now, Toby. Just like I showed you."

When he heard the scrape of flint against steel, Alex stood. He brandished the matchlock wildly and shouted, "Stop right there."

The pirate captain grinned back at him. His long tail lashed behind his legs, and he raised one paw into the air and held it there, ready to signal the order to shoot Alex down. Pirates still poured into the cave, but the sight of gold stalled them, and the tide backed up at the narrow entrance as the cats froze in place to gape at the treasure.

Behind Alex, a telltale hissing said the boy had succeeded in his task.

"Get below, son," Alex ordered. "No argument."

"I knew you'd lead us to it," the *Peahen*'s master crowed up at them. "You old bastard. I know who you are."

"Then you know better than to take another step," Alex said.

That gave him pause. Alex could see the flash of concern, the way the cat's ears lowered.

"Give up, old man." There was less force in the captain's next order, but he stood stock still and as proud as a cock amid the doubloons. "The treasure is ours."

"You're welcome to it." Alex grinned and let his eyes drift

long enough to see the spark traveling against the far wall, following the fuse that Toby had lit. "And may it carry you swiftly to the depths of hell."

His paw flew to the hilt of his knife. Too ornate for his tastes but sharp enough for this task. The spark raced closer to the tunnel mouth, and Alex ducked back behind his gunwale and sawed at the mooring rope for all he was worth.

One of the pirates shouted. A single shot rang sharp and deadly in the cave, echoing even before the round tore through the sloop's hull. Too small to worry about, and much too low to end him.

The kittens, however, were inside that hull, and Alex had to steel himself not to stand and return fire. He had only one shot, and might still need it if . . .

The cave shuddered. Rock exploded at the tunnel mouth as the spark found its home in a case of dynamite left beside the entrance. Pirates screamed and stalactites tumbled from the ceiling, splashing into the sea, the chests, and the deck of the sloop as well.

Alex drove his knife against the rope and felt the last ply give way. The deck jerked as the ship caught for one terrifying moment and then slid easily into the water. The weight in her prow carried her swiftly through the cave's maw. Alex clung to the gunwale as the waves took her, passing her from one swell to the next out to the open sea.

The cave fell away, a smoking hole in the island, boiling over with dust and debris. The last thing Alex saw as they sailed forth was a furious, black-and-white face snarling through the thinning smoke.

What was left of the pirates would have a hell of a time getting out of there, time that would put his craft and his kittens far from the *Peahen*'s reach when the captain finally returned to his vessel.

Alex brushed the grit from his pelt and stood, letting his legs flex with the motion of the sloop atop the waves. The air was full of salt and fury, and he had rigging to attend to, a course to set, and as much distance as possible to eat up before the *Peahen* drew up her anchors.

"Did it work?"

When he turned, two kittens stood beside the sloop's hatch.

They stared at him with wide eyes.

Alex nodded and waved a paw toward the last thing he'd loaded aboard the sloop, a fine, fat chest with a good stout lock upon it. "That needs to get below."

Tabitha's grin stretched wider. "You *are* a pirate," she said.

Toby leapt for the chest, tail puffing. "Pirates only love treasure," he purred.

"Not only," Alex said. He watched them tumbling over each other, prying at the lock with tiny claws. It would have been a nice place to die, surely, but maybe, he'd only needed a reason not to.

The sloop surged over the waves, the sky grew lighter, and behind Alex the Red, the island lay low in the water, weighed down by a belly full of gold and pirates.

"Besides," the old tom purred. "I'm the only one left to look after you lot, and I have a feeling you three are going to prove expensive."

BUCCANEER'S REVENGE

JB RILEY

THE ROAR OF cannon fire was deafening.

Below decks the screams of wounded men added a shrill counterpoint to the crunching booms of the two ships' broadsides, grapeshot and cannonballs pounding into midships and blowing gaping holes through timber and sailor alike in a ceaseless barrage.

Above was worse, a hellish landscape that swirled around men fighting almost nose-to-nose. It was brutal and raw with no quarter asked or given; guts sliced open to spill onto the slippery deck and throats cut without mercy. The British were better armed, better trained, and loyal to a fault. But the brigands had the numbers, and it seemed the very devil was on their side. As the old British quartermaster emptied his blunderbuss into the crazed pirate in front of him, he prayed aloud.

"Mother Mary, deliver us! Save us from Red Beard!"

Below, in the belly of the *Queen Cordelia*, Lieutenant Stewart pressed his lips to the Gunnery Sergeant's ear and yelled as loud as he could. "We need more wicks!" He gestured his cutlass toward the shuddering row of 12-pound guns that were firing, bouncing back in their cradles to be swabbed and refilled with powder and ball, then rolled forward to fire again. The Gunny shook his head. “We can’t spare a man,” he yelled, dragging a bloody body away and gesturing another of his gunner’s mates forward to fill the post. “It’s suicide!”

“It’s worse if we lose the cannons!” the young Lieutenant bawled back. “It’s Red Beard up there, man! We’ll all wish for death if we can’t hold them off!” At Gunny’s hesitation, he bared his teeth. “If none of your lot is man enough, I know who is!” He whirled around, placed his fingers to his mouth, and blew a piercing whistle above the din. “Jack!”

No response. He whistled again. “Union Jack!”

He tried a third time. Nothing.

“Cut!” a loud bell rang and everyone stopped what they were doing. “Tommy! Where’s that darn cat?”

“Not due until this afternoon, Chuck—I told you we were ahead of schedule.” A wiry young man wearing wire-rim glasses, a headset, and a *Buccaneers 5: Red Beard’s Revenge* t-shirt jogged up holding an iPad. “Look, see? Gus is scheduled to be on set at 1:30. He’s got press until then.”

“How come he gets press and I don’t?” asked the buxom blond in the fetchingly tattered dress as she passed through the conversation on her way to the Craft Table.

“Because he has more lines, Honey,” Chuck the director responded, grabbing the iPad from Tommy’s hands with a frown.

“The cat doesn’t have any lines,” Tommy muttered out of the side of his mouth.

“Neither does she,” Chuck hissed back, then raised his voice. “Honey? If you keep hitting the snacks Costume is going to have to let your dress out again, you know.” He handed Tommy the iPad with a sigh. “Kid, lemme give you one piece of advice. Never—and I do mean *never*—let yourself get talked into putting your ex-wife’s sister-in-law’s niece into a picture.”

Tommy didn’t ask which ex-wife, merely nodded and toggled a switch on his belt. “Let’s pick it up in thirty, folks,” he spoke into his headset, which was re-broadcast through the stage set. “And someone find me when the cat shows up.”

I HESITATED AT the front door of the trailer with its star and famous name on the door. I didn’t want to arrive tardy, but neither did I wish to bustle in, nervous. This was my first assignment for *Vanity Fur*, and much was riding on me getting my notoriously mercurial subject to open up and speak freely. Annie Fleabowitz had completed a photo shoot on set the week prior, and Greytom Carter, editor and publisher *emeritus* of Condor Nest Publishing, had proclaimed them superb.

Unspoken but obvious was the expectation my interview must be as well.

To increase my anxiety, there were no recorders allowed. This was old-school, and I would have to take notes by hand—and from those notes somehow write an article that captured the essence of a legend.

This would either make my career or return me to the hinterlands of North Carolina, tail dropped in shame. Kitty Hawk was a great place to be from, as they say, but I wanted the bright lights of Mew York City, and this interview could be my ticket.

A quick smooth of my whiskers, a deep breath, and I knocked on the trailer door.

"A Rebel With All His Claws"
Kit Chaton

PERHAPS THE MOST famous cat of the Current Age sits at his ease at a small table in his comfortable trailer. Impeccably groomed and sipping from a large snifter, his tiger-striped coat remains luxurious, famed whiskers sleek and long. He stands and greets me warmly with a rub to both jowls, then sits again and gestures toward his snifter.

"How about a drink?" That purr of a voice; echoes of movies from the days of my kittenhood. I try to demur but he insists.

"Bah—I won't take no for answer." He gestures toward his elderly valet, hovering attentively nearby. A snifter arrives in front of me and to be polite I dip my tongue, then have to fight the urge to upend the glass and lick it clean. This must show on my face; the great actor smiles. "Single-pail cream," he explains, "from my own private source, aged sixteen hours in a steel tub to bring out those wondrous grassy notes."

I place my snifter on the table with regret and groom my thanks, left paw to ear, then settle myself to the task at hand. "Mr. Asparagus—"

"Just 'Gus'," he interjects.

"Mr., ah, Gus. On behalf of your fans, thank you for this opportunity." I open my notepad and rest one claw lightly upon the first page. "First, tell me about your new film?"

"YES, I *KNOW* it's expensive, but we're going to need at least three days for reshoots because of this weather. Make it happen," Chuck crammed the phone back into his pocket and pinched the bridge of his nose. "Tommy, what's my mantra again?"

"'Ooohhmmmm'," the assistant offered, closing his eyes and breathing out in a controlled push of air.

"Not that one. The other one."

"'I could get away from all this, move to Bakersfield, open a little porno studio'?"

"That's the one." The director removed his *Darkening Army: Pharaoh's Revenge* baseball cap and wiped his forehead. "Now repeat that while rubbing my temples for me, will ya'?"

CHARLES "CHUCK" WOLF, legendary director and producer, offers up a rare smile when I ask about his superstar.

"Gus? Gus is a pro, and let me tell you, they are hard to find these days." We sit in a semi-quiet corner of the massive lot where the non-locations scenes of all the Buccaneers films are shot. "I knew the first time I met him he'd be big."

"Tell me about that first meeting," I say.

"I was filming *Hallows Horrors 3: Witch's Revenge* and he came to read for a bit part. He lit up the audition and I knew then and there I needed to keep an eye on him." The director shrugs. "I couldn't use him for that part, of course, needed a black cat—"

The set's media liaison, a petite brunette with an impressive manicure, jumps forward and whispers urgently in his ear.

"What?" Wolf shifts in his seat to look at her. "I'm not—look, I don't have a racist bone in my body." More whispering. "Fer Chrissakes, Mandy, it was a horror film. The script called for a black cat, it's not typecasting." He waves a hand in irritation. "Anyway, when I needed to cast a High Priest for *Pharaoh's Revenge* I went to Gus and his agent right away. He read for the part and the rest is history."

History indeed. Playing the High Priest of Bast in a low-budget horror movie launched Gus' career. From the big-budget *Converters* series (where Gus' searing portrayal of a shell-shocked Viet Nam vet turned junkyard cat earned him his first Oscar) and box office behemoths like *Mad Manx: Furry Road* to more intimate roles—such as his fearless species-swapped turn in *The Cat of the Baskervilles*—Gus was box office gold.

When Dreamworks Animation announced a live-action version of *Puss in Boots*, there was only one choice for lead actor. The movie won Gus not only his second Oscar but also a Best Song Grammy for "El Gato Mi Corazon (feat. Justin Beaver)" which he co-wrote and produced. The cat from Fox Valley, Illinois was halfway to an EGOT and the sky was the limit.

Wolf's career was revitalized as well; he had found his muse. Their four-film *Buccaneers of the High Seas* series minted money and made the director a major player in Hollywood.

Then *Variety* broke the news Gus was going to serve as financier, executive producer, and lead actor for a movie he described as his dream role; a near-mythic story but one he felt needed to be told. At first he seemed to know his limitations, hiring script doctors and a big-name director to bring his vanity project to life, but then rumours of everything from cost overruns to catfights among the female co-stars hit the tabloids. Gus radiated calm through the pre-release press junket, laughing through late-night interviews with Jimmy Falcon, James Corvid, and Stephen Cold Bear, but the critics smelled chum in the waters and started to circle. The final cut was not pre-screened, always a bad sign.

Meowster and Catmander: The Growltiger Chronicles was released at the height of the summer blockbuster season.

It did not land on its feet, and reviews were scathing.

"Misogynistic in the extreme . . ." "The villains are faceless and the heroes wooden . . ." "An unmitigated mess of gory battles and stereotypes . . ." "This film makes *Ishtar* look like *Citizen Kane* . . ."

A feline Icarus had flown too close to the sun, and his resulting crash to earth made the entire film industry tremble.

Gus removed himself from the public eye. There were rumours of a rehab facility in the Catskills, a pilgrimage to Kathmandu, conversion to Scientology. Then TMZ broke the story that Gus' agent was negotiating a reunion with Chuck Wolf for another *Buccaneers* movie.

Gus has never publicly commented about his most infamous film. Hesitant, I ask if he had anything he wanted to share now. He simply shrugs.

"You have to understand, Kit, it was a tale of a different time. *Growltiger* was supposed to be a film showing the brutality of the Catnip Wars—brutality on both sides, mind you, Chinese and British—and the script team included Siamese writers brought in to manage sensitivity. The whole sampan battle was originally intended as a metaphor for Colonialism, for example."

Perhaps considering his racist reputation, Mel Gibbon wasn't the best choice for director, I suggest gently. Gus raises his right foot high in the air to groom his flank and then reaches for the blue pack of Dunhills sitting on the table between us. Extracting and tamping a cigarette, he lights it with a clawflick against the flint he returns to his breast pocket and smokes, pensive.

Suddenly he checks his watch, then crushes his cigarette and stands abruptly. "I am due on set," he says brusquely, though the paw he extends has its claws politely sheathed. "We can pick this up later."

"HE IDOLIZED GROWLTIGER, you know."

Startled, I turned, arching my back and hissing at the valet.

He moved his ears peaceably. "Easy, Kit." He flicked his tail and sauntered to the table. "Gus was not always an actor. He is a naval cat to the core: in his first life he sailed with Admiral Seymour to open the ports of Canton during the real Catnip Wars. He fought for queen and country, but what he saw—what he did—those dark days still haunt him. When he's deep in the cream sometimes he yowls for old mates who lost their lives in the bombings along the Pearl River."

"How do you know?" I ask, fascinated. The thought came to me that this was a much better story but as I made to pick up my notebook, he flattened his ears and growled. "This is off the record."

I flicked an ear in agreement—though I knew my editor would want my hide for the concession—and the valet settled into the cushion across from me. He loosened his tie, and then spent some time grooming his shoulders and back before chewing between his front toes. Though still in my first life I wasn't born yesterday; I recognized the stalling tactic and tucked my paws under my chest, settling in to wait.

Finally, the valet seemed satisfied with the lay of his coat. He pulled a thin cigar from the pocket of his vest, bit and lit it then puffed until a smooth plume of smoke curled around both our heads. He blinked at me to acknowledge my patience, and spoke.

"Gus and I shipped out together in 1855. In Victoria's opinion the Orient was a mess, and it was killing too much of the spice and tea trade. You have to understand: China had two declared emperors, they were seizing British ships and jailing British crew. Finally, the Colonial Governor called for support. Seymour sailed the HHS Calcutta to answer the call."

The valet leaned back and smiled. "Ah, those were ships, back in the day. None of these clanking monsters full of wire and steel. These were proper vessels, made to sail that route, and the rigging? Oh, sure, we weren't supposed to play in the rigging or the vast sheets of sails but we did anyway, between keeping the rats out of the ship's biscuit and the roaches from the rum.

"Our commander, answerable only to Admiral Seymour himself, was Growltiger, the former Terror of the Thames. He was a fierce bravo cat who had signed onto the Calcutta to avoid lockup in the Tower of London. His crimes had been heinous but his word was good, and once pardoned, he maintained the honour of the Empire just as fiercely as he'd maintained the terror of his reign."

TOMMY SPOKE INTO his headset. "Are we ready to swing her between the ships yet?" A pause. "Why the hell not? Quit frigging with the rigging and get her ready." A longer pause, then he looked over at his director. "Stunts says Honey doesn't want to wear the harness. Says it's—and I quote—icky."

Chuck grabbed his megaphone and bellowed, "Honey, you have to wear the harness, I don't care where it chafes you!" He settled back in his chair and rasped a hand across his chin. "I need a shave. I need a drink. I need a new career."

Tommy, typing rapid-fire on his iPad, snorted then touched his headset. "Stunts says now Honey says—wait, what?" He listened intently for a moment, and then sighed. "I'll tell him. Hey, Chuck? Honey says this all sucks, the harness is going to wreck the boob job she got for graduation, and demands we use a stunt double. She also wants a smoothie."

Chuck closed his eyes. "Get her a stunt double."

Tommy was keeping a wary eye on the vein throbbing in Chuck's temple. "We don't have the budget for another stunt double."

Throb. "Use one of the stunt doubles we have." Throb.

"Um, Boss? All our stunt doubles are big, burly guys. Unless you want to re-write Honey as a bearded lady we don't have a credible female stunt double, and we can't hold production to try to find one."

Chuck's vein had settled into a samba beat. "Why don't you go over and see if any of the girls in craft services want to get their big break," he suggested in a deceptively mild tone.

Tommy fled.

"MOST OF THE time the Siamese were the least of our worries." The valet leaned forward and tapped a claw on the table top for emphasis. "When you sail into a hurricane, Kit, there's no other thing in the world like it. You're terrified of drowning even standing on the deck. The winds will take you, no matter how deep you sink your claws into a surface, and the ship spins like a kitten after its own tail. And let me tell you," he winked, "you're puking up much more than hairballs the entire time. The only thing to do is furl sail, drop anchor, huddle below, and pray to Bast.

"But Growltiger was fearless. It didn't matter if we were in a hurricane or he was leading the charge against the forts in Canton, he would sneer in the face of danger. Saved the life of every cat and man on that warship at least once. Gus worshipped the sand he pooped in. We all did.

"The reviews for that Gibbon movie broke Gus' heart. All his lives he wanted to do right by his commanding officer. He won't give up, but he's in his last life and almost out of time. Why do you think he's doing these ridiculous movies? Gus faced down real pirates." The valet picked up a cruel-looking cutlass from the props pile next to his chair and offered it to me to sniff. It was plastic.

"He needs to raise the money for one more try." The old cat stared at me and I dipped my chin meekly. "Now remember, this is all off the record. I catch you writing about this and you'll never work in this town again." I twitched an ear, accepting his admonition.

The valet's cigar was done, and it seemed his story, as well. He stood and stretched carefully, then tightened his tie and picked up the empty snifters. He refused to say more, not even give his name, and with a firm swat to the nose urged me to leave the trailer.

TOMMY THE ASSISTANT director didn't pause as I asked him to comment. "The cat? He's a cat, what's the big deal? I'm allergic," he threw over his shoulder as he brushed past me.

LIEUTENANT STEWART SAGGED against the poop deck rail. He did not look at the blood-soaked square of cloth pressed hard against his side but instead fixed his eyes on the horizon. "Jack? Are you there, Jack? My sight grows dim."

A meow answered. "We won the day, my brother," the young Lieutenant gasped. "Please. Promise me." He coughed as bloody froth ringed the corners of his mouth. "Promise you'll take my sword and give it to my son, when he is old enough to understand."

The cat rubbed hard against Stewart's boots, once perfectly polished but now covered in gore. Gus sat down on the deck, looked up into the Lieutenant's face, and meowed again.

"I know," Stewart replied, sagging further. "I know you were always proper with her but Mary loves you, Gus. Go to her now. Take care of her." He coughed, spat red, his voice growing faint. "Take care of her. For me." His body fell the rest of the way to lie still on the deck. The cat approached and sniffed at the slack face, twitched his whiskers and sneezed, then sat and began licking his chest.

"CUT! THAT'S A wrap, people. Great job." I blinked back tears, overcome by the strength of the performance, and was not the only one so moved. Director Wolf wiped at his eyes and blew his nose, then walked onto the deck and bent to stroke the tiger-striped back.

"Gus, you nailed it again. We are back, Baby!" The director straightened and waved his hands. "Come on, people, we can break down tomorrow. Time for the wrap party!" He looked at me. "You, kid, what's your name, come on and join us. Maybe you'll get a few more quotes you can use for your story."

Tommy, typing at his iPad, sighed and pulled a pack of antihistamines from his pocket. "Press at an after-party? Like that's a good idea," he muttered, dry-swallowing a handful of tablets.

"Ah, come on, Tommy, stop worrying and live a little. It's never too early to get some Oscars buzz going. Hey Honey, this kid's from *Vanity Fur*, wriggle out of that harness and come talk to him about working with Gus."

SCHEDULES BEING WHAT they are, it was over a week before I sit down with Asparagus to complete our interview, this time over cocktails at the trellis bar of the famed Persian Room inside Mew York's Plaza Hotel. Gus has just been announced as this summer's Artist in Residence at the Gershwin Theatre and—though flawlessly polite as always—he is clearly impatient to begin his first workshop, a revival of Williams' *The Glass Menagerie* set in the gritty streets of Cardiff during the 1984 Miners' Strikes. It is already rumoured to bring him frontrunner status at next year's Tonys.

I attempt to revisit *Growltiger* and the toll it took on him, but Gus simply bats my questions away. Finally, I twitch a conciliatory ear and try a different approach.

"Looking back on your career, the role you return to seems to be one of the British Naval officer. *Growltiger*, of course, plus your work in that East End production of *Mutiny on the Bounty* and your five films as Union Jack in *Buccaneers*. You seem to have an affinity for the roles, and certainly fans respond."

He eyes me narrowly but nods. "The first four *Buccaneers* set box office records," he replies, "and if this fifth one does well I hope there's a sixth."

"Will you ever tire of the role?" I ask. He shrugs and smooths one eyebrow. "Perhaps. It is difficult for an actor to keep a role fresh, after all. But Chuck has many financial obligations—all those ex-wives—and as long as he keeps making these movies and wishes me to play the lead, I will be glad to do so."

"Will you ever revisit your role as *Growltiger*?"

And there is the question. He regards me still and unblinking for so long I cannot but finally blink myself. Finally—with a slight whisker twitch of amusement and a resigned sigh—he gives his answer.

"You have to understand," he starts slowly, "I am the cat I am today because someone believed in me. All my successes started with that simple belief—that I was meant for something greater than a life rummaging alleys or pawning my collar for a measure of gin."

The pack of Dunhills come out and he taps one but does not light it. "It is hard to resist the tales spun by one's own press secretary, the bright light of glory. But in the dark? I am still the half-grown tabby from St. Katherine's docks who chased mice and dreams of glory."

He takes a sip of his Wild Turkey on the rocks. "I am proud of *Growltiger*. I believe it to be a good movie about a great cat, one built as best I could build it." He finally lights his cigarette, leans back in the rattan chair, and blows a long stream of smoke toward the open air. "And understand: any shortcomings are my own, not the source material."

WITH THAT HE would say no more other than I must make contact his assistant when *Menagerie* opened and there would be tickets waiting at the box office. I took it as politeness, made polite responses of my own while thinking of a half-grown tabby from the docks—in his first life and with scarce prospects—lifted up by a Legend now almost lost to fading memory.

I made my exit with slightly distracted thanks and hurried out to hail a cab. I might still have my article to complete and turn in, but I already knew what my next one would be.

It would be an in-depth history (or—dare I dream?—a novelization) of Growltiger: Terror of the Thames, Hero of the Empire.

THE FURGELDT COLLECTOR

JOSEPH HALDEN

"WALK THE PLANK, calico." Captain Powderpuff, white fur stained a red-brown from all her victims, purred at me from the ship's helm.

When the captain stopped using your name, you knew there'd be no more parleying.

Dogs. I could have really used some catnip.

The sea of the Great Lake tossed below, only a thin slice of wood holding me from the murky depths. A trio blocked me way back onto the ship, swords held out and tails raised, drifting in the air like the pondweed that would be me grave.

Tattooed sphinx cats, completely furless, clung to the ship's rails, waiting for me to fall. Those monsters *liked* the water.

They licked their lips, reminding me that plank-walkers doubled as bait.

With their long, sharpened claws, they were ready to pounce and kill the tiger fish that would soon arrive. The crew would feast on the fish once the fish had eaten me.

This circle of life was a wet hairball.

"I can get you a better *furgeldt*, Captain," I tried again, standing tall on two feet and grasping me tricorn so it didn't blow into the dogs' winds.

"No more excuses, calico," the captain said. "They want *your* head for this."

"But you sent me after them!"

It was true. She'd sent me to collect retribution—a *furgeldt* of twenty-two doubloons—from the rival Lake Superior Scoundrels. I'd collected it in the form of one paw, two fangs, and an ear.

That hadn't sat well with the Scoundrels, who claimed the *furgeldt* wasn't owed. Me role as law cat was finished.

"I told you I didn't assign that bounty," Captain Powderpuff lied, shaking her head. "You are sullying the honour of every law cat on the five lakes."

She had set me up.

This felt as rotten as when I'd lost me family, and had become a sister to no one.

She made a swiping motion with her front paw. "Myarr, me kitties! Take a token, then make the calico walk the plank."

One of the pirate trio came forward and plucked one of me whiskers—proof of me demise to show the Scoundrels. Then the trio prodded me forward. I hissed and swatted at them, but soon found meself at the edge.

I wrapped me tail around the plank, keeping me back to the water. I had one last trick up me sleeve: the open porthole with a missing cannon. If I could swing meself there, I could maybe get a weapon and a lifeboat.

"Myarr! Tail up, calico!" Captain Powderpuff shouted while the crew jeered.

Fine. Now or never.

I jumped backward, keeping hold with me tail. I whipped in an arc toward the ship, and slammed into the side below the hole, scrambling to get up. It was slick, but me claws had been studded with silver and dug deep.

Dogs damn it all, the crew poured oil on me. It splashed into me eyes. I sputtered. Slowed.

Just as I got a claw on the edge of the cannon hole, they dropped torches.

I ignited like a bundle of kindling, and couldn't drop to the water fast enough.

The cold quenched the fire, but spelled me doom. I thrashed, but me breath was suffocated and a dark shape—the tiger fish—moved toward me to claim me eighth life.

I AWOKE AS a spirit at the bottom of the Great Lakes with sand in me eyes and a choking hairball in me throat. I gagged and coughed it out. The hairball dissolved into white mist that twirled and fanned out in rat tails. It left behind an orange and aqua strand of yarn that floated to the lake bed. Orange and aqua, like the stripes of me family flag.

This was the final goodbye of me eighth life. I had seen the same thing seven times before.

Now came the long journey to the Catfish Queen, where I'd make me case for resurrection. She would ask about me life—what had gone wrong and what had gone right—and what I planned to do differently this time.

The whole trip, there'd be no bloody catnip.

Usually the Queen granted resurrection to every spirit that came to her, up to nine lives. Nobody knew for sure what happened after your ninth death but some, including me, believed the journey to the Catfish Queen was more arduous the ninth time, and spirits got lost following loose strands of yarn. Going astray was a risk every time I made the cursed journey.

Lengths of yarn, trails in the spirit plane left throughout a cat's life, crisscrossed the basin of the Great Lakes like the roots of a forest. So many different colours: lilac, coral, daisy, and gooseberry, all of them enticing. I wanted nothing more than to get tangled in them.

It took all of me effort to follow the painful strand of me own life, the one that would lead to the Catfish Queen. Staring at the thread brought memories forward from the depths, memories better left unstirred.

A kitten in a world with turmoil everywhere except in the family. Where we'd fought for each other through thick and thin.

Then it all broke in a pirate raid.

We had to split up and survive on our own. Through those dark times, I'd told meself that at the end of it all, I would find everyone and restore what was lost.

But when I found me siblings—Patches, Twinky, and Rubix—they'd already moved on and joined bands of their own. They had no room for me. Like our blood bond meant nothing.

The loss, after so much struggle, was nearly unbearable.

From then on, I avoided thinking too much about the past. Catnip worked wonders for forgetting.

Me strength waned from the biting cold and the effort it took to wade through the painful memories of me thread. I pawed at strands of yarn more beautiful than me own. Those other lives would be much better to follow.

I remembered Captain Powderpuff, though, and the need for revenge helped me stay on me own strand until I reached the gold-knitted gates of the Catfish Queen's cave palace. Cat guards barred the way with scratching-post spears. They held them out as they asked who I was.

"Marshmallow Mittens," I said, looking away. I knew if I let meself touch the scratching post, me freedom would be gone.

One of them sniffed me, then checked me scent against a grid of kitty litter boxes at his side. He found a match proving I was on the "expected" list.

They refused to meet me gaze but let me pass into a high-ceilinged chamber filled with cat statues. I followed signs down a hallway lit by glowing snails, then lined up behind a pack of other dark, misty cat spirits.

We all awaited the Catfish Queen's judgment.

Cat by cat, I moved up the line toward the massive ball of yarn that formed the door to her chambers.

The yarn-door opened and a black cat spirit ran out.

"I deserve another life!" he yelled.

Guards poured out from many doors to corner the feral cat who scratched at them, putting up a valiant fight. That was until a large, striped cat came out with a box. She yelled at the guards to get back, and then threw the box close to where the feral cat was fighting.

The box opened. I fell to me stomach and gasped.

It was the perfect size. I could fit in there so easily . . .

The feral cat couldn't resist. He hopped in and curled up, eyes glazing over as he started to purr. He fit the box perfectly, too. I guessed any cat would have, with all paws tucked underneath, fur bulging over the edges.

"Take him to the dungeon," said the large striped cat. "No one resists the Queen's judgment."

What a mess. The cat wouldn't know his own name by next week. I shivered, averting me gaze as the guards took the box away.

Many more cats got taken away in boxes and I licked me paws nervously. The Catfish Queen had gotten much stricter. Was she even granting nine lives anymore?

Finally it was me turn, and I passed through the yarn tunnel.

The Catfish Queen lay in the centre of the court room's dais. Glowing and undulating jellyfish floated on either side of her. Behind the Queen, light reflected off a cavern lined with bright, gold riches. On the opposite side of the room, separated by another line of jellyfish, a throng of dark, glowing-eyed cat spirits scratched notes into slates.

The Catfish Queen looked as regal as ever. She was beyond fur, with smooth yellow-green skin, plump lips, and wide-set beads for eyes. Her whiskers were long and thick, with one on each side, then several more lining her chin. It was said these chin-whiskers gave her the ability to see truth.

I bowed.

"Your name and life number, please," she said, her voice a purr that shook its way round the world.

"Thank you, Your Highness. Me name's Marshmallow Mittens. I just lost me eighth life."

She waited for me identity to be confirmed, then nodded. "Welcome back, Marshmallow. You are seeking your final life. Tell me what you've done, and what you will do."

This was the worst part. I wanted nothing more than to bury me nose in catnip and roll around until I forgot who I was but if I didn't impress the Queen I'd never have catnip again.

"I was a law cat, Your Highness, collecting *furgeldts* to settle disputes between rival pirate factions. I could buy each side a measure of peace by ensuring blood debts had been paid."

Peace was what everyone liked to hear, but I didn't believe it lasted much longer than I had when I'd fallen overboard.

"And your death?"

"Betrayal." I fought to keep the anger from me voice as I explained what had happened.

"And what will you do with your last life, Marshmallow? I hope, for your sake, that it is not revenge."

Fine, then, me last life is for catnip, I thought.

"No, Your Highness. I want a measure of peace, so I might see the right of things before I become a law cat again. A *better,* more just law cat."

I hoped she couldn't see the truth *that* well today. The words were rough on me tongue. Such talk was cheap and nice, but not for me. What made the words taste like sour milk, though, wasn't that they were lies. I couldn't outright lie to the Queen. The words held truth, but it was a truth I would never taste.

Dog-damn this whole dog and jelly show. I'd need to lick meself clean three-times of this spirit world.

The Catfish Queen stared at me, unblinking, thick whiskers undulating.

"You don't fully believe your words, yet you speak truth."

All I could let out was a tiny purr.

"Your case is very strange. Strange enough I will give you this last chance. I suggest using your life to believe the truths you speak."

All her whiskers moved upward and a wave pushed me back into a bow. The Catfish Queen turned away, and I was carried out by the guards.

I WAS UNCEREMONIOUSLY dropped off at shore by a pair of jellyfish who stimulated me newly-assembled body into life. I hardly recognized me reflection.

Me new body had a coat of black fur with white socks. The only part of me still orange calico was me tail. It seemed the Queen was running low on stock.

First things first. I headed straight for the catnip bar up the shore. I could kill two mice with one paw: see how Kipper'd gotten along taking care of me parrot, Frank, while having some much-needed catnip.

Kipper, the bar owner, hadn't bothered to waste money on paint, which was how you knew it was a good joint. The jutting wooden flag had the place's named clawed into it, *The Frisky Whisker,* and the porch creaked like a braying donkey.

Patrons curled up in beds along the walls, everything tastefully dark except for the odd candle. I felt home at last.

Good old Kipper was bartending tonight. I put me head through a hole in the bar to sniff the day's offerings.

A bit stale and dusty, but it would do.

"I'll take three bowls, Kipper," I said. "And how's Frank?"

"Who are you?"

She had to ask it a lot, what with everyone cycling through nine lives. "It's me, Marshmallow."

Kipper stared at me for a while. "I don't believe you. Who's Frank?"

"Me parrot! Come on, Kipper, it's me."

Kipper shook her head, pawing at her eyes. "Dogs. I thought you weren't coming back. You've been gone awhile, Marshmallow."

Me breath caught. "Is—is Frank all right?"

"Frank's fine—just fed him a few hours ago," Kipper replied.

"Ah, thank you, old friend," I said. "He's not with you?"

"No, I left him at your place. Some of the patrons were getting worked up with a bird around. Don't worry, I still let him out often, and I'm discreet. You owe me."

May Kipper have endless catnip in her next lives. I brought Frank on adventures with me when I could, but sometimes things were too dangerous, and so I left him behind in me secret hideout. Thank goodness Frank was all right.

"Aye," I said. "I'll repay you."

Kipper nodded, preparing me catnip. "So what brought you to the end of your thread?"

"Captain Powderpuff's gang," I said in a low voice. "Can't be trusted."

"I'll keep that in mind."

I frowned at the two bowls Kipper slid toward me. "I ordered three, Kipper."

"Sorry, only two at a time. We're rationing—low stock."

I growled. "Fine. I'll take these and a milk saucer."

Soon I was curled up in a corner lapping up leaves as I rolled me face in each bowl of catnip. Me head rushed, I felt light and tingly, and I turned my mind away from that awful encounter with the Catfish Queen.

In a little while I would go home and check on Frank, then curl up in bed. A lot of time had gone by, but at least some things would be back to normal.

The door banged open, followed by the sound of stomping boots. Everyone in the bar looked up—cats with boots meant they'd lost all or part of their paws from a *furgeldt*. The sorts of cats who weren't fine upstanding felines.

I recognized their scent from Captain Powderpuff's kitty-litter-smelling crew. With torn ears and bald patches, the cats stood on two feet, towering over the bar counter. One of them was a brown and black tabby, while the other had stained yellow fur.

"We're taking your catnip," the tabby said.

Kipper studied them, moving toward the register where she kept her rapier. "You can afford it all?"

"You're giving us a discount," Yellow said.

In a flash, Kipper whipped her sword out at Yellow's throat. The tabby, however, was just as quick, jumping over the counter and landing with his scimitar pressed against Kipper's belly.

"No funny business," the tabby said. "Get the catnip and nobody gets hurt."

Kipper eyed the two pirates again, and then dropped her rapier. She moved a series of hidden wooden panels to pop open a cabinet with sacks of catnip.

Yellow clubbed Kipper and she collapsed into a lump of fur.

Half-stoned and without a weapon, I was in no state to fight them, but all the catnip would be gone if I didn't do something.

Me world swayed as I climbed to the second floor, and then along one of the light fixtures. Just as they caught sight of me, I pounced and knocked the tabby off Kipper.

Yellow swiped at me, but I rolled away from the blur of her sword and snatched Kipper's rapier. I rocked from side to side as we swung and parried one another. Me sword stayed far steadier than me.

I lost balance. Just before I fell over, I batted Yellow's sword away, then reached in and licked her nose. Yes, I fought dirty.

She spat, dropped her sword and pawed at her nose.

I knocked her over. Pinned her with me sword at her throat.

"Gah!" Kipper, awake now, yelled from behind me. "The tabby got away!"

"Kipper," I said, me voice a menacing growl, "how much was that catnip worth?"

"Almost fifty doubloons," she replied.

"That's quite the *furgeldt*," I said back to Yellow.

I lifted me sword and sliced her cleanly in the eye. She shrieked.

"That's twenty," I said.

Then I cut off her tail. "Thirty."

Her right ear. "Thirty-six."

I sliced off two claws. She could manage without them. "Forty-four."

Then I pressed me blade between her teeth to hold her mouth open. Two quick flicks of the hilt, and I had two fangs.

"That's fifty. Your debt's been paid."

Yellow crawled away, bleeding.

I turned to Kipper. "You no longer need to seek retribution. Understood?"

She nodded. "I'm still gonna have to clean it up."

There was just no pleasing some cats.

A few minutes later, Yellow was gone, and so was the mess. I still had the tokens of the *furgeldt*, which I needed to offer to the Great Lake, for use by the Catfish Queen. *Furgeldts* fed the cycle of cats' lives. I'd gotten me new body parts the same way everyone else did.

"Don't suppose there's any catnip left in a secret stash?"

"Sorry," Kipper said. "They got it all."

I cursed and stormed out of the bar.

At the edge of the lake, I said a few words of respect, then threw Yellow's tail, ear, claws, and fangs into the lake. I scratched a note about Yellow's eye, licked me seal onto it, wrapped it around a rock and cast it out, too.

"Meowsers, you're a law cat, aren't you?" a voice said from behind me. "I thought there were none left."

I turned to see a Maine Coon with brown, white, and beige stripes. She had an eyepatch, a well-worn scratch post in place of one of her back legs, and a shiny metal tail and diaper.

I'd never seen anything like her, and that was never good. I lifted me rapier.

"Only a law cat would handle a *furgeldt* like that," she said.

"What about it?"

"You just got back into a new life, didn't you?" She looked me up and down, ignoring me rapier. "Law cats are a rare breed now. I'm sure Captain Powderpuff's behind their disappearance, but nobody believes me."

I didn't know what she was talking about, and I had no reason to trust her. I'd pushed meself pretty hard in the fight, and now that the catnip was wearing off, me muscles were aching.

"You want trouble?"

"No," she said, hobbling behind. "I want your help."

"With what?"

"Captain Powderpuff tried to exterminate the law cats," she said. "She must have come after you, too."

That stopped me. This cat knew more about me than I wanted.

"What if she did?" I asked.

She plopped down beside me, the metal diaper-thing tinkling in the sand. "You must want justice, don't you?"

I coughed like I'd choked on a hairball. "It's not like I can go after her with her whole band of pirates in the way."

"We have to do something. She's enslaved the Catfish Queen."

"Have you had too much catnip?" I asked, secretly jealous if that was the case. "What are you on about?"

"I saw it with my own eyes. I was a spirit working for the Queen, and barely made it out alive."

"This story sounds too long," I said, trotting away. "Good day, and may you bite the fish."

"Where are you going? The Catfish Queen affects us all!"

"I'm sure everyone in *there* wants to hear it," I said, nodding to *The Frisky Whisker*. "They'll be a better audience."

"I can't trust any of them," she said. "I don't know if they're spies for Captain Powderpuff."

"How do you know I'm not a spy?"

"Because you're a law cat."

I sighed. "Look, I just want to go home, and I've got kind of a secret place nearby, all right? The kind of secret place onlookers can't look upon, you see? So you're just going to have to get going, and leave me be."

"Your home is next to this dump?"

"What about it?"

"And it's secret?"

"Yes. Very secret."

"Is it that hole-in-the-ground right there?"

"Ye—what?"

I turned where she pointed. The bushes were torn up, and me sand-crusted trap door was in splinters.

"Dogs, no!" I shouted, running over.

Ducking inside, I moaned. The place had been ransacked.

Most importantly, Frank, me parrot, was gone. His perch, his cage. Everything. Me spine curled and all me fur stood on end.

"Maybe now you want to hear my story," the Maine Coon said behind me.

Dog damn-it.

KIPPER, AND I listened to the cat's story, me lapping at a saucer of milk while Kipper polished the counter.

The cat's name was Nutmeg.

"There was an awful shortage of body parts," she said. "And there was talk of the law cats dying out, with none left to collect *furgeldt*. The Queen felt like minnows were nipping at her fins. I even overheard her say she was thinking of scaling back on the nine lives.

"Around then a message came from Captain Powderpuff, with an offer to solve the *furgeldt* problem. Normally the Queen wouldn't give audience to a living cat, but she was desperate, so she granted passage. Captain Powderpuff insisted on meeting alone.

"A few of us were stationed outside the chamber just in case, though she kept two of her personal jellyfish guards. I don't know exactly what happened in the meeting. I do know that Captain Powderpuff brought a cod dish, one of the Queen's favourites, and later, the Queen's eyes looked glassier than usual.

"Now, see, it had been a long time since I'd lived, but when I had, I hadn't needed to do much hunting. It was because I had toxoplasmosis."

I jerked away, nearly spilling me milk.

"I don't have it anymore," Nutmeg said quickly. "Anyway, in another life when I had it, I infected my prey with it, and they became docile, willing to do anything I asked. They had the same glassy look in their eyes.

"The Queen must have been infected through the cod. I said as much to anyone who would listen. Nobody was willing to do anything, though. Everyone valued their position too much to risk a final death on the Queen's orders. It seemed I was the only one who remembered the importance of freedom among the living.

"That's when they came for me. They put a *leash* around me, and I nearly died. I've never fought so hard in my life or afterlife. I managed to survive that fight, barely.

"I had to scrounge for body parts. Then I begged a friend to take me to the surface as a final favour. Not long after I came back, I saw the first wave of cats coming alive after me. They were all servants of Captain Powderpuff, now, following her directives. You and I might be some of the only cats left who aren't."

Everyone was silent as Nutmeg finished, while I lapped up the rest of me milk.

"Meowsers," Kipper said. "If this is true, then soon it'll be the end of the nine lives."

"Cats might still have nine lives," Nutmeg said. "But eight of them would be as slaves."

"Dogs," Kipper whispered.

I licked the milk stuck in the fur around me mouth. "You figure they have me Frank?"

"Your parrot? Most certainly. They say the Captain prefers birdmeat."

"I'll help get him back, but that's as far as I'm going," I said. "I'm on me last life, and I want to make it a long one."

Kipper looked away and shook her head.

Nutmeg leaned in so her good eye was close enough I could have licked it. "You know there's not gonna be much left to enjoy if Powderpuff takes over, right? You have to think past your next bowl of catnip."

I wanted to scratch her right in that arrogant, judgmental eye. She'd had a cushy gig working for the Catfish Queen, and dared to judge me vices?

This scallywag had a lot of nerve.

"Listen," I snarled, "you're lucky I'm helping you at all. I will help you until I save Frank. After that, you'll have to sucker someone else into helping you win your soft palace job back."

"Fine," Nutmeg said. "Let's get moving then, before they get too far ahead."

FOR A CAT who rarely left the bar, Kipper proved an efficient tracker. Every cat knew her, and either thought well of her, her catnip, or both. In any case, they pointed us in the right direction.

Within three days we were within sight of the pirates. We sailed by the dogs' winds on a ship borrowed with a promise from Kipper to share in future catnip spoils.

We followed and waited.

AT SUNRISE IN a small fishing village, Powderpuff's pirates stormed the shore but there was still no way for us to get close without being seen. The pirates were more vigilant during a raid, even if there were fewer of them on board.

Ashore, sounds of cats growling in anger mixed with the clashing of swords. Pirates strutted up and down the lines of beach houses, spraying urine in dominion over those who'd fought back.

"We have to swim," Nutmeg said.

What? Did she have a whisker in her brain?

"Kipper, you stay while we swim over. If the parrot is alive—"

"Frank," I said.

"If Frank is alive, we grab him, along with any proof of Powderpuff's plot. Let's hope we strike gold."

Before I could protest, Nutmeg jumped in the water.

And she said *I* had too much catnip. She was practically feral.

A pouch opened in Nutmeg's metallic diaper and with a sound like a whale blowing, a black tube appeared around her. Patterned with white skulls and cross bones, it allowed Nutmeg to bob half above water.

I'd never seen anything like it. What other hidden treasures did the Catfish Queen have?

"Come on," Nutmeg said.

We didn't have any other option.

I took a deep breath and leaped. Terror made me overshoot and I landed squarely on Nutmeg's face.

She howled and sneezed in a place I thought no cat ever would. I flipped over and around, barely hanging on to avoid the water.

"You're choking me with your tail," Nutmeg wheezed, "and gouging with your claws."

I hadn't noticed. Guilty as charged.

I twisted and climbed until I leaned against Nutmeg, lifting me paws to avoid touching water.

I couldn't look at her. I didn't care what anyone said: no two cats should ever have to get that intimate.

"Put some paws in the water and help," Nutmeg growled, "or I'm throwing you overboard."

I winced as me back feet slid into the water.

"You're supposed to be a brave and courageous law cat."

"Water doesn't count," I replied.

I shivered the whole way over.

We climbed aboard, dunked two guards who didn't have the benefit of an inflatable raft, then divided up duties.

"You check the stern. I'll check the bow," Nutmeg said. "Meet back in five meownits."

"Catnap time or brooding time?"

I wasn't sure why Nutmeg glared at me. They were very different measures. There was probably a reason I usually worked alone.

I ducked into the cabins at the stern and dispatched several guards. I searched the quarters and found a handful of mice hidden in the rations, but no Frank.

I entered the kitchen expecting the worst—but heard a few muffled squawks and found Frank stuffed into a mouse cage. I wasn't too late, but by the dogs, he didn't look good.

He was much thinner, and he craned his neck to fit the space.

"Thank the dogs' winds you're alive!"

I opened the cage and Frank hobbled his way out. For a few long seconds, he just stared at me. I feared he would never fly again.

"Dogs, what did they do to you? Frank, say something!"

"Dogs' winds! Dogs' winds!" Frank said in a high-pitched squawk.

He hopped twice, then soared into the air.

"You're all right!"

"Dogs' winds! Dogs' winds!"

"Yes, yes. Thank the dogs' winds. Let's go."

Just as we were about to leave, I saw a shadowed crack in the wall next to the cupboards. I stuck me rapier in and pried it open, revealing a huge bag of catnip.

This was the best day ever.

Nutmeg was angry when I met her on deck. "You're a

meownit late," she said. "I found a damning set of orders from Powderpuff along with a map of where she wants all the catnip taken. Did you find anything that could help us?"

"I found Frank and this bag of catnip," I snapped. "What more could anyone want?"

She eyed my findings suspiciously. "Fine. Let's go."

We took one of the pirates' lifeboats to make our escape and had nearly reached Kipper's ship when Powderpuff's pirates pulled up anchor to chase us.

By the time we hoisted the catnip up and scrambled onto the deck, the pirates were firing arrows that hammered the near side of the ship.

"You and your dog-damned catnip," Kipper said.

The three of us—Nutmeg, Kipper, and I—all tugged on the ropes as fast as we could to turn the sail and spin us around.

There was only a ship's length separating us and Powderpuff's pirates now. Thankfully the cannons pointed out the sides, and they couldn't fire those at us without steering away.

That didn't limit their arrows, however. They landed on deck, nearly tearing the sail.

Nutmeg nuzzled me neck with her nose, and I twitched in surprise.

She handed me a parchment. "If I don't make it back, finish what I started."

She didn't wait for me to reply. During a gap in the onslaught of arrows, she ran to the back of the boat. Her diaper opened up to extend two large springs. She crouched and jumped, the springs firing.

She flew and landed in the enemy's sail. Howling, she slid down, clawing gouges that flapped like eels in the white cloth.

I cheered, then shouted at Nutmeg to get back. With their sail torn, the pirates would lag behind until they were out of sight.

Nutmeg stumbled past the few remaining pirates, and jumped overboard. Dogs, what a brave cat.

The pirates scrambled, and a moment later they were dumping oil overboard, coating the water—and Nutmeg—in a black slick.

"Nutmeg!" I shouted. She couldn't die now. She'd helped me

save Frank, after all.

Turning to Kipper, I said, "Turn us around! Swing us past her!"

We'd swung around and were headed laterally past the pirate ship just as the cats brought out lit torches.

Cutting one of the mast ropes and meowling a curse, I took hold and swung out in a low, wide arc.

The torches fell. I glided through the air toward the bed of oil where Nutmeg floundered.

"Grab on!" I shouted.

The world around me ignited. I was going to burn me last life away. There was a sharp pain in me tail, and I saw only bright flashes.

But I was still swinging.

A moment later I thumped to the deck, dragged on by Kipper. When I finally screwed me eyes back on straight, I saw that Nutmeg had clung to me tail the whole way. Her fur was singed but otherwise she looked all right.

In the distance, pirates cursed our names. We'd made it.

THE MAP NUTMEG had retrieved led us right where Captain Powderpuff was gathering all the catnip. The thought of such a bounty made me drool, and convinced me to stick it out with our little crew.

When we reached the hidden cove, there were very few guards. It seemed Captain Powderpuff didn't want a lot of cats there to draw attention. There was a single ship, a small wooden dock, and a small fort nested between the trees that was only visible if you looked carefully.

Strange. Where was the horde, and why wasn't it better guarded?

Nutmeg convinced us to play the part of members of Powderpuff's gang as we approached. It would make it easier to gather information, she said.

If it got us closer to the catnip, I would have shaved meself and pretended to be a sphinx cat.

We waved the bag of catnip when we were within sight. That seemed enough of a signal, and the patchy-furred goon let us dock.

"Ah, nice to see a genuine pirate," he said as Kipper and I

carried the bag of catnip ashore. "I've seen too many of them mindless followers come by today. No personality. Though I can't complain too much; it's making the looting easy picking."

"Myarr," I said. "Where do you want this?"

"Through the door, into the metal trough," he said, walking alongside us and pointing.

He held the door open and we found ourselves in a large watery cavern cut into the island. In the middle of the water was a large ball.

A hatch was opened in the ball, and a trough angled in above and from the side.

We walked up the ramp running in a spiral around the rim of the cavern, and poured in the catnip. To my great disappointment, we were now high enough to see that the large ball was empty of catnip.

Dogs damn it.

As we poured the nip, we saw a nook with several suits in it—they looked like body-shaped blankets with a fishbowl where the head was supposed to be.

"Underwater suits," Kipper said.

"Meowsers," I breathed.

"Yes," the patchy cat said, nodding toward the nook with the suits, "all the others love those things, but going under water still gives me rat pimples. Above the water is a pirate's life, I say."

I nodded, patting him on the back, once, twice, then a third time to knock him off-balance and into the water.

"Help!" he shrieked, flailing and splashing.

"Where's the catnip?" I shouted.

"At the palace! The Catfish Queen's palace!"

I heard Kipper sigh.

"And where's Powderpuff?"

"She's there too! Please, help me!"

I looked at Kipper. She nodded. All right. I guess there wasn't a *furgeldt* owed.

I helped the pirate out, then tied him to a barrel of food. He'd be able to escape once he'd eaten all the food. It was one of the tricks they taught you as a law cat when you couldn't permanently punish someone.

We called out to Nutmeg, who joined us. She was in awe of

the suits, and had them figured out faster than a falling cat flipping onto their feet.

"We can attack the palace," Nutmeg said as she tried on one of the suits. "With this letter, there's no way the spirit guards will stay loyal, knowing the Catfish Queen's been betrayed."

I sighed. Catnip seemed farther and farther away, and the last thing I wanted was to be making another visit to the Catfish Queen so soon.

"Frank, what do you think?" I asked.

"Nature's depth! Nature's depth!" he squawked, flying around the opening of the ball.

"Fine," I groaned.

IF YOU'VE NEVER tumbled to the depths in a rolling metal ball, while wearing a suffocatingly tight suit, you're lucky. It's about as much fun as being in a whirlpool.

Frank couldn't get enough of it, though. He squawked, "Nature's depth! Nature's depth!" the whole way down in his tiny suit. I was too busy flipping over meself to see if Kipper or Nutmeg enjoyed the journey.

When we reached the bottom, we came into view of the knitted gold-trimmed exterior of the Catfish Queen's Cave Palace. A myriad of cat spirits lined the periphery, armed with scratching posts, chew toys, scimitars and boxes. There were so many spirits I doubted we could overcome them.

"Delivery for Captain Powderpuff," Nutmeg called through the short end of a cone.

"Stop where you are, and open the hatch," hissed a large tattooed sphinx cat.

"Dogs," Nutmeg muttered.

She stalled while we adjusted our suits and readied our weapons. This was going to be a very short and awkward fight if we didn't get some cats on our side.

We opened one hatch, then the other. Water poured in.

The sphinx cat hissed as soon as she saw us. Her tattoos glowed, and her claws enlarged to twice, then three times their size. She looked like she held jet-black knives in each hand. She clacked them together and bared her teeth.

"Wait!" Nutmeg cried. "Can you not see she's enslaved you? I have proof right here—"

Out of a compartment in her underwater suit, she pulled out the thick parchment from Captain Powderpuff. I was glad the ink didn't run.

"Look at the ruthless orders Powderpuff gave!" Nutmeg shouted. "And how the returning hordes are forced to join her army without question!"

Cats stirred, looking at one another and murmuring. Nutmeg walked closer, letting them read more carefully. More cats looked over their shoulders and around as though seeing things for the first time.

The sphinx cat roared. "Lies, all of this! You will turn back now, or be destroyed!"

Nutmeg rolled up the parchment, then nodded to the cats she'd managed to convince.

"So be it."

The cat spirits turned on one another, and there was total pandemonium. They bit and tore at each other. It was a slightly more even fight, but we were still outnumbered.

Nutmeg and I took on the sphinx cat, who moved much faster than we did without fur or a suit. She scratched at us, and soon there were several shallow tears in our suits, bubbling trickles of air.

Nutmeg launched herself right into the sphinx cat's mouth as she tried to bite her. The sphinx cat gagged, and I sliced her open like a tomato.

One down, a hundred more to go.

I looked over and saw Kipper fighting off a pair of spirit guards wielding scratching posts. She went misty-eyed when one of them hit her. Frank and I darted over and pried her off before it was too late.

Nutmeg went on fighting spirits with a sword in each of her front paws, and a blade on her tail sticking through the bottom of her suit. Maybe I'd get an upgrade meself if I made it through this.

Slowly, we advanced. We might be able to win.

Then a loud jet of water and bubbles sprayed out from behind a rock at the knitted periphery. It rumbled and slid away to reveal a passage with a train of cats marching in darkness.

No. They weren't cats. Not anymore.

They were skeletons brought back to life without all their

parts. Captain Powderpuff was abusing the Catfish Queen's powers, creating these lumbering perversions.

I gasped when I realized what they held for weapons. Not even Powderpuff would do such a thing, would she?

Dogs. No, there were no words to describe this horror.

The cat skeletons held balls of yarn. Beautiful, glowing balls of yarn—the gathered threads of their lives. A tendril from each looped around and into the cats' sternums. Captain Powderpuff was going to make them toss them—throw their lives away—just so we'd be entranced.

The worst part was that it would probably work. If they threw those enticing balls of yarn, I don't think any of us would be able to resist. We'd play with those poor cats' life stories like they were toys, and Powderpuff would win. She would sweep the litter box with our fur.

The skeletons groaned, a low mix between a purr and a choke, then threw their yarns at us. Bright trails criss-crossed the battlefield and cat spirits everywhere dropped their weapons to pounce on them.

One ball rolled closer to me, and I felt the muscles in me legs twitching.

Frank landed on me shoulder and cawed, "All skeletons. All skeletons."

Skeletons were surrounding those of us who'd been incapacitated by the yarn.

"All skeletons. All skeletons."

We would all end up as skeletons sooner or later. If Captain Powderpuff won, the culmination of our lives would be to make a weaponized toy. Something to be used and discarded.

The threads were so beautiful; a gorgeous blend of shimmering orange scintillated with the underwater waves. Me body stiff, I took halting steps toward it, feeling me mind grow fuzzier as I closed the gap.

Nearer, I saw a deep aqua spiral wrapped around the thread and jerked in recognition of me family colours.

The family that hadn't cared when we'd lost everything.

Huddled together around a large milk saucer at the end of a long day. Sleeping curled around one another in overlapping spirals. None of this had mattered.

So much time, so much love, invested in something that

vanished so quickly.

Although I'd become a law cat to prevent the kind of injustices that had destroyed me family, I spent most of me time with me head buried in catnip to avoid thinking about the losses that piled up over nine lives.

Until now.

Lumbering toward me, shoulders undulating, came me brother Patches with a deep gouge across his eye socket—an early scar from a violent brawl.

He halted in front of me and groaned.

"Dogs," I said, me body tensing. If it wasn't for that scar and the yarn, I wouldn't have recognized him. "I'm . . . so sorry she did this to you."

Patches' head bobbed slowly.

"I don't want to fight," I said. "But I have to stop her. I would ask for help, but I know how far that'll get me."

Patches trembled, jawbone quivering until his rattling voice spoke. "I would help if I c—could."

"Sure you would." I tightened the grip on me rapier. "Just like the Mittens would always be together, and always stand up for each other, right?"

Patches' head sagged. His jaw worked but he made no sound.

"That's what I thought. Before you were all talk and no action, and now you barely have any talk. You know, if the Mittens were still together, we might have been able to stop Powderpuff before it got this bad."

Patches' teeth clicked, and his ribcage shuddered. "We grew up, Marshmallow, and times changed."

I picked up his sparkling thread with the tip of me rapier, readying to cut it. It was a cruel thing to do, but then again, so was what they'd done to me.

"Times changed," I repeated. "That's a rotten mouse of an excuse. You gave up on us. You abandoned our family, like you never cared at all. Like it meant nothing."

"It pained me too, to see it end," Patches said. "But by the time you came for us, it would have been too hard to go back. We would have been hunted down if we had. Not all of us were as strong or as dedicated as you, Marshmallow. But that doesn't mean it meant nothing. For me . . . it was a memory I dared not tarnish by trying to remake a cheap imitation. Things that end aren't without value."

Me eyes stung. Other skeletons loped closer to us, and with each step they took, Patches quivered. It seemed he fought the influence Powderpuff exerted over his bones.

"I c—can't hold on much longer," he said. "Kill me, Marshmallow. Sister. Before it's too late."

"How could I do that?" I whispered, gazing again at the brilliant lines of yarn snaking the landscape.

"C—cut me thread."

I lowered me rapier, letting his sparkling thread fall to the basin. I thought I could do it—I thought I would do it—but no. I couldn't and wouldn't.

The scintillating yarn-filled battlefield was spotted with knocked-out cats. In a few moments, I would join them, unable to see past the lustre of the yarn to me true purpose.

Except now, I couldn't see anything *but* the bigger picture. Me whole life stretched before me, an uncoiling and extensive web. Me hips ached from clenching me legs. In one sense, I was scared to act for fear of making things worse than they already were. Of losing more than I already had. However, Patches' words echoed in my mind:

Things that end aren't without value.

How much had me life been spent trying to fight off endings? How much time had I spent trying to preserve what I had by enforcing law through *furgeldt?* How long had I buried me head in the sand to avoid thinking about what me own ending might look like?

It was another shameful realization, one I didn't know if I could ever tell anyone. I knew now, though, and I couldn't shy away from trying to do better.

In the end, if nothing worked out, it wouldn't mean that what I'd tried was worthless. Worth was a treasure buried somewhere else, deep inside.

I sheathed me sword, and picked up Patches' thread. The urge to play with it was overwhelming, and me breath shook as I gathered energy.

Looking up and meowing, I twirled Patches' thread like a lasso. Then I wrapped him with it, the glowing tendril cinching around his legs. He fell onto his side.

"W—what are you doing?" Patches said, immobile.

"Taking control of our future," I said. "*My* future."

His head tilted back and he purred with the sensation of being surrounded by his own yarn.

Take care, Patches, I thought.

Maybe we'd meet again when this life was over.

I ran across the battlefield, picking up yarns and lassoing skeleton cats.

I reached Nutmeg, who was enraptured with a ball of lemon-coloured yarn. I pressed meself dangerously between her paws and shoved the yarn out of her grasp.

She hissed and swiped at me. I wrapped around her as she scratched and tore. I hoped I blocked her view of the yarn.

"Why did you get up this morning, Nutmeg?" I said into her ear.

She slowed for a moment. "Yarn!" she snapped.

"No. You still have your own yarn to spin. Look up. You remember how important it is that cats stay free?"

"Free," she repeated. She stopped scratching me, her paws hanging in the air.

"Yes. Freedom. We have to fight for it now."

Nutmeg's glassy eyes gained definition. Her gaze met mine. "Yes," she said finally.

"Help me. Wrap them with their yarns," I instructed. "And let's free the others."

Nutmeg did, and since we moved much faster than the skeletons, we soon had most of them lassoed and bound. Frank even tied a few by flying around them with a tendril in his beak.

We had to fight some of Powderpuff's forces along the way, but most of those retreated into the palace.

Many of our forces, including Kipper, had been knocked out and there was no telling how long it would take them to wake.

Leaving a few behind to care for the injured, Nutmeg and I pressed on into the palace.

We fought a smattering of guards in the hallways, then pushed our way through the giant ball of yarn and into the Catfish Queen's courtroom.

The Queen swam tilted slightly to the side, her eyes a thick-misted white. Beside her, in an underwater suit, stood Captain Powderpuff.

"It's over," Nutmeg said. "Surrender, Powderpuff."

Captain Powderpuff hissed and pulled a long black cylinder from a sheath at her side. She pointed it at the ground in front of us, and then squeezed it.

A brilliant spot of green light appeared magically on the ground. Nutmeg and I gasped. The light demanded attention, swatting, toying, catching. I wanted so badly to hold that between me paws, to sniff it and look at it from every angle.

Nutmeg dropped to her belly and sidled up to it, making furtive swats.

That light held the promise of everything much grander, everything brighter than me own life. It was what I'd been looking for at the end of every ball of yarn: a brilliant coalescence of energy, spirit, and possibility. Was this another one of the Catfish Queen's treasures?

Frank swooped at Captain Powderpuff, and for a moment, the green spot flickered off. In that moment, I saw the same path laid out before me, one well travelled: one of burying meself in avoidance and ignorance of everything I needed to do to take control of me life.

"Powderpuff," I said, brandishing me sword and straightening me tricorn. "Stop your cheap tricks."

She pulled out her scimitar and pointed the green dot-maker away. Nutmeg followed mindlessly after it.

It was only Powderpuff and me.

"Myarr!"

We parried, sliced, and thrusted at one another, nicking each other until blood misted the water around us. Thankfully our suits were sealed separately at the arms and legs, because otherwise I'd have already drowned.

I targeted the hand holding the dot-maker. After losing a large patch of fur and suit in a dangerous lunge, I slashed her paw and tackled her. She dropped the dot-maker, stumbled, and fell head first onto it. Under Powderpuff's glass helmet, the dot-maker cracked in two.

Powderpuff roared, rolling up and on top of me. She had her sword at me throat a moment later. "No more lives for you, calico."

Nutmeg, no longer under the trance of the green dot, bounded on Powderpuff with a thump, pinning her with her metallic diaper. She looked at me, licking her paws and rubbing some of her wounds.

"Sorry about that," she said. "It was so shiny."

"I know."

"Queen! Attack them! Myarr!" hissed Powderpuff.

"No," I said, getting up and moving to the Catfish Queen. "This ends now."

Maybe it was time for me to see Patches again. So be it.

I took off me glass helmet, holding me breath as the water flooded in around me face.

"Marshmallow! No!" Nutmeg cried.

I ignored her. I licked the Catfish Queen all over her face, and slowly, the white mist disappeared from her eyes.

"W—what happened? Where am I? Who are you?" she said in her depth-rumbling voice.

"Powderpuff gave you toxoplasmosis," Nutmeg said, looking between me and the Queen. "You've been in a trance."

The Catfish Queen took several moments to take in her surroundings before nodding. "Thank you both. You have done a great service to all felines today."

I nodded. Me vision narrowed as me breath ran out.

I hope Kipper takes care of Frank, I thought. There was no way I could make it back to the surface now, but at least things would be all right.

Nutmeg ran up to me and dropped the glass bowl on me head. It was no use with all the water inside.

"Queen!" she yelled. "Help her!"

The Catfish Queen floated toward me, and with those long, thick whiskers, she pulled the water out of the bowl.

I gasped for air and fell to me knees.

"Thank you," I managed as I finally caught me breath.

Frank rubbed his glass helmet against mine, and squawked. Life could be grand, even this far under the cursed water.

The Catfish Queen had given me a tenth life, as far as I could see. I had to make good use of it.

"As law cat," I said, standing, "I have to ask. How many doubloons is that green dot-maker worth?"

I pointed, and the Catfish Queen recognized the smashed cylinder on the stone floor. "Ah yes, the laser pointer. A very rare treasure. It is difficult to put a price on it. If I had to, I would estimate its worth at five hundred doubloons."

I strode over to Powderpuff, smiling as I pointed me rapier down at her. “That’s quite the *furgeldt* to be paid, Captain.”

Cat Out of Hell

Leslie Van Zwol

THE ANCHOR SPLASHED into the waves, taking my heart, then my lunch along for the drop. The ship lurched to a robust stop.

"We're here, cats," announced Captain Cambrie. As though the rest of us hadn't already deduced the successful arrival without the unnecessary announcement; and people say I'm dramatic.

I bit my tongue, keeping my sass to myself. The Captain was a short and stout feline, made entirely of teeth and muscle, and no one challenged him to a fight they weren't enthusiastic to lose.

A murmur slithered through the crew—all puffed tails and tensions as high as mine, suddenly sparked to a fever pitch with the first resounding hurrah of, "We did it!", followed by the more subdued and gut-wrenched follow-up, "We did it . . ."

My eyes shot to Penny Prior, standing firm at the wheel, chin high, whiskers straight. She was a striking puma, wild and furious like the ocean. Penny was no damsel, nor was she looking for friends. She was twice the hellcat of any of us, and just as alone on the ship as I was. Meeting her marked the first time I'd felt comfortable in my new skin, instead of like a monstrous abomination. In her I saw that they . . . that *we*, could be beautiful.

Fate it seemed, despite my wishes for the contrary, was on our side. The Queen would get her prize, a crown of legend, and the crew would continue to dance on the edge of the regency's payroll, stretching their claws somewhere between the law and gallows; they knew who to pay off, who to piss off, and who to cut off. As for me, I fit the job description—a linguist with a penchant for the obscure. Where I came from, the language in question was just dead, and the skill was nothing more than an easy elective in Ancient Egyptian logographs to boost a failing grade. But we weren't in my world, and here the language was mystical and unknown. Luckily for these pirates, they were plus one broke asshole who read a book he shouldn't have and woke up in a world full of bipedal cats, willing to take a paying gig with no questions asked.

I wiped my mouth with my sleeve, determined to not have vomit on my chin for whatever came next. Back in my world, I'd barely been able to grow a beard or chest hair—now, I was fumbling through being entirely fur-covered. Needless to say, I wasn't taking the transition well.

"Steady yourself, lads," Lieutenant Kimera snapped, a yowl slipping on the coat-tails of the whistle of her sibilant. I had a hard-enough time telling the cats apart, and she was practically a clone of Captain Cambrie: a grey-furred bobcat with a tuft around her neck like a lion's mane or an expensive flyboy's collar. Though their body-shapes differed, it was near impossible to tell through trousers, blouses, ostentatious jackets that reached to the floor, and innumerable belts and buttons that adored their attire. The only distinctive feature to know for sure was to get on their left side and spy Kimera's telltale scar over her eye that clouded it blue.

The moon stretched its silver fang, yawning from behind a thick cloud and a wave of icy light set the deck aglow.

The crew's murmurs grew as the ivory light cascaded silver tendrils over the dark spires of craggy rock jutting out from the sea.

The massive black rock had the strongest fuck-off vibe I'd ever seen, sending a chill down my spine to the tip of my tail which now imitated an oversized powder puff. I waited for the chorus of laughter from the hardened pirates, but we all felt it. The wind picked up and sent an icy breeze to ruffle our whiskers and mainsails, the smell of death clinging to the air strong and sour like a devil's pact. I had to find a way to avoid that island.

I took the moment of awe that fluttered through the crew as an opportunity to turn tail and get out, but then there she was, arms folded, right in my path back to the longboat. Penny. The silver moonlight made her golden fur shine. Her head was tilted to the side, giving her embellished hoop earring the inch it needed to rest on her shoulder.

I felt my face go slack and sweat soak my shirt. She grinned, knowing she had my number and the skill to play me like a fiddle. Her lips parted as her smile grew broad and beaming like the moonlight, putting her gold-plated fang on full display.

The breath was out of my lungs now and my shoulders slumped. So, when the Captain clapped his large paw on my shoulder, he almost sent me sprawling with how slack my muscles were, infected with defeat and resignation.

"There ye are, ol' Nikki," he said with a wry chuckle. His hand hung on tight, his claws slipping into the soft fur of my shoulder, a message received.

Anxiety suffocated all the words in my throat and I gave him a thumbs up. Though a strange custom for this world, it got a snort out of him and he released his death grip.

"There's a good lad." He gave me a shove forward and I stumbled over my own feet, but stayed upright, albeit barely.

The crew were already well on their way to the longboats when Penny slid in on my left, her eyes aflame in amber glow. Taking the sleeve of my shirt in her hands, she hauled me faster. "Where did you think you were going? Running scared on a longboat while their backs were turned? Fool of a cub."

She ignored my stifled protests, moving through the larger crew members with ease. Fighting her was like telling the tide not to come in. "They would've caught you before the boat hit the water."

"You have any better ideas?" I wheezed, trying to keep pace with her.

She stopped and spun me until we were nose to nose. I swallowed, nerves spiked with adrenaline.

"If you were going to play the coward, you should have done it a week ago, while we were at sea. There's no room on that boat," she hissed, her thick accent adding a sharp bite to the words, "for a cowardly cat!"

"Ah, Nikki," the Captain said, cutting himself through the tension and putting a steadying hand on my shoulder. "You'll go in that one. *One Sink Betsy*."

Another raw gulp and I got into the aforementioned *One Sink Betsy*, tucking my knees to my chest and choosing the middlemost spot furthest from any stray waves. Penny sat on the bench in front of me, her eyes drilling into the side of my head as I looked anywhere but at her.

"Drop the longboats, cats," the Captain ordered, his voice booming into the night.

Another deathly breeze whipped through and I shivered, pulling my shirt collar tight around my neck.

The lines went loose and we dropped. This was how I would die, with my eyes squinted shut and a shriek locked behind clenched teeth.

Her hand was on my thigh, claws digging in, holding me in my seat. I don't know where my arms were, but I felt my forearm hit something more than once. My torso whipped around like a snapped rubber band. We hit the water and I lurched forward, my head slamming into something hard like brick.

Taking a steadying breath, I opened my eyes, trying to answer Penny's angry glare with a reassuring smile. Then, I lunged as fast as I could for the edge of the longboat to send whatever was left in my belly out to sea.

Like I said: in a corner of the university library, fighting off an impending nap, I shouldn't have read that book. It was a weathered text bound in twine and stained in blood. It even had a fucking sign on the cover clearly stating the Ancient Egyptian loose translation of "*DON'T READ THIS BOOK, MORON.*"

Months later I was still here—caught somewhere between trying to claw out a new life as the man I'd always wanted to be and the same old Nikki Selfish who was three percent too lazy and stupid to find the way home.

I retched again.

"Should've taken the nap," I groaned, taking back my seat. The crew had already started to row, and my body swayed in time with the momentum of the waves.

"You need to pull yourself together," Penny hissed.

I gave her a shrug and flopped my head to the side so I could look past her at the impending doom-cliffs. I didn't want to look at her face, at the disappointment in her eyes. That wasn't how I dreamed she looked at me.

She grabbed my shirt-collar, gave it a shake at half-strength. "I mean it."

With a sigh I steeled myself to face her. "We both know, given the chance, I'd fly off this boat to Never-Never Land and leave you all here to die. Don't pretend I'm something I'm not." I brushed her hand away with a flap of my mine. "I'm not anymore, and neither should you."

Penny straightened, releasing her iron grip, and turned her glare from me to the cliffs, letting her waves of frustration settle into determination.

My nausea boomed and busted in time with the waves and I found myself, finally, longing for the days of university. For days in the library, for my simple, lonely, meaningless, depressing life. I'd lied my way into university and I stupided my way out here.

My anxiety was out of steam, giving way to apathy, and with it came the cold noose of depression tightening around my neck.

The job's stakes weren't as Ragnarok level high as the Captain had made it sound. Though, not seeing the will of the Lion Queen to fruition would be akin to the same conditions. The end of our world, at least, in an off-with-their-heads sort of way.

Thunder boomed in the distance, and the flash of lightning blossomed through the stark clouds billowing towards the sea, threatening the horrific ambiance of fog. Against all common sense, the crew rowed onwards, into the maw of the cliffs, with a baritone hum that kept their strokes in rhythm.

The waves leapt up over the edge of the longboat and sogged me down to my boots. I shivered as we disappeared from the moon's watchful eye under a rocky umbrella of the small island. Everything grew dark with beams of crystal moonlight scattering like diamonds on the water and the damp stone. The further we rowed, the more the craggy rocks seemed like teeth jutting up from the sea from a giant, unseen mandible.

Another wave crashed into my mouth, which must've been agape. The onslaught of saltwater seared my tender palate and I coughed relentlessly to the raucous laughter of the crew.

Jackie-Boy, a hulk of a fellow, patted me on the back, wiping a joyous tear from his eye. A tall, burly midnight panther with edges of tiger-stripes slipping out from the greyer parts of his belly and face.

The longboat shook to a stop and I almost toppled out of my seat. We were land-struck now and everyone was on their feet grabbing shovels and ropes, bags of gear needed for treasure hunting. I didn't want to be the one to mention the entire cave looked to be made of unyielding rock and the shovels would be useless. Instead, I minded my own business, moving onto blessed land, like a grudging storm cloud drifting through the crew's sunlight radiance.

Someone grabbed my shoulder and held me firmly, likely stopping me from straying too far away from the pack. Penny, always the killjoy of my heart, shook her head and pulled me back towards the crew, dragging me to the front of the orderly line like a riptide as they moved into the small cavelet in the rocks. She wasn't going to let my slacker tendencies come between her and her paycheque. There was something about her that spoke to more of a story, one I couldn't help but obsessively want to read, but every attempt to get through her glacial exterior had been met with a prompt rejection. But if my name was misery, so was hers, and we both didn't mind a bit of company.

I had to duck down, and my eyes gleamed, adjusting to the lights and adding clarity in the darkness.

The walls closed in on us and I felt like I couldn't breathe. The joyous yowls and hums from the crew hushed as we descended down into the belly of the world, under the sea. The tunnel sloped downwards, and I was glad for my sure-footedness and clawed feet that could grasp onto the wet stone. Even though I was the clumsiest of all the cats, I still held my own, tripping only a handful of times.

Penny kept a firm hand on my shoulder, equal parts steadying me and reminding me with pointed claw that I wasn't running anywhere. Each time the tunnel narrowed, my breath seemed to squeeze in with it until only panicky gasps could squeak through and my world dwindled to the pinprick pain of her claws in my skin. Bastet be damned, when we finally broke out of that crawlspace I could've kissed her if I didn't think she'd have slapped my skull off my neck.

The walls were polished onyx veined with quartz that shimmered like tiny stars in our eye-glow. But I could see it now, my purpose on this voyage: the entire room was carved with images I'd only ever seen on a computer screen, or stone beneath glass.

I broke from Penny's grasp, forgetting the fact there was enough ocean above to drown us in seconds, and smooshed my face into the wall. My fingers traced the pictographs like braille, and images translated into words, and then sentences. Without light I could only see a few hieroglyphs at a time, but this was my moment and I'd do it all by feel if I had to.

"Light 'em up, toms," Jackie-Boy rumbled, and the flicker of flame lit the room like an obsidian fire opal.

The walls glittered like black diamonds. I took a step back, now able to see a larger section of the logographic script. My breath stopped to see something so unaltered, untouched, in a natural habitat. I was like Plato in fucking Atlantis!

An intake of breath to my right drew my attention. Penny was standing, awestruck, tips of her fingers pressed to her lips, eyes so wide I could see the white corners amid the glow of her cat eyes, her pupils slits of black like a line of calligraphy.

I moved to ask her what was the matter when a strong arm landed on my shoulder.

"Which way do we go there, Nikki, m'boy?" It was Kimera, though I had to do a double take, seeing, for a second, the Captain in her face. I forced a confident grin.

"Lieutenant, I'm just reading the symbols now."

She nodded, eyeing the crew who were now drunk on the excitement of the hunt, loud and boisterous. "Calm your tails. There's no bird in your teeth just yet!" she hissed. Leaning down to my ear, she whispered, "Don't keep them waiting, Mr. Selfish."

I gave a curt nod and slid my eyes over the images, easily finding Bastet among them. She was more predominant than the rest, always shown larger and with more care taken to her carvings and the subtle overlying hematite glaze added to her headliner status. The images sprang to life in radiant firelight. My fingers traced the large red circle that sat atop her lioness head—also glazed in the crimson light. She was missing her token sistrum, and the breast of her dress was carved in a flowing Rosetta pattern, but everything else was consistent. My brain was working overtime, glitching on the few details that didn't feel quite right.

Jackie-Boy had slid alongside Kimera with a few cabin boys. His voice was hushed and he leaned into her ear. "Some of the lads are concerned about Prior. After what happened in the last cave . . ."

"Save it," Kimera hissed. "She's as stalwart and sturdy as the ship itself. I won't have ye bring my choice of crew into question, Jack."

Out of the corner of my eye I could see him wince, but lean in again.

"She's just . . . Bastet's sake, Kimera, you know what she's like when she gets the fits. It unsettles the crew."

"She's been fine, and a good medic in place of the Doc, Bastet rest his soul."

My eyes drifted back to Penny. She was pacing now, clenching her fists tight until her arms flexed, and then releasing. Her gaze fixed on a point blocked from my view by Jackie-Boy's wide shoulders.

I pointed down the pathway to the right. "That way," I said, hastily. The crew moved like a wave, flooding the hallway I'd indicated. Kimera pushed her way to the lead, grabbing every crewman who tried to push ahead of her by the scruff with clawed fingertips.

Penny lingered, and so did I, following her locked eyes now that Jackie-Boy's massive chest no longer blocked my path. My eyes hung on the images, mesmerized by the beautiful inlay of red that stained every carving. Impressions from a childhood dream carved into daylight: cats, crocodiles, crane, hawk, ibis . . .

"Mr. Selfish," Kimera shouted over the murmur of voices. "To the bow of the line."

I swallowed, suddenly transfixed by one image, the one directly in front of Penny. It was carved in such immaculate detail that it felt like it was staring back at me with a midnight glare. The brimstone eyes of the jackal drilled into the back of my skull. This was not just a dog. No, this wasn't just a tail-chasing, cat-shaking canine—this was *the* psychopomp.

My stomach felt heavy, like I'd swallowed a brick of iron.

"Mr. Selfish," she called again, her voice further down the path. "Now, if you please."

I startled, biting my lip. My feet led me away from the image and I tried to shake the iron taste from my mouth. I stopped midline, feeling the pull from behind me, like a tether back to the carving. Tearing my eyes away, dazed, I fumbled through the crew. Penny slid past me, her touch electricity on my skin as we both fell in line. My limbs were heavy and my mind in a haze, as though I was pulled from a trance or sobered up from taking too many drugs.

It occurred to me, after the fact, that every cat who passed the image had hissed and spat. One younger fellow even jumped straight up, to the chuckles of the older crewmembers.

"Come on," Penny said with urgency, clawed fingers dragging me to the front of the line.

There were no dogs in this world, aside from a few wild breeds that roamed on four legs. So, then, what in the hell was the weigher of souls, the protector of rifts, doing here?

I stuck to Penny's side, who seemed less inconvenienced with my presence than usual. Trusting her to lead, I sharpened my eyes and looked for any other signs of Anubis on the trail as we journeyed deeper. But once we left the ebony chamber the world turned back to soil and rock. It seemed the ornate design was limited to the bubble of obsidian at the entrance.

With no sign of the jackal-god to spark my attention, I was now painfully aware of the crew giving Penny a wide berth. No one strayed too close, like ships steering around a dangerous reef. I'd assumed hers was a self-induced isolation, but after hearing Jackie-Boy, I knew I'd been wrong. I tried to imagine what he'd meant by *fits*. Penny was the opposite of an open book, but I hoped I would've at least noticed if she were sick.

Between the dampness of my socks and the erratic brain-itch spurred by the jackal, Penny breathed a short reprieve from my obsessive attention. The tunnel was filled with a foot of water and my boots invited it inside like an eager host. It distracted me, threatening to pull my sharp cat-eyes away from my fanatical task of examining the walls for any sign of the jackal.

The path broke out into another small cave and the torchlight exploded, sending the chamber ablaze in red light as it met with the prismatic facets of more rubies than were housed in the Smithsonian, all imbedded into a lone, golden altar.

The crew stared in awe, some even letting out a purr of approval. Everyone was squirming, unable to stand still. Tension built like accelerant; one flick of a spark and the whole thing would explode. These were the people on the fringes of society—where the sea was their mistress, judge, jury, and executioner—and they abandoned all civility when offered something worth coveting.

Yet, to their credit they didn't rush in like a mob on Black Friday. Kimera was at the front of the pack, and her attention was on me. Fifteen sets of eyes followed the blazed trail of her eyes like a spotlight. My weight shifted from left to right, and I broke the stare, feeling the heat rise in my cheeks, and tried to scrub off my stupid-boy dope face.

"The pictures, Nikki," Penny hissed. "What do the pictures say?"

"Oh," I said with a dumbfounded breath, suddenly more embarrassed I'd missed my cue than a crowd staring at me. The inlet was mundane, a small amphitheatre filled with a good layer of dirt over black stone. Moving closer, I studied the roof. The lip of the entrance blocked the light from reaching the top, but a few stubborn beams reflected off the lower reaches of obsidian stalactites which shimmered like a rain of stars.

Returning my attention to the floor, my eye caught the edge of the brown dirt near the doorway, where our careless entrance had disturbed the dust. The edges of pictures peeked out at me. Filling my lungs I exhaled deeply, further unfurling the powdered carpet.

There was no artistry to these scarce, discordant images. The lines weren't clean, the images convoluted like someone had shredded a book and tried to weave the torn scraps of paper together to tell a tale.

"I don't know what I'm looking for," I growled, panicked eyes flitting between the symbols.

The crew still hadn't moved, but I could feel their stares boring into me with anticipation, hoping it wouldn't turn to claws if I took too long.

"Anything that says *no*," Kimera answered. "The only thing that dwarfs our lust is an omen. Nothing's worth the price of our blood and lives. Cats don't like to bleed."

"Spoken like a crew familiar with curses," I offered absently, and wasn't rebuffed. I looked at the symbols on the floor: nothing told a story, only spoke of the greatness of Bastet, and outlined her majesty in all of her forms. It was more like a photoshoot of Bastet in Vogue, poses and outfits showcasing style and beauty. The Beyoncé of the Egyptian pantheon. I gave a shrug and a nod to Kimera. "Nothing says *no*."

They tore in to the room like hungry hyenas, skin on everything, touching, rubbing, smelling. My feet were petrified like they were stuck in poured concrete, leaving me stranded in the entryway while the crew revelled.

A ruby sheen danced around the room like a vampiric disco ball. All fifteen of them were crammed into the hollow, not dance-club-on-a-Friday levels of shoulder to shoulder, but a pretty tight squeeze just the same. Though, no one in the room seemed half as bothered by the crowding as I was looking in from the outside. They all radiated pure joy as they worshiped their bounty.

An uncomfortable groan pulled me from my trance and I glanced to my right, a pace or so behind me. Penny was also not revelling in the treasure, standing like her feet were frozen in place. I gave a last longing look at the crew who were now removing rags wrapped around what appeared to be treasure.

I wanted to be a part of what they were doing, even though the instinct to brush the gems on my cheeks leaving my mark on them like some garish graffiti tag reading "Nikki Selfish Was Here" felt so uncanny to me. But the pull of curiosity and Penny was stronger, and I needed to know what kept Penny from sharing in the crew's revelry.

"What's wrong?" I asked in a whisper, sliding the two feet back to her, while still keeping an inch of distance my high-school dance teacher would have been proud of. Her nose wrinkled and I forced a nervous laugh. "Don't you want to see the treasure?"

Penny shook her head and folded her arms over her chest. She took a breath as if coming to a decision. Then she looked at me. I forced down my own panic that I was about to get a face claw and held still.

"That picture back there . . . the one you were blocking the way to look at. Like, it was something vexin' you. Why'd you do that?"

"It just didn't make sense," I paused, fighting the urge to say something suave and nonchalant. "It's a type of picture that belongs somewhere else. Usually in a burial chamber or some spiritual place that marked a rift. Why'd you stop?"

Her chest dropped in a sigh and she ran her hands over her face. "I used to dream of it . . . of *him*. In a black desert of endless night. But you start telling folks you're dreaming of a bipedal dog with a voice that cuts like a butcher's knife, and they start throwing around words like hysteria and the madhouse. So, I stopped talking."

I let the silence give her room to breathe. Not wanting my interest to make her feel weighed or studied, I let my attention wane from her, though my thoughts mulled over her admission. The crew was making short work of everything. A cabin boy was sprawled on the floor with a small ruby kissing each facet of the crimson gem, pausing to smile between each display of affection.

"His name's Anubis," I offered, after letting the moment simmer at a comfortable temperature. "He's a god in the Egyptian pantheon. He's a guard, of sorts . . . he protects the barriers between realms and ferries the souls of the dead after weighing their judgement."

Penny scoffed. "Seems like jobs better suited to a cat."

I gave a small snort. "Yeah, well, he seemed to do fine in the stories."

The remaining dust on the ground had been flourished away by the eager footsteps of the crew. My eyes trailed down to the floor, seeing the symbols more clearly than I had from my previous post, and spying others freshly exposed further in the chamber. The images were different with more context, still drawn in the red ochre paint by an unskilled artist . . . but one stood out above the rest, more detail and more paint making her bold and brazen in comparison.

A woman's form with a lioness's head. The sun above her head was filled in with red, brilliant bold, and in her hand was an ushabit blade I'd mistaken for a sceptre. Not drawn with a hasty smear of paint but accentuated on the sharp side to represent a blood stain. My mind traced all the lines I'd dismissed as shoddy, seeing them in a new light. Another splatter of red dripped under the weapon, a pool of blood and not just a careless smudge. The quivering lines clarified into blood, seeping from her mouth that was grinning with rapturous delight, splashed across the shendyt tied around her waist—it was everywhere. At the base of her feet were limbs, all dripping in a pool of red ochre.

My mind twisted, realizing I had combined two images into one. *It was a common mistake*, I heard my professor say with a chuckle, *to mistake Bastet and Sekhmet*. Pieces moved into place, the peaceful nurturing mother being replaced with the voracious war-queen. Both two sides of the same coin.

A reflective beam from the stalactite shot into my eye, and instead of beautiful spires of rock all I saw were glimmering, sharpened teeth waiting to crunch down. The horror was in my eyes, pupils dilated, adrenaline running rampant in my veins, my heart jumping so hard it tried to break through my sternum. I lunged towards Kimera, towards the crew, my crew. Words were babbling out of me, nonsensical and in the wrong order—just like the warnings painted under their feet.

I fell, tumbling to the ground, just shy of crossing the threshold from the hallway to the altar room. Everyone looked at me with baffled expressions. None of them understood my inane babble, because in my panic, I'd reverted to my native language, unknown to the cats.

The room shuddered and the spikes of teeth came crashing down. I couldn't look away. Maybe my instincts truly were broken because I held the gaze of that young cabin boy on the floor, not even knowing his name to cry out, as the fangs came down, impaling him while I was lost in a horror-locked stare. Blood splattered, staining the walls, staining the floor in a colour not so different than the red paint used to pictograph the room.

I tried to scramble to my feet but there was something heavy pressing down on my spine. I twisted, expecting the fatal sight of a spire impaled through my own back, but instead came to meet the gaze of Penny, wide with fear, staring back at me.

"Did you do this?" she demanded, adding force to the weight compressing my ribs.

"What? No!" I stammered, the breath rushing out of my

lungs.

"Did you cast a curse or . . ."

A few groans and whimpers spilled out of the room and her attention jolted to the crew. She shoved off me and ran into the darkness; the spires of rock had crashed into the floor at odd angles, crossing over each other, making a maze of rock.

I stayed on the floor, at the edge, watching Penny use her claws to climb and jump from gap to gap. "Hang on for Bastet's sake!" she shouted.

The cracks in the floor bowed and boomed in wavelike contractions like some hungry muscle gulping down the blood of my friends. Was it a trick of the light, or had I stumbled into madness?

Penny emerged from the crooked bite with Kimera slung over her shoulder, cutting through the mess of bars like water. I got to my feet, moving like a zombie to help them through the barricade.

I tried to grab Kimera's arm that was not slung over Penny's shoulder, but I only grasped at air. There was nothing except blood, muscle, and bone protruding from the gaping wound in her shoulder. Instead of looking for what was no longer there, I grabbed the folds of her vest and pulled her through to the other side. Her weight was beyond my strength to bear so I maneuvered her body to the floor with Penny, who was scrambling to stop the bleeding.

More groans were coming from the dark; the maladroit jaws were inefficient and hadn't given them the mercy of a quick end. The crew was wounded, pinned in place, but not as dead as I'd first surmised. Penny's head shot up and the impossible task became clear. Kimera was likely to bleed to death without attention, but so was everyone else.

My face was cold as I ran a blood-slicked hand over my forehead to clear the sweat. My hands tremored, and I could hear Penny's voice, though it sounded like she was yelling at me through a hurricane gale.

"Bandages!" she said again, shouting and shaking me out of the clutches of my waking nightmare.

My vision swam, but I met her eyes. Jade wells of threat that had nothing on the sea.

"Bandages, take them." She shoved the cloth into my palm

and turned back to the tomb, disappearing into the gloom.

I swallowed and tried to lengthen my inhales. My body went through the motions, pressing the cloth against the gaping spot where Kimera's arm used to be, my eyes trained on the swimming shadows where Penny had disappeared. There was just enough light from the discarded torches that I could see in the hallway, and it glimmered off the stretched fangs. I lolled my head to the side, glancing upwards at the top of the maw, unable to purge the image of a mouth from my mind. Like the bloody pictographs, it was now impossible to not see. The light flickered casting a glow on more shimmering spears dangling from the roof. All crooked and gnarled at opposing angles. Another set of teeth would turn their groans to silence.

Looking back to Kimera, I watched as her blood drained in a stream, meandering back into the hungry pallet. Penny's voice lulled a soothing rhythm from the dark abyss.

No, this wasn't done. This room was hungry, ravenous, and it wasn't finished yet. There was a whole other layer of teeth, threatening to drop like a guillotine.

Giving Kimera an apologetic look, I rushed to my feet, running to the edge of the room. "No, no, no. Please, please don't do this . . ." My mind was racing. Sacrifice, blood. "I volunteer. Willing blood's got to be tastier, right? Take me instead."

A musty, warm wind whipped from the stone, stale as the tunnel, smelling of iron and sweat.

A taste so sweet. You know what I need. Give it to me.

The words were a whisper and they snared in my ears. Yet whether it was the itch of the heat, the smell, or something intrinsic in my cat DNA the words ground into my insides like sharp talons, and my knees buckled.

"Avarice. You need blood, and sacrifice" I flipped my forearms over and rolled up my shirt sleeves. I ran my shaking fingers over the soft fur on my wrists, digging through the undercoat to my skin, tracing the scars a younger me had made with a discarded pair of sewing scissors.

Bleed for me, Nikki Selfish.

"Instead," I repeated, letting the word linger in the air for clarity. "Instead of them. Not in addition to."

I took the knife from my belt and traced the blade down my

forearm, opening my flesh like a blooming red rose. Cutting a few more times for good measure, I pressed my forearms flat on the warm floor.

The stone came up to meet me, affixing to my wounds like the tentacles on a cephalopod. The warm wind blew again, and I cried out, feeling something coil and stretch up through my lacerations, diving into my skin, lapping my blood from the inside a snake's tongue.

It bulged under my skin as it took a tour of me from the inside. I squeezed my eyes closed, tears streaming down my cheeks, letting vertigo drag me to the ground.

I felt so undeniably empty. Drained. Hollow. My eyes shot open, feeling the hot air breathe again, an apparition of crimson floated over me, running her fingers over my lips.

Speak my name, Nikki Selfish.

Her ghostly mouth drew into a smile and I watched her fangs lengthen.

Consciousness dithered on the edge of my vision. Her fingers were intoxicating, her presence awe-inspiring. My head lolled to the side to see Penny sliding through the teeth with Jackie-Boy slung over her arm. I smiled.

My eyes fought to stay open, each inhale more laboured than the last. But I tried to keep that smile on my face as the last of the air seeped out of my lungs. "Hell no."

THE WORLD WAS black, lit by an unending horizon of twilight. Wind whipped black sand in chaotic blasts as I tried to orient myself in the ebony desert. There was no sound, no smell, no taste, only empty hollowness. I couldn't even feel the wind on my skin, just the irritation of it spinning me around like a feather on an updraft.

I hadn't spoken Sekhmet's name. It wasn't part of the deal, seemed like a bridge too far at the time. Did the crew survive her wrath? I probably shouldn't have pissed her off on my way out, but I wasn't interested in giving a blood-hungry goddess exactly what she wanted.

The desert breathed again and I flinched, putting my hands to my face instinctively. But this time, the wind moved like a god-breath blowing into the sand. I tumbled and twirled crashing into stone. Around me rose pillars of obsidian, archways for giants, and the more the wind blew, the more rose up from beneath the sand. Things moved in the vortex, eyes of red, emerald, ivory, amber beaming out from the windstorm at me. Then, out from the wall of sand moved a giant shadow, coming to rest in the eye of the storm where I'd fallen.

A giant made of black glass, a man's body with the head of a jackal and amber eyes that held me down by my throat.

Anubis, weigher of souls, guide of the damned, the doctor of mummification strode towards me, the wall of sand parting like a beaded curtain for him. With a wave of his ankh-tipped sceptre the storm abated, settling around two crooked archways. The span between them glistened like untouched midnight ponds.

Then his gaze fell to me, and my legs moved, walking towards the archways. On a whim, I angled towards the one on the right and stepped through the blackness.

THERE WERE NO period bells like there had been in primary school, but my mental bells always rang at mealtimes. It was lunch.

I took in a deep, disorientating breath, and sunk my fingertips into the book on the table. *That* book. Gasping, I sat bolt upright and glanced around. I was in the university library, my stomach rumbling, and my brain aching from last-night's binge hangover. Holding up my hands, my flesh-toned hands, I examined my furless forearms and cackled.

Rocketing to my feet, I grabbed the book and rushed out of the library, grinning as the lunch rush all congregated at the campus coffee stop, Sips Ahoy. I was back, I was home, and I was alive. The smile melted from my lips: I was alone.

I could hear Captain Cambrie in my mind, his booming chortle as I walked on his ship, "Ahoy there, Mr. Selfish. Welcome aboard the *Curiosity*. How about we just call you Nikki?"

His jovial demeanour was replaced with an anguished grief-yowl that echoed off the windows spanning the walkway, silencing the hum of the students. If Kimera didn't escape the temple, if he'd lost his crew . . .

Was it a dream, this other world? I shook my head, remembering the twilight desert and the weighted stare of

Anubis. There had been two archways. Two possibilities. Anubis wasn't a malicious god, he was a judgement god: a protector of the place between worlds. He'd fixed me with his heavy gaze, and I'd felt dissected. Was he watching now?

More stomach-twisting "what ifs" came to the forefront of my mind. What if the crew was gone? And, oh Bastet be damned, *Penny*. Would she carry all those bodies out herself? Would she leave mine behind? Was she all alone down there surrounded by the corpses of the closest people either of us had to friends, alone with an enraged apparition of Sekhmet?

The hum of the lunch crowd came back and I realized where I wanted to be, where I *should* be. Steadying myself, setting my shoulders, I flipped open the book, bypassing all the warnings and read the words aloud. Hell, I incanted them, giving myself over to the moment, even throwing my hand up at the end like a goddamn wizard.

And nothing happened. Students edged past me, whispering to each other, not making eye contact with the crazy man. I waited for half a minute and then read through the passage again, quick and quiet this time, showmanship tossed to the wayside. Despair tore at my heart. No, it was real, I knew it was.

"I want to go back!" I shrieked, uncaring of who heard me as I manically flipped through the book. "Please! Let me go back."

Then, a hole burned in the world, and a giant ebony hand picked me up by my throat and tore me through the breach.

My head swam, the world fell dark, and I felt hot blood flood my nose. I saw an image of the black desert, of the jackal god holding his infamous golden scales. I watched the scale plates shift to an even weight and he nodded.

Then a world of hurt swept over me. Pain blazed through my veins and I groaned. Nothing hurt so bad as living, and I wouldn't have traded it for all the comfortable afternoons in the world. My eyes shot open to the onslaught of rain and fog, and the image of Anubis faded into the darkness, his scales bending and stretching like an apparition settling into the familiar silhouette and bloodstained tawny fur I'd have recognized anywhere. The crash of ocean waves was like music accompanied by the hum of sombre sailors rhythmically rowing a longboat towards, what I hoped, was a ship called *Curiosity*.

THE PERFECT KIBBLE

KRISTA D. BALL

JUDICIAL COMMITTEE HEARING

New Sky Station

Investigation into Malcolm Critch, owner and operator of *Space Tortie* and his role in the HMS Dartmouth incident of February 19, 2019.

Interview date: April 22, 2019

JUDICIAL COMMITTEE MEMBERS

Jared Holland, Chief Judicial Arbiter

Daisy Attar, Judicial Arbiter

Dunn, New Sky Clan, First of his Generation, Judicial Arbiter

Anna Wells, Judicial Arbiter

Michael Nansen, Judicial Arbiter

INTERVIEWEES AND WITNESSES

Malcolm Critch, owner and operator of *Space Tortie*

Tinky aka Tinks, feline owned by Mr. Critch

TRANSCRIPT EXCERPT

Holland: The arresting officer's report noted that you *repeatedly* stated that you did not fire upon the patrol ships during your initial interview. Is this accurate?

Critch: That is correct, sir. It was all just a terrible accident and I feel awful about all of it.

Holland: This terrible accident, as you call it, did over three million dollars' worth of damage.

Critch: As I said, sir. A terrible accident of which I feel horrible about. Horrible.

Wells: A accident that you feel horrible about, and yet you insist you did not cause.

Critch: That's right.

Wells: Then, Mr. Critch, whose fault was it?

[Sound of a cat meowing]

Holland: Mr. Critch. Why did you bring your cat to this hearing?

Critch: The court summons expressly stated to bring any witnesses I had.

Dunn: And you brought your cat?

Critch: Like, she was there, so she's a witness in my mind.

Holland: Let the record show that Tinky has been verified to be a feline by the station scanners and the veterinarian onboard. As well, she was interviewed by a medium and a shapeshifter expert. All confirm Tinky's identity as a feline and no other magical or supernatural forces are influencing her.

Critch: Yes, sir. As I said from the very beginning, she's just a cat. Nothing weird or magical at all, or suspicious, no sir. Just a cat who is a jerk. But I love her. Yes, I do. [unintelligible cooing sounds] That's a good girl.

Attar: Your just a cat, as you say, caused three million dollars' worth of damage to the patrol ship, the HMS Dartmouth.

Critch: Like I said, she's a very typical cat.

Holland: Mr. Critch, I feel as though you are not taking these proceedings seriously. Are you aware of how much trouble you are in?

Critch: Yes, sir. I am very aware. I've not been allowed on my ship in weeks. I've been living with strangers because of it. If today goes well, I could lose my licence. You could confiscate my ship. You could fine me the three million dollars. You could even take my cat from me.

Nansen: Sir, we're not going to take your cat. We are here to determine if this was an accident and what, if any, action needs to be taken. We are not here to judicate on pet ownership.

[Short pause while Mr. Critch coos at his cat]

Holland: Mr. Critch, for the record, please state what you do for a living.

Critch: These days, I'm an ice hauler. Melt and purify, then process the leftover particles. Then I re-freeze the water into ice blocks. I have a 98% filter and a small metals processor onboard, so my ship is super efficient, like you know what I mean? So, when I sell the water and the extracted metals, I get high prices because the stations don't need to do much more work with my stuff. It's why I can keep running as a small ship.

Nansen: What is your circuit?

Critch: Before the accident, I mean not the one with me blowing a hole in the patrol ship, but the other mining accident, ya know the one? On New Beijing?

Nansen: Yes, everyone is aware of that accident.

Critch: Right. Well, before then, I used to do the entire circuit between all the ice asteroids and the mining platforms, but these days I only do New Sky to New Beijing's platform.

Critch: There's one big rig with New Beijing and just four of us small ships for now, so no competition. And I have the metal processor, too, you see? So everyone leaves me the dirty ice and they mine the edges. I can pull just about anything out, so I grab the really bad ice. And, what's great is that I make extra money off all the other crap I pull out of it, so I still make enough to get by.

Holland: I don't show any employee records with your papers. Do you take on contractors?

Critch: No. It's just me and the cat.

Holland: Tell us what led to the events of the incident.

EIGHT HOURS BEFORE the Incident

Sweat dripped off Malcolm's forehead and his t-shirt was stuck to the small of his back. He'd take off the wet shirt, but that was a great way to end up covered in scratches from crawling around the tanks. No, he'd just have to deal with the heat. Two more months and he'd have enough to install an air conditioner down here without needing to use credit. He could wait.

"Press the button, Tinks!"

Tinks yawned.

"Oh, come on, Tinks! I don't want to be down here anymore than you do."

The chubby tortoiseshell cat's yawn caused her ears to pin against her head.

"We're almost done. Just get on the plate."

Tinks let out a stream of low meows that, to the well-trained feline owner, was a litany of complaints.

"Oh, nobody in this room cares. Just get on the button already."

Malcolm suffered through several more grumpy meows, much louder than the last, but she dragged her fuzzy self over to the pressure plate that he'd installed on top of the grunge and gunge run-off tank. She dramatically collapsed, still meowing her complaints.

"Keep that pressure . . . there . . . good . . . and release!"

His monitoring gauge kept rising.

"Tinks!"

Tinks let out an annoyed yowl.

"Get your fuzzy butt off the pressure plate before you blow the system."

Tinks spread her hind legs to began grooming. The gauge beeped its increasing situation.

"Tinks! I mean it! Move!"

A dramatic meow, a stretch, and finally the cat stepped off the plate seconds before the ship-wide emergency alarm would have shrieked. He watched the gauge numbers decrease, changing colour from red to yellow. He let out a relieved breath. If the alarms went off, he'd have been stuck trying to use a broom handle to both press the plates whenever he needed to check the systems *and* to get Tinks out of the ceiling vents.

The numbers finally fell back to green.

"Okay, Tinks. That's locked off and we're good to go with the gunge tank. Let's make sure the main processors are doing fine and then we can get some sleep."

Malcolm shouldered his tool bag. He dropped the gunge tank tablet back into the cat-proof slot he'd installed on the side of the tank.

"Come on, Tinky! Let's go check out the processor. Tinky!

Come on, kitty! Let's go!"

He whistled for her to follow, and she leaped across the tanks and made it to the processor's control station first. When Malcolm rounded the corner, Tinks collapsed on the keyboard to sprawl luxuriously. She made piteously little coos.

After putting his tool bag on the floor, he pulled out a small plastic container. He put two tiny treats on top of the processor tunnel in front of her. He tapped where the location of the treats were until Tinky jumped up. She gobbled her goodies and began a long series of yowls.

"I'm not listening to it. And if you ate your kibble, you wouldn't be so hungry."

When more yowls echoed through the room, he said, "I don't care that they changed the shape. It's still the same food."

The yowls of protest continued the entire time Malcolm confirmed the processor was working properly and the metals and debris were being separated properly into each of their various deposit tanks.

Tinks finally got two more treats just so Malcolm could hear himself think.

JUDICIAL COMMITTEE HEARING – Transcript Excerpt

Nansen: How do you manage that ship by yourself? Do you have robots? Ghosts?

Critch: That's why I'm only doing the New Beijing run now. It's a lot less stress with just me running things.

Most of my ship is automated. I rigged it up myself so that I could run it. Don't worry. It's all been inspected by New Sky. I have the papers. Well, it's not real paper. It's a file, but you know what I mean. I can email it to you.

Holland: We have your papers.

Critch: Oh, okay.

Holland: So . . . ?

Critch: Yes?

Holland: Your schedule?

Critch: Oh, right. Once I tether the ship, I'm locked into place until I've cut through everything in my area and it's all in the tank. Normally, that can take hours, but if it's really dirty, it can take days. My systems are set to automatic. Alarms will go off if anything goes wrong. I do routine checks every twelve hours to make sure everything is running fine.

Nansen: Do you often have problems?

Critch: Nah. It's all pretty smooth. A lot of the equipment is new, and the old stuff was all serviced when the new filter went in. Ya know? New Sky station rules and all that. So, I've not had a thing go wrong. I just need to keep ahead of things. Make sure the filters don't get clogged. Repair any mining drones that run into problems. That sorta thing. All wear and tear really.

Holland: The attending physician onboard the *Dartmouth* said you were so exhausted that you collapsed in the evacuation transport and didn't wake for twelve hours. Is that true?

Critch: Oh, that was just stress. I crashed hard from all the adrenaline and all that. I mean, ya know? I'd thought I'd killed people and all that, so I was pretty amped up out of my mind with worry.

Holland: And then?

Critch: Well, when it was clear no one died and my cat was okay, I crashed. That's just normal, I think. There's nothing wrong with that, is there?

Wells: So just to be clear for the record. Would you consider yourself well-rested that day?

Critch: Absolutely.

FOUR HOURS BEFORE the Incident

"For the love of . . . Tinks! Get off my face!"

Tinks complied, mostly because Malcolm rolled her off him when he flailed about trying to catch his breath and cough up a hairball. She tapped his wrist gingerly. "Meow."

Malcolm checked the time on his phone before collapsing back on his pillow. "Oh come on, you can't be hungry again. You ate two hours ago."

More tapping. "Meow."

"Oh please. I'm going back to sleep."

The meow turned into yowling. Malcolm rolled on his side and pulled the covers over his head. Moments later, a heavy pressure collapsed over his face, cutting off his oxygen. He managed to throw the cat off his face, and sat up, flustered, and struggled to breathe.

He picked up his phone and squinted at the time. "Why are you acting like this?"

Cooing.

"Oh, buzz off. I'm not falling for this."

More cooing. Also a headbutt. And a butt-butt.

"Get your . . . Tinks! Stop rubbing my butt against the side of . . . fine! Fine! I'll get up. I'm up! God, you're annoying."

Malcolm turned on the light and squinted at the searing pain blinding him. He blinked several more times to glance at the display panel on his bedside. "Ah crap. We're nearly done the last extraction. I might as well stay up."

"Meow."

"Yeah, whatever. I'll get you some food. Three-eighths of a cup, though. That's all you're getting."

Yooooooooooooooooooooooowl.

"You should have thought of that before you decided to stick your head in the food bin and gain three pounds. You look like you swallowed a volleyball."

Yooooooooooooooooooooooowl.

"If you don't lose the weight, I can't take you back to that vet you like with those nice shirts because she'll blame me for making you fat."

Silence.

"Three-eighths of a cup it is."

JUDICIAL COMMITTEE HEARING – Transcript Excerpt

Wells: So you admit you were tired because your cat woke you up?

Critch: I was sleepy, sure, but a coffee and some toast, and I was fine. Plus, ending extraction is the least dangerous part of the entire operation.

Holland: Please explain the process.

Critch: See, the ship automatically untethers as soon as the asteroid is too small to use the main drill. The laser drones cut what's left, the clean-up drones use a magnetic net to grab whatever it can from around the ship. Then everything is back inside. The processor runs the final checks. Then, I start the journey back out. I can sleep for the trip and usually leave autopilot to handle the rest.

Nansen: Do you autopilot out of the debris field?

Critch: Oh, no way! I mean, no, I can't, ya see. So, what it's like is that, um, well, you have to pay attention just to make sure you don't need to send drones out to move something out of the way. Because, like, well, ya know? Stuff will shift around in space. And you are removing a few giant chunks of ice, so it makes sense that other stuff will fall in to fill up the hole you made. So you have to be careful clearing the field. But after that, it's just autopilot until you hit the perimeter checkpoint. That's when you have to be awake.

Attar: And you were awake during the departure from the field, but then you went back to sleep for the journey to New Sky?

Critch: Yup. I mean, yes.

Dunn: Why did you go to New Sky? Your logs show you'd just been there. Normally, you'd carry on to New Beijing, according to your own testimony.

Critch: There was just a small emergency onboard.

Holland: What kind of emergency?

THE INCIDENT

Malcolm yawned when the warning klaxon sounded. He blinked his eyes, disoriented at his unfamiliar surroundings. He'd fallen asleep on the main bridge. Granted, the chair was really comfortable, but even still. He craned his neck to the left, waiting for the crack and pop of tissue across bone. Then he repeated the gesture on the other side. He wasn't rewarded with the delicious release of stiffness nor the satisfying pop.

Malcolm looked about the screens in front of him, blinking to focus his eyes. He made eye contact with the blinking red light first. Red equals bad. He tapped and read the warning. They were approaching the security perimeter and he was getting the automated message to turn off autopilot.

Malcolm yawned again and began the process of turning everything over to manual. He had an emergency takeover app on his cell phone, where he could run the manual controls using voice control until he made it to the bridge. However, he also risked crashing the main computer and having to run the entire ship from his cell phone until the system rebooted, and that took forty-minutes.

He'd just do it manually and all proper-like.

"Tinks? Where are ya?"

Silence.

"Tinks?"

A meow echoed above him.

"Get out of the air vent! I told you, there's no mice left in there."

Meeoooooooooow.

"That was one time! And it was only because I agreed to haul that load of lizard supplies to New Beijing."

Meeeeeeoooow.

"We're going back to New Sky to get you some cat food. I said I'm sorry they changed the shape of the kibbles!"

Yowl.

"You can't be that hungry if you won't eat your food. Now get out of there before you get hurt!"

Malcolm stepped up on the desk and reached inside the vent, hoping to grab Tinks by the scruff and haul her out.

"Attention, captain of the *Space Tortie*. This is the *HMS Dartmouth*. You must cut your autopilot before you enter the perimeter for your own safety. Please reply that you will comply."

"Computer: voice reply. Hi, HMS Dartmouth. I'm in the process of doing so. Just give me another couple minutes."

"*Space Tortie,* is there a problem with your systems? It shows you have deactivated the autopilot but have not engaged manual control. Your ship is dead in space."

Malcolm was reaching. He got Tinks' front paw. "Come on, you little . . ."

"*Space Tortie?* Is everything okay over there? Do you need drones dispatched to tow you into dock?"

"No, *Dartmouth*, just . . . just, stupid cat!"

"Say again *Space Tortie?*"

"Get your fuzzy butt back here or I swear to God I will skin you alive!"

"*Space Tortie,* are you threatening violence? *Space Tortie?* What is happening over there? Are you in danger? *Space Tortie?*"

Malcolm grabbed Tinks by the armpits as she howled at the top of her feline lungs. He swore and insulted her and grunted from the effort of trying to move a fifteen-pound cat that absolutely did not want to move. Just as Malcolm got her head out of the vent, she let out a high-pitched shriek.

"*Space Tortie?* What was that? I am dispatching drones and a military police force."

"Dartmouth, I'm fine. I'm just . . . ow!"

Tinks used Malcolm's head as a springboard to leap to the control panels. She landed with a thud on the keyboard.

"Warning: mining laser activated."

Malcolm lost his balance and hit the console underneath him. His head swam with the screaming anger of his ribscage.

"*Space Tortie,* I am dispatching assistance. Remain calm and . . . why have you engaged your cutting lasers?"

"Computer, activate emergency collusion evasion."

"Warning. Cannot comply," the computer said calmly.

"*Space Tortie?* What is happening?"

Malcolm moaned and rubbed his head. He thought he was going to vomit. "Ow. Computer, emergency stop. Emergency stop."

"Cannot comply."

"Why not?"

"Meow."

"Tinks! Get off the damn keyboard!"

"*Space Tortie!* Stop firing! What are you doing? Cease fire! Cease fire!"

YOOOOOOOOOOOOOOOOOOOWWWWWWWWWWWL.

Transcript Excerpt

Holland: And that is when the mining lasers all went off at once, while your ship was rocking back and forth, destroying eight tugboat drones, disabling two rescue pods, and carving up the exterior plating of the HMS Dartmouth.

Critch: That is correct. It was just a horrible, terrible accident.

Dunn: So you are saying that this entire incident was nothing more than your cat being upset because the kibble you bought her had changed shape?

Critch: Pretty much. I mean, yes, sir.

Dunn: Do you realize how incredibly unrealistic that sounds?

Critch: Have you ever owned a cat, sir?

Dunn: No. Historically, my people eat cats.

[Hissing sounds fill the room.]

Dunn: Mr. Critch, are you certain that cat is just a cat?

Critch: Of course she is. Your scans even said so, right? I mean, I wouldn't lie to you now, would I? No sir. She's just a really bad cat. I mean, she's good at being a cat, but she's just trouble.

Holland: Mr. Critch, give us an hour to discuss our next steps.

THREES HOURS AFTER the Judicial Hearing's Conclusion

Malcolm didn't speak to Tinks for the entire trip back to his ship. True, she was asleep in her carrier but he was too upset with her to speak in any case. He off-loaded his wagon full of cat food, including four different large bags of food she'd eaten previously, as well as nineteen different small bags of various brands, shapes, and quality. He also off-loaded four cases of canned cat food, two cases of tuna, one case of salmon, and another case of smoked mackerel. If he was lucky, Tinks would like one of those.

He brought Tinks and her carrier to the little kitchenette and he put her on top of the table. He opened the carrier door. She lightly snored.

He poked her until she woke up. "We have to talk."

Tinks rolled over to expose her tummy. Her back paws curled.

"I mean it, Tinks. I was fined ten thousand dollars for failing to drop out of autopilot and the improper storage of cargo. They counted you as the cargo, by the way. I lost three demerit points off my operator license!"

"Oh, stop your whining. You get fifteen points every three years."

Malcolm glared at his cat. Tinks was washing herself and completely unconcerned by the voice coming from her collar.

Malcolm scowled. "Ten thousand dollars!"

"It's not my fault you didn't tell them about me."

"Um, yeah. Exactly how do I explain that I picked up an alien who has possessed my cat because it's the only way you can survive in our universe?"

"Just like that. Now, Tinks wants her belly rubbed. Give that tum-tum a rub."

"No. She's just going to kick me and then bite my hand. Now, seriously, you can't use Tinks to do crap like that again, man. I'll be in enough trouble if they find out who I used to be. I am trying to be legit here. I can't be legit if you're firing my cutting lasers at patrol ships."

"That wasn't me."

"What do you mean, that wasn't you?"

"Seriously, my friend. That was Tinky."

"Tinks? Was that really you?"

Purring sounded through the room.

Malcolm sighed. "There are days I regret ever leaving Earth. Come on, Tinks. Let's see which of the new foods you'll eat."

All Cats Go to Valhalla

By Chadwick Ginther

"Well, we're fucked," Kills-the-Sky muttered at the far-off storm.

If only his name meant he had the power to rule a storm, like Thor, instead of being a noted bird hunter.

A soft mew from behind him, and Kills-the-Sky turned to see a ginger cat named Sunchaser.

Sunchaser asked, "When will we make landfall?"

"Soon," he lied. His tail entwined with hers, his green eyes met her golden ones. "Land is on the other side of those clouds."

Satisfied with the lie, Sunchaser wandered off, their tails clinging a moment before she was gone. "I'll tell the others."

Kills-the-Sky looked back to the seething clouds. "So totally fucked."

They were a long way from home, and further from safety. Once that dark bank of clouds reached the ship it would capsize, and then they'd all drown.

That is, if the nightmare didn't get them first. After the nightmare had killed the cats' human servants, it had seemed unconcerned with them—perhaps cats didn't dream the way humans did?—but there was no telling how long that would continue.

While the hold had normally been filled with trade goods or

war gear, this time there was only their servants' provisions and the box which had imprisoned their nightmares. Kills-the-Sky and the cats guarded the hold from rats. The hold was their purview, and as the leader of the ship's cats, *his* purview. And he had failed. Failed so mightily. He stared into the hold at the opened chest and hissed his annoyance into the wind.

Kills-the-Sky didn't know how the nightmare had escaped her imprisonment and it didn't matter. A number of cats had begged Kills-the-Sky to open the box during the voyage, so they could sleep in it, or play with whatever was inside, but he'd held to his duty. They protected the stores from rats and he'd done the same for this prison. For all the good it had done.

With their servants dead, Kills-the-Sky and his cats would die too. No cat could tow the oars, or cut into the wind with the sail. Even if the cats knew how to sail the ship, it'd be no help. Great rends marred the square woollen cloth from the top to the bottom, as if Jólakötturinn, the Yule Cat, had shredded it in a fit of pique. Cats were as adept with a needle and thread as they were at manning the oars. Frayed fabric was a toy, not something to mend.

Kills-the-Sky licked sea salt from his fur, feigning nonchalance to the other cats roaming on their listing vessel. They looked up to him. They needed him. But they were fucked.

Kills-the-Sky's ear twitched. The barest whisper of a padded foot over wood from behind him.

"Quite the pickle," a tortoiseshell named Fairweather said, watching the sky from the oarsman's seat beside Kills-the-Sky.

Kills-the-Sky didn't catch the reference, but he gathered the cat's context. "One could say that."

"So stoic." She patted Kills-the-Sky. "We both know we're fucked."

Kills-the-Sky hissed and clawed at Fairweather. She dodged the swipe and didn't retaliate. Her back was up, fur on end, and her tail swished warily, teeth bared in an incongruous smug smile. She was the most recent cat to join them on the ship, and a bit odd, which among this crew, was saying something.

"Do cats go to Valhalla?" Fairweather asked, her mismatched eyes glittering, and her anger gone like a summer squall. "Inquiring for a friend."

"*You* won't," Kills-the-Sky said. "Since you're so afraid to fight."

"There are some fights one can't win," Fairweather said. "Even you."

Kills-the-Sky didn't answer. Still, Fairweather's question prickled Kills-the-Sky's whiskers. A question he couldn't answer. A question he wasn't certain he *wanted* answered. Valhalla didn't sound like the place for a cat to him. Odin was more of a dog man anyway, and the less said of Thor and his goats, the better, but there *were* ways into the Hall of the Great Servants, if one dared. At least Kills-the-Sky had been told so by his grandsire, Sleeps-with-Swords. Better, the old cat had said, were the ways into Fólkvangr, the realm of Freyja. Freyja loved cats. To the skogkatts, those felines with the divine in them, *she* was the first among the Great Servants, for she paid them their due. To laze in the bright sun of her hall, being doted upon, was far superior in Kills-the-Sky's opinion to dodging the spit and kicks of Odin's *einherjar*.

"You're not going to bring up your bloody grandsire again are you?" Fairweather's playful teasing took on an edge of waiting violence. "*My grandsire* was Sleeps-with-Swords. *My grandsire* climbed to Asgard. *My grandsire* was a skogkatt. *My grandsire* fucked Freyja."

Kills-the-Sky's muzzle twitched. He'd never said that last one. Maybe his grandsire had, but never to him. Fairweather had a surprising amount of disdain for a cat who was dead long before she was born. Stranger, she had even more disdain for Freyja and the other Great Servants.

Fairweather must've been satisfied to have had the last word. She'd disappeared from the deck while Kills-the-Sky hunted a retort.

A cloud glided over the sun and an old woman appeared on the deck beside him in the passing shadow. Kills-the-Sky blinked and the membranes flicked over his eyes, showing the woman for what she was, a nightmare. A mara. Her dirty, cracked nails dripped blood. Lank grey hair hung to her waist covering a distended belly full of the fears of dead sailors. The rest of her body gaunt, yet corded with ropey muscle. Flashing wild eyes, a sweaty sheen over her skin, moist beads tracing the cavernous lines of her face, as if she'd been running all night. She reeked of horse, lathered beyond endurance.

That sheen of sweat a salty wave, waiting to break over Kills-the-Sky. He saw their doom in her face. Since his youth, he'd dreamt of being dragged down under a tide of rats that wouldn't stop coming. Drowning under a wave of teeth and fur, choking on his own blood instead of water. Maybe the dream was why he'd preferred hunting birds to rats.

The mara's gliding steps, toenails barely touching the wood, were as loud to Kills-the-Sky as the clacking of shod hooves over stone. She stopped and squatted on the chest of a dead servant, his face frozen in a scream; the filed runes in his ochre-stained teeth had been no protection. Kills-the-Sky had never learned that one's name—he hadn't liked cats. Had threatened to feed Kills-the-Sky to his hounds back home, kicked at him when he thought no other sailors were looking, and threatened to take his pelt for a fur collar. He would be the first to be eaten, if the mara and storm left him alive long enough. And good riddance.

Their sailors—most of them—had been good servants. Kills-the-Sky missed the captain. He, for all his violent bluster, had known how to treat a cat. Offering scritches under the chin or pats when desired, treats when demanded, and otherwise left them to hunt and bask in the sun when they chose.

Kills-the-Sky hopped from the rower's bench, soundlessly landing on the deck. The mara turned a baleful eye to him and glided away to another body, the sound of hoofbeats following in her wake, until she squatted on its chest, kneading her clawed fingers into it and staring into its clouded eyes, looking for something. But what?

Slowly, Kills-the-Sky stepped onto the first sailor's chest, keeping a wary eye toward the mara. He prodded the corpse with a paw. The sailor's rictus, terror-filled face stared unblinkingly at the sky. Kills-the-Sky found no answers in the dead face. It wouldn't be much longer before the ship cats took to feeding on their dead sailors.

They'd already killed all the rats.

THEIR SERVANTS HAD found a new world. Their tales of the hunting, the danger, the sheer expanse . . . Kills-the-Sky couldn't wait to see it. And now he never would. It was there the servants had been taking the nightmare, to keep it far from home and hearth, as far as wind and sea would take it. Hoping it would never find its way back.

A great yowl rose from the far end of the longship. Kills-the-Sky ran toward the clamour, darting from stem to stern. One of the other cats on the ship, Sunchaser, was dead. Murdered. Not just murdered. Left for Kills-the-Sky like a prize. His eyes narrowed. Or a taunt. If not for the trickle of blood from Sunchaser's mouth, it looked as if she were sleeping in the sun one last time, splayed out to absorb the heat. Except her head was turned around the wrong direction.

She'd been a good hunter. Stealthy. Perceptive. What on the ship could've done this to her? This was no cat's kill. Sunchaser hadn't died like the servants. She hadn't seen death coming and feared it. She'd been ambushed. Or betrayed. It seemed as if she'd been killed by a man's hand and presented as a trophy here. But by who? And where were they?

As he dragged the body over the side, three other cats, Wintermute, Ghostkill, and Blacklock helped him. They said nothing as they pushed Sunchaser over the edge into the sea. She'd always had a way of finding a sliver of sun on a cloudy day, never at peace otherwise. Pacing endlessly, mewing her annoyance until the rest of the ship shared her displeasure. No sun for her final rest today. None ever again. Still, it was more ceremony than they usually received from the servants. Maybe the currents would take her home.

Kills-the-Sky didn't know what could have killed Sunchaser.

That wasn't good.

He didn't like things he didn't know. But the mystery gave him purpose. Something more than waiting for the sea or the nightmare to claim them. Kills-the-Sky stared at the advancing line of black clouds and the sea that'd swallowed Sunchaser.

The storm might be better.

ANOTHER CAT, TREESPEAKER, a ginger with a bent tail, and green eyes, had taken to playing with his dead servant's bag of runes, batting the carved stones and bits of antler across the deck and pouncing on them. The servants believed the future could be revealed, the past unveiled, and the present exposed by the position and symbols of the cast runes, playing at understanding the secrets of the Great Servants. Treespeaker had always been fascinated with the runes. Maybe he'd seen something, or heard something of their fate in those tales Kills-the-Sky could use.

Kills-the-Sky padded to his side. "What do the bones tell you?"

"The bones," he said gravely, pushing one with two crossed lines upon it toward Kills-the-Sky, "tell me nothing. They are only rocks."

Kills-the-Sky let out an exasperated sigh. Time wasted. Time they didn't have. Sunchaser's killer, whoever they were, could've found another victim. Who would they target next? The ship was large—to a cat—but not so large one could hide forever.

The only creature still walking the ship with hands that could strangle a cat was the mara. It'd only been a matter of time before the mara turned their nightmares on them. And yet, something about that didn't feel right. So far she'd shown no real interest in them.

Wind ruffled his fur and Kills-the-Sky turned, glancing over his shoulder. The clouds were closer, the gusts more prevalent. With Sunchaser gone, it seemed the sun itself had gone with her. Kills-the-Sky knew that wasn't true, and yet . . . and yet . . . The mara would only be walking more as the storm grew closer, and then, the *real* nightmare would begin.

The last nightmare.

NIGHTMARES COULD BE found anywhere, in anything, and any place, but in Kills-the-Sky's experience, they liked the deepest darkness best. The shadows. Solitude. *That* was where the mara could best dig their claws into you. She appeared on the deck only in the shadows cast by the mast and sail, and disappeared when they sun crept past them. Kills-the-Sky preferred the sun, but he was well accustomed to hunting in the shadows.

All Kills-the-Sky wanted was to solve this mystery before the sea claimed him. Before it claimed them all.

"I will go below to hunt her," he said. "And I will end this."

He padded to the ladder to the hold, and measured the jump just as Fairweather swiped at him, swatting his tail. The surprise almost drove him over the edge and into the hold. He hissed and swiped back. Fairweather rolled on her back and made a purring, an almost human laugh. Kills-the-Sky wrinkled his whiskers. They'd all have been better off if Fairweather had stayed at home with the servants too afraid to take the voyage.

We'd all be better off if we'd *stayed there too.*

Kills-the-Sky snuck into darkness while Fairweather waited under a rower's bench, swiping at any cat passing by. She made him so *tired*.

Kills-the-Sky leapt into the hold and felt a chill when he landed on the box that'd held the nightmare. He kept a wary eye to the shadows. The sealed box had been left open to the elements where any and all could spot the prison and reassure themselves the nightmare had been contained. Not that their placement or concern had saved them.

Two pinpricks of light, a dull glow from the mara's eyes, presaged her stepping into Kills-the-Sky's sight. Cat and hag circled the rune-etched prison box. Each taking the other's measure. The nightmare returned to the chest where the servants had locked her away, drifting in the air, talons dragging over the wood, perched like a vulture.

"Why did you kill them?" Kills-the-Sky demanded.

"Who?" The single word dropped like a turd in the sand. "Your 'servants?'"

"No, not them. We expected that. They expected that. Sunchaser."

The nightmare blinked. "The cat?"

"Yes."

A dismissive snort. "Not my work."

Kills-the Sky choked back a rising yowl of frustration. Her eyes bored into him. "You're not hunting us?"

"Not yet."

"When?"

"Dreams become nightmares," she smiled, cackling, and snapped her fingers, "like that."

Kills-the-Sky looked from the mara to her useless prison. The rune wards had been scratched away. The nightmare's own talons, perhaps? Or a servant's knife? The gouges were too deep and broad to be a cat's work. The sliver of sun was obscured. Fairweather peered in from the tops of the steps, a halo of sunlight ringing her head. The nightmare's eyes shot up, and she glided away in a rush. Galloping hooves rang in Kills-the-Sky's ears as her stink washed over him like a wave, flattening him to the floor.

With another cat's life in the balance—even Fairweather's—Kills-the-Sky grew bolder, padding closer. He swiped at the mara, but his paw passed through her like she was shadow.

She laughed.

She *laughed.*

The nightmare locked eyes with Kills-the-Sky, and he heard the dying screams of the first man she took and then the next and the next, so hungry, a feast she could've stretched for months was gone in a night. When she chuckled, he heard those pained shrieks in the pause between every guttural laugh. The mara turned back to the ladder.

The nightmare stretched a taloned finger toward Fairweather, coming just shy of broaching the threshold into the light. Then the ship rolled on a wave, pitching Fairweather into shadow. The mara's hands clutched her ruff until the ship rolled back and the grasping hand evaporated and Fairweather fled.

Other than Kills-the-Sky, only Fairweather paid any attention to the nightmare, and she kept a nervous distance from her.

What do you see that others do not, Fairweather?

Kills-the-Sky's ears twitched, and his eyes narrowed as he watched the young cat bolt under a rower's bench.

Now he had a second target.

FAIRWEATHER PROVED HARDER to stalk than the Nightmare. And Kills-the-Sky's failure had cost.

Another cat dead.

Treespeaker, this time. Same method as Sunchaser. His runes scattered around his body in some deliberate pattern that meant nothing to Kills-the-Sky. Lightning flashed in the coming clouds. No time for another funeral. Not if they wanted to find the killer before they all died.

THE NIGHTMARE CAME back on deck when the sun went behind a cloud. Whether they saw her or not, all the cats kept their distance. Smart. But for now, she was not Kills-the-Sky's problem. Cats may dream of the sun, but they're not afraid of the dark.

Kills-the-Sky watched, silently from beneath the rower's bench. The nightmare turned back and looked at him. She licked her lips. He knew—*knew*—he'd be first when her hunger returned. It was his ship. The dreams of cats may be small to her, but his were the biggest among them. A world where his family had spread across the world. Where they no longer had to pretend to be pets, where they walked the heavens mighty as the Great Servants claimed to be, in the days when they hunted men, not for them. Their proper place once more.

Too late he was pulled from his thoughts to realize it wasn't the shadow of a cloud that'd fallen over him, but the mara.

Kills-the-Sky's breath caught, and he felt the hag's full weight pressed on his chest but when he strained to look, it wasn't her on him, it was a wave breaking against the longship. A wave with teeth, and it pulled him under until he couldn't see. Couldn't breathe. Couldn't feel anything but pain.

A dream turned to nightmare. The mara's work. He knew this, and yet, for all the knowing, couldn't make it end. Couldn't rise. Couldn't wake. Couldn't scream.

SOMETHING BRIGHT SEARED Kills-the-Sky's eyes. One last patch of sun had burned through the clouds before the storm fell.

The biting wave receded, leaving a dark-haired shadow looming in its place. Its mannish shape had hair curving over its head by wind, like horns, and broad feet that could crush the swiftest cat and a tongue that whispered faster than Kills-the-Sky could understand. Cat after cat fell under the shadow's hands.

Kills-the-Sky's grandsire, Sleeps-with-Swords, was full of tales like this. He'd boasted he'd climbed to Asgard, and from there, to Freyja's hall, Sessrúmnir, to pilfer from the tables of the Great Servants and their dead believers. That he'd grown to the size of a bear to wrestle Thor, stolen fish from Heimdall, and bested Loki in a flyting. Or how he'd flown to the stars to harass Hati and Skoll, where he'd lost an eye to Hati and an ear to Skoll.

He'd been a liar and a braggart, but to Kills-the-Sky, Sleeps-with-Swords had been a hero. A skogkatt—an elf-cat, a dwarf-cat, a god-cat. Perhaps there'd been truth to the old cat's tales. Kills-the-Sky had believed the stories as a kit, but as his years rolled on, and Sleeps-with-Swords was long dead, it seemed a milk-tale.

Now he wished it *was* true. That he could follow his grandsire and climb the mast until he reached the World Tree and the Great Servants. He wished his grandsire would show him a way out of this nightmare. He wished he could *be* his grandsire. But a ray of sunshine had banished the nightmare and dream both.

"I'd hoped she would finish you," a familiar, yet strange voice said from behind Kills-the-Sky.

He sprang to his feet. Fairweather regarded him with her mismatched eyes smouldering; a man's shadow stretching from her cat's body.

"You are the last. The last of his seed. I told him he would pay. To the last kit. To the last person who'd cared for his scions. That what he stole would be replaced in blood. *His* blood.

"I'd have tried to get you to open the nightmare's prison, that would've been more pleasing to me, but you're as stubborn as Odin, and harder to kill than Baldur."

There was something half-remembered from a curse in Fairweather's eyes. Especially when they looked back at him as if belonging to a serpent or a bird but no cat.

"*Loki.*"

Hate filled Kills-the-Sky. An ancestral grudge he didn't know he bore. A connection to his grandsire. To the forest. To *power*. He shuddered as the hate swelled within and grew until the hold felt very small, and Fairweather—Loki—even smaller. Kills-the-Sky put his paw forward and saw it was large enough to crush a cat. Or kill a god.

The trickster's eyes widened, and he bolted. Kills-the-Sky knew then who had released the mara to kill their sailors. Whether the god of mischief released the nightmare, or had the deed done for them, it didn't matter. Only the result mattered.

If Loki had trapped the cats on this ship to die, Kills-the-Sky would ensure the trickster remained trapped alongside them. It would be small comfort to eat the trickster before he drowned, but when one faced death, small comforts mattered most.

Kills-the-Sky gave chase. He knew every nook of the vessel. Still, he didn't want to lose sight of his target. Loki ran well, the body of a cat as natural to the trickster as if he was born to it. Kills-the-Sky's new form was fast. Faster than Loki, and he gained ground on the trickster.

Another cat—Bugeater—sought to stop Loki. Whether Bugeater sensed the danger, or, wrongly assumed Fairweather wanted to play, he pounced. Kills-the-Sky roared in warning. Too late. Contorting his body at the last moment, Loki rolled onto his back and lashed out with his hind legs.

With a startled *mew*, Bugeater was launched off the longship. Kills-the-Sky didn't hear the splash, but he knew Bugeater was lost. Kills-the-Sky couldn't stop the ship without the servants, and they had no means to rescue Bugeater even if they did. Another cat lost because of him. *No. Because of Loki.*

Another score to settle.

Fortunately, Bugeater's sacrifice wasn't in vain. The ambush and response had slowed Loki. Kills-the-Sky closed. The rest of the cats joined the chase, harrying and slowing the trickster, wordlessly following Kills-the-Sky's lead.

When he thought they had Loki cornered, the trickster laughed—a very human sound from his cat's mouth—and sprouted broad brown wings the colour of dried blood, taking to the sky.

Kills-the-Sky bounded to the mast, ran up it, and sprang backward into the air, colliding with the bird. He sank his teeth into the nape of the trickster's neck and rode him to the ground. The blood tasted thin, not rich, as he'd expected. Cool, like a body left out in winter, but not yet frozen. Fishy and foul, and yet clear and crisp all at once. Loki thrashed and shifted from shape to shape, but Kills-the-Sky kept his teeth deep in flesh, and his claws deeper. The trickster's attempt to save himself was going to hurt.

"Let me go," Loki wailed.

Kills-the-Sky wanted to retort but kept his teeth stuck in the trickster's neck. Instead he raked the trickster's flanks with his hind legs.

"I see it in you," Loki said through gritted teeth. "You're like your grandsire. You can travel to Asgard. Suckle at the teat of Heiðrún. Leave me go, and I'll show you the way."

Kills-the-Sky cared not for mead, or goats, or goats with mead for milk. He *did* care for the Lie-Father's insistence that his grandsire's stories had been true.

"Leave your cats behind. Save yourself."

The trickster's words had a strange sibilance to them, a call from port on a foggy night, offering a path home. A path Kills-the-Sky wanted to take, but couldn't. Port wasn't home. The *ship* was home. And Loki was a fucking liar. Any salvation Loki sought would always be his own.

"I think you'll die with us," Kills-the-Sky said.

The rest of the ship's cats surrounded them. Eyes glittering like gemstones, tongues dancing over whiskered muzzles. They hissed and yowled, scratching the trickster, nipping gobbets of flesh, feasting.

Clouds swallowed the last spear of sun that'd freed Kills-the-Sky from the mara's clutches. Rain peppered the deck, a harbinger of the storm to come. His breath misted like they'd sailed straight into winter, and rime crusted his fur.

The mara.

"Such delicious fears you have. Almost as savoury as Loki's," the nightmare said. She licked her cracked lips. "You *know* doom. And you seek to dodge it. One of you may today, but not forever."

Loki shuddered, looking at the mara. *So that's who she'd been looking for*. The ship cats saw her for certain now, and backed away.

"Trade my fears for yours," Loki pleaded to Kills-the-Sky. "My fate for yours. You'll want no part of what she's planned for me. And at least the storm won't kill you."

"I'll still be dead."

"It's a chance. A chance is better than nothing."

Kills-the-Sky thought on Loki's words. And the mara's. *One may dodge fate. A chance*. Loki was right. Kills-the-Sky didn't want to admit it, especially since he'd placed the cats in this forked stick to begin with when he'd gotten caught in his own trap.

Kills-the-Sky released Loki's neck and repeated, "We will take his place. My fears for his."

"You intrigue me," the mara said.

Kills-the-Sky patted his bleeding flank where Loki had scratched him, and laid a bloody paw on the deck at the mara's feet. "He came for my blood. It's yours. *If you can take it*."

Loki stood smirking, victorious.

"One day, trickster, you *will* see your doom," the mara said, voice a growl. "I *will* bring your nightmares to truth."

The trickster, human now, with a crooked grin and icy eyes, flashed two fingers, the middle on each hand. The gesture meant nothing to Kills-the-Sky. Nothing other than: Loki had won. Kills-the-Sky's cats were beaten. *He* was beaten. Loki changed his shape again, diving off the boat, taking the form of a salmon. "Good luck getting into Valhalla."

"We'll find you from Freyja's hall, from Asgard, or from Hel, and you'll never sleep true again."

The mara nodded along with Kills-the-Sky's words. "Hel will have you home one day, trickster."

Loki's fishy grin grew wider. "But not today."

The hag disappeared, and breaking from the storm, another ship, a husk with broken masts and tattered sails, appeared; outrunning the wind, moving faster than any oars could propel it. Kills-the-Sky's nose wrinkled. The oncoming ship stank of Hel. The wind carried it, corruption. Decay. *Wrong*. Kills-the-Sky heard the rustle of serpents writhing and the skitter of rat feet over wooden planks. It was teeming with rats. His ears twitched. The wind carried squeaking and the sounds of a seething river of vermin.

"Naglfar?" Kills-the-Sky whispered. He'd heard the name fearfully mentioned whenever the servants had been stuck in fog. The nail-ship. The end-ship. The last voyage for man or giant who had fallen into Hel's clutches. Had Ragnarök come? Had they missed the End of All Hunts while they drifted at sea?

"Nothing so grand." The mara's whispered words tickled Kills-the-Sky's ears. He looked for her but could not see her. "Now there's no one left but you. The price for trusting Loki."

Kills-the-Sky refused to accept the trickster's victory. The rain fell in earnest. The cats understood their peril now, mewling at the sky in protest, as if to change the weather with the sheer force of their displeasure.

His low rumbling roar carried over the water like thunder. "If this will be our end, it will be such an end. One the Great Servants cannot dispute!"

The cats formed a wedge with Kills-the-Sky at its tip, a feline spear aimed at the rats. They took the high ground of the rower's benches and waited for the press to come to them. The Hel-ship was woven serpents still snapping where their heads protruded from the weave. Kills-the-Sky tried to push the boat away, but the serpents had sunk their fangs fast into the wood of the longship, creating a bridge for the rats.

The whole vessel rattled in warning and although Kills-the-Sky had never seen snakes with the pattern of these scales, he knew—somehow he knew—their bite meant death. Those fangs weren't the only ones promising death. A rat army, gaunt fur-shrouded skeletons, surged onto the longship as the ships collided. The river of rats flowed below them, covering the bodies of the servants and devouring them. Bloated bellies distended, they turned from the skeletons to the cats.

For all they looked like starved and desiccated corpses, they had to be alive because they still hungered. Their eyes burned with it.

There'd be no easy victory. It was cat against rat to the end and the odds were against them. Kills-the-Sky swatted a swath of vermin to the side and off the ship. They squeaked as they sailed, their cries growing louder after they splashed. Kills-the-Sky couldn't gut them fast enough, and gaunt as they were, the tide of rats were still near as big as each of his fellow cats. They'd never kill them all. Each rat was but a drop in a sea.

But they kept killing anyway.

He lost himself in the killing. In the work. The job. It was his purpose. His reason for being. He killed until not even the entire ocean could wash the blood from his fur.

He'd been outnumbered before, but never so greatly.

Seen storms, but never like this one.

At least the pounding rain and waves slapping against the hull drowned out the dying cries of his companions.

A rolling wave washed the deck clean of rats, but there were more on the Hel-ship. Always more on the Hel-ship. An entire Hel's worth, and the serpent gangplanks still clutched the longship giving them a bridge to launch another wave. Only two other cats lived. Wintermute and Blacklock.

Maybe he could spare them the worst.

Kills-the-Sky launched himself across the gap between the vessels, breaking the gathering rats, and slashed at the serpents clutching his ship. Some, severed, were lost to the sea. Others detached, snapping at him, striking flanks, and back, and throat. A few, quivering under the weight of the longship, held fast. Rats scurried over their serpent bodies, still trying to swamp the cats under their numbers.

Kills-the-Sky ignored the sharp needle pains of the serpents' fangs and the burning fire they spat into his body as he slashed at the final moorings holding the ships together. His limbs felt heavy as stones.

Maybe it was the wind, but it seemed the Hel-ship screamed as a wave pushed the two vessels apart, sending the longship adrift again. There was a sound, like thunder, and the Hel-ship rolled over, dumping Kills-the-Sky into the ocean. The shock of the cold water was almost enough to drive the poison-induced lethargy from his body. Almost.

As water entered his lungs, a golden hand reached down and grabbed his scruff to pull him up. He stared into a smiling face. Freyja's face. Blacklock, Bugeater, Treespeaker, and Sunchaser—all of the ship's cats—at her side. The rats floated atop the water until a wave slapped them under, and they didn't surface. Kills-the-Sky smiled a hunter's smile.

They had done it.

He had done it.

Wintermute and Blacklock boarded Freyja's chariot after him. Towing the Great Servant's chariot in a shimmering harness, Kills-the-Sky saw his grandsire, leading the way to take them home above the clouds and into the sun. And when they got to the halls of the Great Servants, after Freyja doted on them for a time, Kills-the-Sky would find Loki. He would tree the trickster and bring him to ground. But for now, the sun felt good on his face, and a scratch under his chin, and Kills-the-Sky purred himself to sleep.

Cat at the Helm

Rose Strickman

"That hedge witch!"

Malcolm started back from his breakfast food dish as James threw down the latest issue of *Wizards Quarterly* with an angry snap. He glowered at the open page. "That two-bit hedge witch!"

"What's Therese done now?" James's wife, Lillian, wandered into the dining room, sipping a mug of coffee. Malcolm sauntered over to rub against her ankles, and she bent down to give him a scratch.

"Been cited as one of the top ten thaumaturgists of the year!" James ran his hands over his face and through his hair. "For her work in MagioGames. I ask you, since when did prostituting the arcane arts to the unwashed masses count as thaumaturgic greatness?"

"Oh, you and your endless feud!" Lillian came over to wind an arm around his neck. "Good thing Enrique's off with his family for Thanksgiving, and not here to see you make a fool of yourself over your silly old quarrel." Enrique was James's apprentice in the thaumaturgical arts. He could be a mixed blessing.

"It's not silly and it's not old." Malcolm leaped lightly into James's lap, and his wizard petted him absently. "Therese McGayvern is a charlatan and she's lauded and feted and—"

"Stop being such a baby." Lillian swatted at him good-naturedly. "You've been mad at her ever since you had that public fight at the Wizards of America Holiday buffet." She let out a whistle. "That *was* something spectacular."

"I suppose it was." James smiled shamefacedly. "Well, she hasn't enacted her vow of revenge yet, so I guess that's one mark in her favour." He closed the journal and shoved it away. "I'll stop ranting about it, I promise. For now."

"Good, because I've got a list of things we need to buy for Thanksgiving . . ."

Malcolm jumped down. His humans sounded like they'd be at it for a while, and the autumn day beyond the window was bright and crisp, enticing him beyond the house. He slipped out through the cat door, into the greater wilderness of the suburban neighbourhood.

When he returned, a large package sat on the doormat.

Malcolm crouched down and sniffed at it cautiously. It smelled like any other package—cardboard and tape and packing material—but there was something else, something that raised the fur on his back—

The door opened, and Malcolm leaped back, hissing. "Malcolm!" said James. "What's the matter—" He stopped, looking down at the rectangular package. "Hello, what's this?" He bent down and picked it up to take inside. Nerves still jangling, Malcolm followed.

Lillian had shrugged on her coat and was dealing with her purse. "Come on, James, let's get to the store."

"Just a sec." James set the box on the table. "We got a package."

"Really?" Lillian came closer, peering. "From who?"

"It doesn't say." James made a slicing gesture with one finger, and the tape magically split, the box flaps springing open. "But I . . ." He trailed off, mouth going slack, as he stared into the box with suddenly vacant eyes. Beside him, Lillian went still.

Crouched at their feet, Malcolm let out a low growl as he smelled the sudden, overwhelming waft of magic coming from that box, high above his head. He mewled, scrabbling at James's leg, but his wizard paid no attention. Instead, moving with eerie slowness, he and Lillian both reached into the box and removed what looked like long veils made of net.

"Look," said James in a flat, toneless voice, "there's the manual."

"Yes," agreed Lillian, just as flat and toneless. "*Pirate Adventure*. Should be good."

"Let's get started." Moving like zombies, the couple headed off to the living room, carrying the veils and the little booklet.

Malcolm yowled, clawing at James's jeans, lashing at his feet, but nothing he did made a difference. James sat down on the sofa and opened the manual. "'Place the veil on your head, fully covering your face,'" he read aloud. "'And say the magic words, "Let the adventure begin!" This will initiate your magio-reality adventure on the high seas!'"

"Sounds like fun," said Lillian, still zombified, sinking down onto the sofa beside her husband. She hadn't removed her coat or purse. "Let's do it."

Malcolm let out his loudest yowl, scrambling back James's pant leg and sinking his teeth into his wizard's unprotected flesh. For the first time ever, this brought no reaction; Malcolm might as well have been gnawing the sofa leg for all the notice James took. His ankle bleeding, James lifted the veil and placed it over his head.

Immediately, the net adhered to his face, head, and shoulders, a shimmering caul. Strange lights flashed dimly within it. Beside him, Lillian was already similarly shrouded.

"Let the adventure begin!" the bewitched couple said in a ragged chorus.

The lights flashed brighter and more frequently. Lillian and James both twitched once, then went still.

They didn't move again.

MALCOLM DID WHAT he could.

He scratched at his humans' legs until the blood ran. He climbed up to their shoulders and yowled into their veiled ears as loudly as he could. He leaped about the living room, knocking things over with huge crashes. Nothing. Lillian and James sat on the sofa, the enchanted veils flashing, like a pair of corpses.

Malcolm retreated under a chair, ears laid back. He mewed softly with distress and misery. When were they going to wake up? Aside from anything else, Malcolm was getting hungry, but

James and Lillian didn't move to feed themselves, let alone Malcolm, as the afternoon waned and eventually it grew dark.

Miserably, Malcolm stole some bologna from the kitchen and curled up in his cat basket, afraid to go back into the living room, where the bewitched pair sat, heads wrapped like mummies, and the lights flashed and flared.

THREE DAYS LATER, nothing had changed.

Malcolm ranged around the house, hungry and increasingly desperate. His litter box stank and he had eaten all the food he could get at, even foul things like crackers. Luckily, he could still get outside, but he hadn't managed to hunt down more than one small mouse. And even putting hunger aside, it was dreadful seeing his humans like this, two inanimate forms on the sofa, heads wrapped in evil dreams.

Malcolm was prowling the staircase, fur up and ears down, when the front door opened. "Hi!" called Enrique, hauling his wheeled suitcase over the lintel. "I'm back."

Malcolm let out a howl of joy and relief, and ran to greet James's apprentice, back from the Thanksgiving holiday. He rubbed himself against Enrique's legs, purring ecstatically. He'd never been happier to see anyone in his life.

"Hey, Mal," Enrique said, reaching down to scratch his ears. "Glad to see you too, buddy." He straightened, looking around. "Where's James?"

Malcolm mewed sadly and turned to lead Enrique to the living room. Bemused, still hauling his wheeled suitcase, the young man followed, only to reel back, face whitening, as he beheld James and Lillian.

"Good God!" he cried. The suitcase fell from his grip, clattering to the floor.

Malcolm leaped up beside James, mewing plaintively. Enrique bounded forward, yanking the veil off his teacher's head. It came off with a wet-sounding *splurt*, clinging to James's head all the way, only reluctantly letting go.

"Wha . . . ?" James, his face white and wizened, stared in blank bewilderment at the world beyond the veil. "Enrique . . . ?" He tried to move, and slumped sideways. Malcolm leaped after him, climbing onto his shoulder.

Enrique, meanwhile, was having his own problems. The veil,

still glowing with sullen lights, was clinging to his hand and oozing up his arm like a great, malignant mollusc. Yelling, eyes huge, he peeled it off his arm, shaking his hand frantically.

The veil finally snapped off his hand and flew stickily through the air back toward James.

Malcolm noticed none of this, still perched on James's shoulder, purring in anxiety. Gaze fixed on his wizard, he didn't see the veil coming toward him and James. He didn't hear Enrique's shout of warning. Indeed, Malcolm noticed nothing, right until the point when the veil, aiming for James, snapped onto *him* instead.

The veil lit up as it latched onto its newest victim, moulding itself onto Malcolm's entire body. Malcolm let out a yowl, writhing, before the spell sank into his mind and he went still, flopping off the sofa onto the floor, a small, helpless package.

"SHIP SIGHTED, STARBOARD side!"

All over the *Sea Witch*, crew members raced to their battle stations. The first mate turned to his captain and saluted smartly.

"Orders, Captain Malcolm?"

"Meeerr . . . ?" Malcolm looked around in bemusement. He wasn't used to any human but James, Lillian, and Enrique paying him the least attention—but now a whole gang of them was staring at him, awaiting his command.

Something else was odd, too. Malcolm looked down at his little blue jacket with red lining, bright with brass buttons, from whose sleeves his front paws peeked. A black tricorn hat balanced on his head and a miniature rapier hung at his side. Part of him wanted to scratch the awful bindings off, but the rest of him knew this was perfectly normal. This was what he always wore—he was Captain Malcolm of the *Sea Witch*. And they had a ship to plunder.

Malcolm twitched his tail imperiously. "Meow!"

"Right away, Captain sir!" His first mate saluted again, and began relaying Malcolm's orders. Malcolm, meanwhile, curled back and washed himself as best he could around the coat.

Leaping lightly upward, he prowled along the railing, easily keeping his balance on the swaying ship. The sun sparkled on the shining sea, and the waves skipped and splashed eagerly.

There it was: the *Demon Queen,* the great black ship of his only rival and deadly enemy, Captain Lillian, the Pirate Queen. He'd been hunting her for years, and now her ship canted to starboard, her hated sigil flying high. Malcolm purred with pleasure. At last. He was going to capture the *Demon Queen* and run his rapier through Lillian's heart.

Wait.

Malcolm sat down, curling his tail around his paws in confusion. Why would he want to kill Lillian? She'd always been nice to him. He remembered her feeding him, and long winter afternoons cuddled on her lap . . . He flicked an ear impatiently. What was he thinking? He wasn't some housecat! He was captain of the *Sea Witch*, the Pirate King, about to destroy his only rival!

His *Sea Witch* pursued the *Demon Queen* across the main, drawing ever closer. Malcolm could see the tiny figures of its crew now, swarming all over the deck and rigging. Cannon mouths appeared in its portholes, and shots rang out. Sea water fountained where the balls failed to hit their mark. Malcolm snarled, and the *Sea Witch* ran out her own cannon. Malcolm's men shouted in triumph as ragged holes appeared in the *Demon Queen*'s side.

But Malcolm's own ship was suffering damage too. He spat out orders, and his men raced to pump out the bilges. They drew ever closer. Malcolm could hear the creak of the *Queen*'s rigging now, the flap of her sails. He mewed a command, and some of his men ran to grab the grappling hooks while others readied their swords and pistols.

The *Demon Queen* hurried away, sails turning, and Malcolm issued the order quickly, before she could slip off. The men whirled their hooks above their heads before letting go. Some of the hooks failed to catch hold of the other ship and splashed into the water, but most of them caught. Even as the *Queen*'s crew raced to try and throw off their imprisoning hooks, Malcolm's men began reeling them in.

On the poop deck of the rival ship, haloed by the sun, Malcolm could see the hated figure of Captain Lillian. He growled and his fur stood up as she unsheathed her sword, bellowing a command to her men. The *Demon Queen*'s crew rushed to pull out their own swords and cutlasses, snarling and jeering, ready to defend their ship.

The *Demon Queen* was now so close that the two ships were almost rubbing each other, and Malcolm's men began leaping onto the *Queen* or swinging from ropes, to land with swords drawn. Cries of pain, rage, and bloodlust rang out as the battle commenced.

Unable to contain himself, Malcolm scampered out along one of the grappling lines and onto the *Queen*. His small size allowed him to duck the swords of Lillian's men, to slip under their clumsy feet, and leap over their kicks. His gaze was fixed on Lillian, who flashed her sword.

"Come on, James, bring it!" she shouted.

James?

Halfway up the ladder to the poop deck, Malcolm faltered. What had she called him? He and Lillian had been rivals for years, fighting for supremacy of the ocean—why would she call him by the wrong name? Lillian stepped back too, blinking in her own sudden confusion, and another burst of memory came: rubbing himself against Lillian while she worked at her desk, running to greet her when she came in through the front door—

A bullet whizzed over Malcolm's head, and the memories disappeared. *This* was real: the battle, and his enemy before him. Growling, he advanced.

Lillian snarled and swung her sword. Malcolm swung his, and the weapons met with a great silver ring, at a ridiculously steep angle given their differences in height.

Malcolm looked at his paw, holding his rapier. There was something very—wrong—about this. The unnaturalness of his holding a weapon in his paw—of holding *anything*—howled through his mind. He let out a cry, leaping back—but though he used all four legs, he still absolutely *held* the sword in his front paw—and this was wrong—wrong—

"I'll have your head, you dog!" shouted Lillian, swinging her own sword.

"Meow!" Malcolm forgot his predicament in his sudden indignation. Dog? He was clearly a cat!

Perhaps Lillian realized this, for she suddenly faltered, blinking. They stood and looked at one another, veiled by the smoke of the battle, isolated amidst its tumult and cries and spills of blood. "You—you're not James," said Lillian. "You're—

you're—"

"Mew?" said Malcolm.

"Malcolm!" cried Lillian in realization.

"Mewl!" Malcolm cried in joy, and, to his utter relief, found he could no longer hold onto the rapier. He leaped forward, hat falling off his head, to twine around Lillian's ankles, purring.

"Malcolm." She bent over and picked him up, cradling him against her tan greatcoat. He rubbed his face against hers, breathing in her warm, familiar scent. Though a part of him still screamed that he was a pirate captain and here was his deadly enemy, that part was growing fainter and farther away, the longer he cuddled near Lillian.

"Malcolm," whispered Lillian, "I think we're under a spell. Can you lead us out?"

Malcolm writhed and bit at his awful coat. Lillian hastily pulled it off him. "Can you, boy?"

Malcolm, happily freed of his pirate clothes, ruffled his fur proudly and impatiently. Naturally he could do *that*. He was a wizard's familiar, wasn't he?

But then Lillian stiffened, and Malcolm realized that an unnatural silence had fallen. The pirate crews—atoms of the spell—had all ceased fighting. As one being, they turned to stare at Malcolm and Lillian, faces blank masks of malevolence.

Lillian stepped back. The pirates all stepped forward.

"You must fight," said a spell-creature. "You must fight and you must kill each other."

"You must fight." The spell-creatures stumbled up the ladder. "You must kill."

"Malcolm," whispered Lillian, backing up, eyes darting. "Now would be a good time to find that way out, Malcolm."

Malcolm sniffed. He could smell—yes, there was the gap in the spell. He leaped out of Lillian's arms, up onto the prow, and Lillian, still watching the approaching pirates warily, clambered awkwardly after him.

The ship's figurehead nodded over the ocean. It was shaped like a female demon, tentacles writhing, a crown on her head. And yes—there was the point where the spell came together—the seam—where a small cat and perhaps a desperate woman could slip out.

"Fight," chorused their pursuers. "Kill." They were crowded

onto the poop deck now, a mass of murderous intent. Lillian let out a moan of fear and dropped down after Malcolm, onto the figurehead.

But too late. One of the pirates lunged after her, grabbing her hair and shoulders with nails like claws. She shrieked, trying to beat the spell-creature back, but more were swarming around her, dragging her back, and now one was after Malcolm. It fell onto the figurehead beside him with a wet-sounding *splat* of gooey flesh. It reached for him—

Malcolm spat and lashed out, but his claws merely dug into the pirate's rubbery flesh. They spilled no blood and made no impression on the spell-creature. It grabbed hold of Malcolm and lifted him up, ignoring his wails and screams—

And then the light came.

A vast, blinding light filled the sky, like sunrise, only a thousand times brighter. The pirates all stiffened, going wooden and doll-like, as the light invaded, burning up the sky and the ocean, dissolving the ship. First the sails, then the rigging, then the body of the ship itself, all gone, all evaporated, and Malcolm and Lillian spun away, whirling into the light . . .

MALCOLM OPENED HIS eyes. He was lying in Enrique's arms, utterly spent. He felt tender all over, even his fur and whiskers hurt, but the veil was gone and he was back in his own house. He let out a soft mew.

James bent over Lillian, who was lying on the sofa. "Lillian?" His expression was stark with anxiety as he peered into his wife's face.

She moaned, stirring. Her eyes slowly fluttered open. "James?"

"Lillian!" He embraced her, shuddering with relief.

"James . . . ?" Lillian's voice was slow and thick. "What . . . ?"

"We got the veil off you—and Malcolm too." Enrique, still holding Malcolm, nodded at the wall, where the two veils hung shrivelled, an iron nail driven through both of them. Malcolm stiffened and spat at them. "It wasn't easy—they kept escaping and getting back onto you."

"I . . ." Lillian lay back, horrified realization flooding her eyes. "Oh, God, James, I . . . I think we were meant to kill each other in there."

James, still weak, slumped down on the floor beside the sofa. "That *bitch*," he whispered. "I'm going to *kill* her!"

"No, you won't." Lillian tried to sit up but failed, slumping down on the cushions. "*I* will!"

"Wait a second." Enrique looked down at Malcolm thoughtfully. "I've got a better idea."

JAMES LAID DOWN his copy of the Wizards of America monthly newsletter with a happy sigh. "Terrible," he said contentedly. "Just terrible."

"What is?" Lillian came by, carrying her morning coffee. Christmas was coming, and outside the house, a cold rain lashed. Within, however, all was bright and cosy.

"Therese McGayvern." James's face was utterly seraphic. "She's gone mad."

"*Has* she?" Lillian cracked a wicked smile. "How unfortunate."

Enrique clomped in. "What's happened?" Malcolm rubbed against his legs, and he bent down to give him a pet. Malcolm purred.

"It's all here." James spun around the newsletter for his apprentice. "Very sad. Therese McGayvern was rather fond of playing with her own products, it seems. She slipped on one of her own veils—the pirate adventure one—and then . . ." He gave a long, sorrowful sigh. "Something wrong with the spell, it would seem. She thinks she's still in the pirate adventure, even after they took the veil off her."

"And not only that," said Lillian, eyes sparkling, "but, apparently, she also thinks she's a cat."

"You don't say," drawled Enrique. Malcolm uncoiled from the boy and leaped up onto the dining table.

"Indeed." James gave Malcolm a pet. "They've got her at the New York thaumaturgic hospital. Apparently she's trying to wave an imaginary sword *and* mewing. Such a sad fate, for such a brilliant mind. What a tragedy."

"A tragedy," agreed Lillian. The three wizards all grinned at one another, and turned to beam lovingly at Malcolm.

Malcolm sat down and licked the place on his side where they'd shaved his fur to line the insides of one of the veils they'd sent back to Therese McGayvern. He still hadn't entirely forgiven them for that indignity, even if they had fed him chicken for a week afterward.

Still, Malcolm thought as, one by one, they all gave him an affectionate scratch, thus was life for a wizard's familiar. He purred and rolled over, exposing his stomach. It sounded like his humans were appropriately grateful, for once—and now Christmas was coming. This surely meant cooked meat, and all the lovely enticements of the Christmas tree . . . Malcolm's purr increased in volume.

The alternate pirate adventure reality had been an interesting place to visit. But he definitely didn't want to live there.

A Royal Saber's Work Is Never Done

BETH CATO

I HAD PICKED many a lock in my youth, but never upon a heaving ship. I gripped the coarse iron bars with one paw while I twiddled a sharpened claw from the other within the mechanism. My contortion was sure to pain my shoulder something fierce tomorrow, if I hadn't been born into a new life by then.

The wooden hull's groans masked the sound of my cell door clicking open and shutting. In the darkness, my fellow female prisoners—my village neighbours, my friends—appeared to either be asleep or consumed with abject misery as I crept by. I imagined the toms were in much the same state in their cells nearby.

Rage shook me. Mamaya had long been Belgray's enemy across the sea, but nothing Belgray had done could justify this action against innocent civilians: sailing in from the fog, kidnapping our village entire, and hauling us across the Blue. Our king was an offensive individual, truly, but I knew of no direct act of war. His mother, now—Queen Tabitha had goaded Mamaya many a time, but always with intelligence and force to back her words.

I liked to think that I had contributed in both respects.

"Elin." My name was a hoarse whisper. Layla's eyes gleamed

at me from her cell nearest the door. "What do you plan?"

Adventuro bless her; she hadn't assumed that I intended to sneak out and abandon the lot of them. "I dare not release everyone. We're out-armed and trapped."

She nodded. My respect for her grew. Layla was scarcely more than a kit, but already maintained the rocarac rookery nearest the village. Few cats had the kindness and patience to train the mighty passenger birds, much less to tolerate the stench of their nests.

"Are you going to try to get away, then?" No accusation bent her tone.

"Perhaps. Or procure arms. We must be ready for anything."

"I'll let the others know."

Her faith both comforted and frustrated me. I hated the idea of abandoning them, though I knew it was likely the most prudent course. If—if—I could reach Belgray's shores, King Hayden could send aid. His air-filled brain would surely recall his visit to our village last year. Perhaps that'd make him more inclined to help our cause.

Or he might recognize me and promptly execute me before dolling up for another one of his ludicrous midnight balls.

That thought accompanied a mighty heave of the ship. I dryly swallowed. I'd never taken on sea duty as part of being Royal Saber, in part because of my tendency toward sea sickness. The emptiness in my gut—and sheer obstinance—must help me endure now.

I listened at the door, my stubby tail drawn close to my body. Snores wheezed on the far side, the sound sharp against the creaking of wood. I opened the door to find a sailor dozing in his chair. I sneaked by on shoeless paws.

I checked on other rooms along the passageway but found nothing of use. Two sailors approached, causing me to hide for a minute. I then edged upstairs.

Here I found the crew berthing, abundant with snores and mutters, fragrant with piss-pots and worse. I also found clothes. These sailors tended toward young, so none should recognize my face from my Royal Saber days. I slipped the trousers and overcoat over my careworn nightclothes. The enlisted sailor's belt with dagger felt especially satisfying on my hip. A cap completed my look.

Now, I looked like any other sailor but for my continued lack of sea legs.

I took the stairs to the deck. Dawn hesitated at the sky's edge. Movement drew my eye past a multitude of sailors and to the majestic black rocarac perched at the forecastle. Not only did a saddle still attire the massive prey bird's back, but a small passenger carriage rested just behind it. I was awed. Rare was the rocarac trained to ferry passengers to galleons; the many sails above me were vulnerable to the average bird, and certainly to one the size of a village granary!

I recognized the red coat of an admiral—that explained the finery of the rocarac and carriage—and I stared a moment before realizing why he looked vaguely familiar.

Adventuro help me. It was Durant.

I acted casual as I turned away, retreating into deep early morning shadows to recover my wits. Durant would know my face, my very scent. And here he was, an admiral now! Well, Queen Tabitha had sent him undercover as a Mamayan spy some fifteen years ago. He'd had time to work upward in rank.

Two officers chatted not ten feet away. "And if we find no white hairs? What becomes of the prisoners then?" His ears flickered flat against his head. "Still strikes me as pointless, grabbing even the oldest mollies and toms—"

"Do you want to attend to a mob of wee kits?" the other officer retorted. "The older ones will take care of the younger, until we don't need them anymore."

The realization of their intent knocked the wind from me.

For five-hundred years, each member of the royal family had birthed kits with three white hairs at the tips of their tails. This was seen as a blessing by Adventuro himself, the first of his line, deified due to the greatness of his rule.

King Hayden's tour had brought him to our village for several nights. How he'd spent them, I could well guess, but I'd kept my distance to avoid recognition by him and his party. Royal Sabers didn't retire, after all. They died in service to their monarch.

Hayden hosted three white hairs in his tail, yes, but he was no king in my eyes, and not worth my life.

Many of my old skills had gotten rusty, but I always kept an ear tilted toward gossip. There'd been no mutters of a royal kit.

King Hayden had refused marriage as of yet, and the lack of an heir vexed court and commoner alike. If an illegitimate kit had existed in the village, that news would've been yowled from the rooftops.

I needed weapons. Many. When the sailors tried to grab our kits, they'd pay for their effort in blood.

Our kits. This was my village, my home, a place that'd accepted me grudgingly at first, then in full. My cottage offered shelter to any in a storm, a tea kettle always ready to whistle, a medicine kit packed for needs ranging from veterinary to midwifery—and I could expect the same from any of my neighbours in turn.

My paws pattered down the stairs, my head down. Three sailors approached, our bodies angled to squeeze me in the narrow space.

The ship listed.

The sailors readily compensated for the tilt. I did not, my shoulder meeting the wall between the last two cats. The last sailor's gap-toothed mouth parted in surprise.

"No sea legs? What 'ere!" he cried.

The time to playact was done. I unsheathed my knife as I spun around. My elbow crunched into the nose of the yowler as my blade came around to meet the steel of the second sailor. His quick attack reaffirmed the excellent training of Mamaya's forces. The ship's next lurch bowled me into him, a move I wish I could credit to my Royal Saber training, not landlubber clumsiness. He toppled and flattened the sailor behind him.

All three cats screamed alarm as I bounded over the downed sailors and to the open deck. Cats rushed my way. I'd lost my cap, baring to them my strange tabby face. More cries of alarm rang out all around. I ran for port side. A white-furred molly swiped her knife, an attack that would've cost me the end of my tail, were it not already gone. I countered with a kick that jolted through my arthritic hip.

A gun cocked behind me, its range close enough for deadly accuracy. I turned to face Admiral Durant. He looked as much the gentlecat as ever. The tricorn hat suited him, but even after all these years it panged me to see him in Mamaya's colours.

I'd begged the queen to not task him with such a role. "You don't know how long he'll need to stay undercover in Mamaya!"

"He'll stay as long as needed."

And so he had. These days, I was unsure if King Hayden's new Sabers even knew Durant had once been ours under a different name, during a different life.

"Well, well." He lowered the pistol as the crew mobbed me. I barely checked a cry as they forced my forepaws to the small of my back, my knife wrenched from my grip. At least death would spare me the pains I'd otherwise awaken with tomorrow. He waved back the other cats as he grabbed the ropes that bound my wrists. He bent close, his mouth a snarl. "I wondered where'd you'd gotten to." Despite his fierce expression, the words embodied tenderness.

"Did you now?" I kept my tone airy, even as nausea struck me anew. Sailors were dashing to the hold, undoubtedly to rouse the villagers. Other Mamayans loaded their guns in readiness of the coming confrontation.

His whiskers kissed my cheek. I shivered. "I'm glad you escaped that royal buffoon, Belinda. Mamaya has killed a score of Belgray's Sabers in recent months. King Hayden treats them like storybook characters adventuring to suit his whims."

The sound of my born name—so long unused—rang like five seconds of a brilliant symphony. "I found a genuine home, Gregory." To his credit, he didn't even flinch as I spoke his former name. "A quiet, tight-knit village. I make cheese. The fishing is excellent, by shore and boat." I knew that would appeal to him.

Yearning flickered in his eyes. Our Queen had once said I was his one weakness as a Saber; she was still right.

"Don't act too nice to me, Gregory," I murmured, even as his closeness made me ache to purr. I couldn't act nice, either. We were enemies. Captor and captive.

"I won't. I can't." His expression hardened, black whiskers flared. "Is there a royal kit?"

"My answer means nothing. You'll check the wee ones' tails nevertheless." My heart caught in my throat as my neighbours began to stagger to the deck, their forepaws bound by a jingling line of chain.

"Would it be so terrible if Mamaya had custody of Belgray's heir?"

Twenty years ago, my "Yes!" would've emerged in a roar.

Now—Adventuro help us all—I didn't want to answer at all. I was old enough to know Mamaya wasn't an evil entity, wise enough to know that the hairs on a tail said nothing about a cat's divine worthiness to rule.

"Our audience has gathered," I murmured, my ears flattened against my skull. "You must act the admiral." We both knew that may well mean my death.

Durant stepped back, motioning a lackey to grip the rope at my wrists. "Take her to the others," he snarled, dismissing me with a wave. The sailor shoved me repeatedly. His final push knocked me into the middle of the villagers. They braced me upright as I glared hate at the admiral and his dreck.

Durant struck a fine pose. "Morning greetings to you. I am Admiral Durant. I will be forthright. You are here because rumours tell of a royal kit in your midst."

Beneath the dawn's pink blush, the villagers' fear promptly shifted to indignant rage.

"And you believe those fools?" shouted Cagney, the butcher. His thick grey body strained against the chain.

"What're you going to do to our kits?" cried Saria, her two shut-eyed wee ones clutched to her shoulders despite her heavy manacles.

"We haven't even heard mutters o' such a tale!" Renaldo the shepherd sounded almost angry to be denied such alluring gossip. Old toms like him jabbered worse than any molly in town.

"You all right, then?" Layla whispered to me. Her yearning gaze fixed on the rocarac lounging near the prow.

I was more right than I expected to be, considering our plight. By Durant's order, ropes restrained me rather than chain, and he'd sent me to rejoin my friends. Either he'd set me up for a mighty fall, or he'd provided me—and my village—means of escape. Layla's skill was another asset. Not even Durant would expect a peasant here skilled with rocaracs.

"Cast your shadow over my hands," I muttered to her. She obliged, casual as could be. This molly was made of Royal Saber stuff, no doubt.

I shifted the angle of my paws. My right pointer claw found the rope and began to saw.

"Step forward, if you hold a kit below a year in age," Durant continued. My companions bellowed more protests and questions; none stepped forward. The sailors shifted, ready to attack. The villager's jailer stood conveniently close, a key circlet upon his belt. I took note of the nearest weapons. I was happy to see they'd been outfitted with Mamaya's latest line of automatic pistols, capable of three shots in sequence.

"My kits have all-white tails! We needn't even be here!" cried Saria.

Durant's gaze was cold. "You know the stories, likely better than I. The three royal hairs, even against white fur, are distinct. Adventuro's blood makes itself known."

It did indeed. The tip of my mostly-white tail had been amputated when I was too young to remember.

I sawed through the rope fast as I could while keeping my body still.

"We're halfway across the Blue! What'll happen to us after you confirm the cockamamie nature of this whole scheme?" growled Renaldo.

Durant motioned to the ship captain and his sailors. "Get the kits."

Pandemonium roared. The ropes fell from my wrists. I lunged for the jailer. I unholstered his pistol with one paw while grabbing the key with the other. I levelled the gun on Durant as he faced me. His expression of steel, he granted me the tiniest of nods. Nearby sailors dove for cover.

I fired. Durant dropped, his left leg shot from beneath him. I fired twice more in quick succession, one striking another sailor true, the other penetrating a mast. I tossed the empty gun aside.

The jailer, slow to react, turned to afford me an excellent angle at which to unsheathe his cutlass. I cut him down before so much as a yowl emerged.

I tossed the key to Layla. "Get those kits and their families off this ship," I snapped as she reached for the lock. "You'll probably need to fly all day to reach the—"

I dove for cover. Bullets followed me, splinters gouging my hind paws. I bit back an agonized yowl as I rolled behind barrels to come face to face with two Mamayan sailors. Seconds later, they were down, my breaths ragged.

The villagers roared as they joined the fray. More bullets pinged and voices cried. From the crow's nest came a booming voice, "—a ship! Belgray!"

I fended off several more sailors before I dared look toward sea. Adventuro be praised! Belgray pursued us!

I motioned to my comrades. "We must form a protective line at the rocarac." Even though the bird would provide our means of escape, I knew the sailors would be hesitant to risk hitting the near-priceless creature. No point in surviving this melee to end up hanged by their own military.

With a glance toward the still-prone form of Durant, I provided cover as the villagers scrambled across the deck. A minute later, I dashed to Layla.

"What do you want me to do?" She glanced at me amid her checks on the bird's harness. Terror and determination lit her eyes, even as her whiskers trembled.

"Ferry our cats to the ship. As you approach, direct the bird to dip its right wing three times in sequence. That'll signal an emergency request to land. A white flag with a blue circle on it will give you permission to do so." I would not discuss the alternatives.

The white fur of Layla's throat bobbed as she dryly swallowed. I turned to the villagers who hunkered nearby.

"We will evacuate in orderly fashion." I met their eyes. "About ten adults can squeeze into the carriage. That means all of our kits board first, with at least one close family member in attendance." Hurried decisions were made before me, cheeks licked, weapons exchanged. The first evacuees hurried aboard, kits clutched to chests and dragged by arms. Layla climbed into the saddle atop the beast.

"For Adventuro and Belgray!" I yelled, with a salute to those in the carriage.

"For Adventuro and Belgray!" chorused my motley fighters.

The bird rose with a heavy flap of wings. The carriage clanked and dragged, then all were airborne.

Part of me wanted to watch its progress with hope and dread, but a greater part of me didn't wish to be shot or stabbed in the back. Gunfire from my side peppered the air, but we had essentially reached a stand-off, with Mamayan sailors clustered around the cabin and us at the forecastle. Someone sobbed softly nearby, while another cat keened.

A cannon's report caused me to twist around in fear—had

Belgray fired upon the rocarac?! No—at Mamaya. The cannonball splashed into the surf off our prow. Their next shot would be more accurate.

I grimaced. If the rocarac were allowed to land, the Belgrayan vessel would soon know more villagers were aboard. Perhaps that would cause them to hold off their attack, perhaps not. King Hayden was not judicious in his choice of commanders.

Tension lingered in the quiet as we faced our rivals. In the new stillness, Durant crawled to take shelter behind the main mast. I silently thanked Adventuro.

Minutes of forever passed until heavy wings flapped overhead again. Wind eddied my fear as the bird returned to its perch, the empty carriage scraping the deck as it settled to a stop.

"Our village wasn't the only one kidnapped!" Layla cried out as soon as the noise ended. "Mamaya raided much of the coast. War's been declared!"

No mercy upon our captors, then. I directed villagers to board. This trip focused on the injured, and included two of our dead.

"Belgray be praised!" said an elder, sobbing as he scurried over.

Be praised, indeed. I hadn't been sure if they would let the rocarac land, or hold off fire while we evacuated. How sad that their assistance came as a genuine surprise to me. I'd come to expect so little under Hayden's rule.

I latched the door of the full carriage and took cover nearby. The carriage filled, the rocarac set off. Eight of us remained.

That meant we had room for one more.

"Our turn next, eh?" said Cagney.

"Yes, and then Belgray will send this ship to the krakens. But first of all, I'll see if we might gain a valuable hostage."

Marvia followed my gaze toward Durant, her seal-point ears flaring down. "Is that worth the risk? A lot of open deck between here and him."

"Eh, an admiral'd be worth a ton of kibble with a war on." Renaldo spat onto the deck. "Try not to die. You've been making fine cheese."

"I intend to make more." My paw brushed my comrades'

backs as I passed behind them, a wordless display of gratitude.

I'd promised to live before, and kept my word. I could only hope to again not be proven a liar.

I'd been raised to believe I was an orphan of lower nobles, but as a castle ward, I'd often been flattered by Her Majesty's attention. The truth of my lineage only emerged just prior to my adulthood ascension ceremony. Not long after, I told Queen Tabitha of my intent to be a Royal Saber.

"You need not die for me," she had fumed. "I wanted you to know a safe life of privilege, not—"

"I promise, I won't die," I said, full of youth and stupidity. "I want to serve Belgray. I want to serve you, have an excuse to be near you often."

I adored her. I always had—but then, so did most everyone in the kingdom. "The most beloved monarch since Adventuro," it was said, and the words resounded as truth, not propaganda.

I think to her surprise as well as mine, she loved me, too.

"Oh, why can't you use your brain more than your heart?" she'd cried.

Despite my advanced years, my heart remained my weakness.

I grabbed a fresh pistol from the deck, loaded it, and weaved my way toward Durant. Many of the Mamayans had retreated below; they'd be readying their cannons and preparing for a nastier battle than what we'd offered.

"I come to parley!" I called out as I approached, loud enough for both sides to hear.

"I suppose I shouldn't return the favour by shooting you, then?" Durant's voice was only for my ears.

I scampered the remaining distance to join him. He sat, legs stretched out. "I was careful to shoot your prosthesis." He'd lost part of his lower hind paw soon after infiltrating Mamaya. They'd outfitted him with an extraordinary prosthesis that flexed to almost give him a natural gait. Thanks to me, however, the end was now a jagged stump of metal and wood, the boot and its faux paw gone.

"I accept your apology, such as it is." He sighed, the motion fluttering his long grey mane. "I argued against this foray, you should know. Belgray isn't the only kingdom with a fool upon the throne. I don't see things going well here once you're evacuated."

"You may be the commanding officer, but you needn't go down with the ship," I said softly. "There's room in the next carriage—"

"No thank you. I know how Belgray treats military prisoners these days. I would prefer to keep what paws I have."

I bowed my head. I knew what he said was true, and yet . . .

"If you ruled," he said in the barest whisper, "so much would be different."

The blood in my veins turned to ice. "You know." I closed my eyes, pained. "Of course you figured it out. You were always the best of us."

"I could argue with you on that point, but I won't. It'd be futile." He sighed. "You and her were alike in many ways."

The queen's plea rang through me again. *"Oh, why can't you use your brain more than your heart?"* Yes, we had been much alike.

My paw clutched his, a touch familiar yet changed with time. "Court's pettiness and intrigues would've killed my soul. I've lost much over the years, but not that."

"Your cheesemaking has restored your soul, then? Made it strong for your next life?"

"Yes," I said simply. My ears swivelled. The rocarac made its return. "Survive. Come home."

"I don't even know what that means anymore." His voice, raw and pained.

"Find out."

"You survive, too," he said. "Not simply today, but whatever comes next." Yes. If my past as a Royal Saber became known . . .

With a final squeeze of paws, I crept away. No one fired at me. The Mamayans reserved their bullets for worse opponents.

Ten minutes later, I sat aboard the carriage, my stomach lurching as we swayed into the air. Below us, cannon fire began in earnest as the ships drew alongside. Layla had been advised to keep aloft for now. Smoke clouded both ships, their sails rippling.

"I have a favour to ask all of you regarding my role today," I said to my cabin-mates.

"You need us to keep our traps shut?" asked Cagney. "Aye."

I blinked at him. "Well, yes."

"I told as much to everyone else as they boarded," added Marvia, "They understand."

"Understood what, exactly?" I asked.

"That you're no mere city cat, come to the coast to enjoy the last years of this life," said Cagney.

"That you're someone King Hayden might want back again," growled Marvia.

"And he's not getting you back!" Renaldo's fur stood on end. "You're ours now."

The immensity of their support felt poignant as a hug. They knew me for a Royal Saber, and they intended to protect me—and here, I was the one trained to protect them!

The sound of exploding wood boomed from far below; boomed through me, body and soul. I glanced out the window. The Mamayan ship had taken a direct hit and began to sink at astonishing speed. Toppled masts and tattered sails almost obscured the view of dark figures dashing about the deck, but I could still make out Durant in his vivid red.

I could look no more. I leaned against the headrest, my age and aches finding my bones in an instant. Tears slipped down my cheeks. No one questioned my tears; they thought they understood.

The true source of my grief—like so much in my life—must stay hidden. I kept it as close to me as my shortened tail.

THE SMELL OF cooking mutton lured me up the path from the cheese cave to my cottage door. The deep grey sky and persistent rain had called for stew since dawn's break, and ah, that scent was bound to torment me all afternoon long.

At my doorstep, I began to shrug off my oil slicker, then paused. A stranger came up the long drive.

I grabbed my rifle from where it leaned a foot away. My vigilance—and that of all the village—had increased in the months since our return, though Mamaya had made no further forays to our shore. Adventuro be blessed, the war had been going well for Belgray—as well as wars can go, anyway. To my shock, King Hayden had been sobered by Mamaya's brazen attack. I didn't know if his newfound dedication to his duties would last, but even the temporary change came as a comfort.

I studied the approaching cat. A heavy limp dragged their

stride. To my puzzlement, they carried both a traveller's pack and a fishing rod.

Even when their eyes met mine from feet away, it took a moment for the truth to sink in.

"You shaved back your fur," I blurted.

Brassy eyes stared at me from beneath a wide-brimmed hat. "Indeed I did." Durant's thick, puffy cheeks and downy mane had been rendered as short as my own fur. Durant—that name could be his no longer.

I nodded as a strange sense of exhilaration flowed through me. "A wise precaution, though when my village was captive, I imagine most never saw past your admiral's coat and cap."

"'There are always cats who remember a face,'" he said, quoting one of our old treatises.

I barely knew his face now, much as I had memorized it during nights in our years past. "How did you survive?"

"Among the flotsam and jetsam. I washed up to the far south, quite ill. My recovery was long. I wish I could've sent some word your way, but . . ."

"No, I understand why you could not. You were in Belgray, all this time." I shook my head in awe. "Your leg—"

"No more fancy prosthesis for me. I'm making do with a peg leg, as a Belgrayan commoner should. I am physically recovered."

We need not speak of the wounds unseen, not now. "How does it feel to be back here?"

"Strange, yet familiar." He considered me as he said the words; my thoughts had already summed him up in the same way.

I motioned to the rod in his hand. "If you can stand to delay your fishing, you could come inside for hot tea with milk." The proper Belgrayan way, not like those heathen Mamayans who drank tea plain. "You're old like me. Our bones need warming time and again."

"Indeed they do. I can wait to fish. This rain doesn't look to let up soon. Besides, it smells like you've already got a fine supper underway."

"The pot holds more than enough to feed two." I set aside my rifle. "I welcome fish for supper tomorrow, and in days to come."

He stepped beneath my thatched roof's overhang to remove his hat. As he shook water beads from his whiskers, I realized again that I didn't know what to call him now—nor did he know what to call me. We had much to catch up on. Years of our lives yet to do it.

"Welcome home," I said, and I opened the door wide for him.

Biographies

Rhonda Parrish
Editor

Like a magpie, **Rhonda Parrish** is constantly distracted by shiny things. She's the editor of many anthologies and author of plenty of books, stories, and poems. She lives with her husband and three cats in Edmonton, Alberta, where she can often be found playing Dungeons and Dragons, bingeing crime dramas, or cheering on the Oilers.

Her website, updated regularly, is at rhondaparrish.com and her Patreon, updated even more regularly, is at patreon.com/RhondaParrish.

Megan Fennell

The Pride

Megan Fennell is a legal assistant by day, and by night (and evening and weekends) writes genre fiction, paints, Taiko drums, and dabbles in local theatre. She is the pun-slinging, whimsy-wielding half of the co-writing power duo V. F. LeSann, which is comprised of herself and Leslie Van Zwol. Her two tabbies were not consulted for this piece, as they prefer guerrilla warfare tactics over nautical combat.

S.G. Wong

The Comeback Kitty

S.G. Wong writes crime and speculative fiction and is known for the Lola Starke novels and Crescent City short stories: hard-boiled detective tales set in an alternate-history 1930s-era "Chinese L.A." replete with ghosts and magic. She is an Arthur Ellis Awards finalist and a Whistler Independent Book Awards nominee. A past volunteer and Board member with varied organizations, Wong currently serves as National Vice President of Sisters in Crime and is based in Edmonton, Alberta where she can often be found staring out the window in between frenzied bouts of typing. sgwong.com

Rebecca Brae

The Motley Crew

Rebecca Brae lives in Alberta, Canada with her husband, daughter, and growing pack of animal companions. She is an artist, lover of diversity, fog enthusiast, and proud geek who aspires to one day live in a cave by the ocean (with wifi, of course). Her background in Criminology and Classical Studies informs her writing in unexpected and occasionally horrifying ways. Rebecca has co-authored two urban fantasy novels with her husband, *Chaos Bound* and *Curse Bound*, and is eagerly awaiting the debut of her fantasy novel, *The Witch's Diary* (2020). Learn more at: www.braevitae.com

Grace Bridges

Whiti te Ra (Let the Sun Shine)

Grace Bridges is a geyser hunter, cat herder, editor and translator, and Kiwi. The current president of writers' organisation SpecFicNZ, she is often found poking around geothermal sites or under a pile of rescued kittens. She is a multiple nominee and two-time winner of the Sir Julius Vogel Award from the Science Fiction and Fantasy Association of New Zealand, an editor and mentor for Young NZ Writers, and has edited dozens of published books. Her own novels include Irish cyberpunk, Classics in Space, and the Earthcore urban fantasy series based in New Zealand. More information and free stories at www.gracebridges.kiwi.

Lizz Donnelly

The Growing of the Green

Lizz Donnelly is a writer, knitter, cat lady, baking enthusiast, and occasional actor. She writes speculative fiction of all lengths, essays, and even the odd short play. Her work has been published recently in *Speculative City, Brave New Girls Volume 4*, and *Grimm, Grit and Gasoline*, among others. She is the founder of The (K)indred Experiment, an extracurricular writing club for middle school students. You can find her on Twitter @LizzDonnelly and on Patreon, where she blogs monthly about books, shares new fiction, and is undertaking a year-long project of reading exclusively female authors in 2020.

Blake Liddell

The Cat and the Cook

Blake Liddell is an Australian writer with a love for the fantastical. She writes fantasy, horror and science fiction, delighting in poetic prose and quirky characters. She lives with her large orange cat, who may be part Bengal, part sabre-tooth tiger.

Frances Pauli

Pirates Only Love Treasure

Frances Pauli writes books about animals, hybrid, aliens, shifters, and occasionally ordinary humans. She tends to cross genre boundaries, but hovers around fantasy and science fiction with romantic tendencies.

Her work has won two Leo awards, a Coyotl award, and her short story, "Two Minutes in Hell", was the third place winner in the Arcanists Monster Flash Fiction contest.

She lives in Washington State with her family, a small menagerie, and far too many houseplants.

JB Riley

Buccaneer's Revenge

JB Riley lives in Chicago and writes technical proposals for a major US-based corporation, but has loved reading and writing speculative fiction ever since discovering *The Chronicles of Narnia* at Age 8. When not trawling the shelves at the local used bookstore, she enjoys travel, hockey, beer, and cooking.

Joseph Halden

The Furgeldt Collector

Joseph Halden is a wizard in search of magic, an astronaut in need of space, and a hopeless enthusiast of frivolity. He's shot things with giant lasers, worn an astronaut costume for over 100 days to try and get into space, and made his own soap. A graduate of the Odyssey Writing Workshop, he writes science fiction and fantasy in the Canadian prairies. Find him at https://josephhalden.com/

Leslie Van Zwol

Cat Out of Hell

Leslie Van Zwol works for justice by day and moonlights as a writer, traveller, and dancer. She likes her fiction like she likes her drinks: dark and peaty, and is most frequently recognized as the brazen-half of the pawsome co-writing duo V. F. LeSann, which is comprised of herself and Megan Fennell. She also declines to disclose the quantity of Claritin consumed to abate her claw-ful allergies during this purr-larious endeavour.

Krista D. Ball

The Perfect Kibble

Krista D. Ball is an Edmonton author of over twenty books, including the popular *What Kings Ate and Wizards Drank.*

Chadwick Ginther

All Cats Go to Valhalla

Chadwick Ginther is the Prix Aurora Award nominated author of *Graveyard Mind* and the *Thunder Road* Trilogy. His short fiction has appeared recently in *Earth: Giants, Golems, & Gargoyles, Over the Rainbow: Folk and Fairy Tales from the Margins*, and *Abyss & Apex.*

Rose Strickman

Cat at the Helm

Rose Strickman is a sci-fi, fantasy, and horror writer living in Seattle, Washington. Her work has appeared in anthologies such as *Sword and Sorceress 32, From a Cat's View*, and *Well Said, O Toothless One*, as well as online zines such as *Aurora Wolf* and *Luna Station Quarterly*. Malcolm has other stories to tell!

Beth Cato

A Royal Saber's Work is Never Done

Nebula-nominated Beth Cato is the author of the *Clockwork Dagger* duology and the *Blood of Earth* trilogy from Harper Voyager. She's a Hanford, California native transplanted to the Arizona desert, where she lives with her husband, son, and requisite cats. Follow her at BethCato.com and on Twitter at @BethCato